MYSTERY RANCH

**Center Point
Large Print**

**This Large Print Book carries the
Seal of Approval of N.A.V.H.**

MYSTERY RANCH

MAX BRAND®

CENTER POINT PUBLISHING
THORNDIKE, MAINE

This Center Point Large Print edition
is published in the year 2007 by arrangement with
Golden West Literary Agency.

The text of this Large Print edition is unabridged. In other
aspects, this book may vary from the original edition. Printed in
Thailand. Set in 16-point Times New Roman type.

ISBN: 1-58547-897-0
ISBN 13: 978-1-58547-897-2

Library of Congress Cataloging-in-Publication Data

Brand, Max, 1892-1944.
    Mystery ranch / Max Brand.--Center Point large print ed.
        p. cm.
    ISBN-13: 978-1-58547-897-2 (lib. bdg. : alk. paper)
        1. Large type books. I. Title.

PS3511.A87M97 2006
813'.52--dc22

2006024373

CHAPTER I

Just before this century began, when the world began to feel old and sin-worn in the latter nineties, when ladies pinched their waists and gentlemen padded their shoulders, before civilization was flavored with gasoline, and when newspapers held forth against the trusts, John Templar came out of the desert.

He cared not for trusts and his shoulders were not padded, neither did he journey in a rubber-tired phaeton; above the waist he was clad in a blue flannel shirt with his brown elbows punching through the sleeves and salt marks of perspiration on his back like tide marks on the shore; his black felt hat had turned green; his bluejeans were battered white at the knees; and his conveyance was a roach-backed mustang with a look of a Christian martyr and the soul of a Christian devil. About his lean belly was a belt heavy on the inside with gold dust which he had washed with his own hands, and with his own hands he had kept it, for the outside of that belt was garnished with large cartridges and at either hip it was balanced with a single-action Colt, each hand-polished with much use and innocent of sights. The age of John Templar was twenty and an unimportant fraction, and he weighed in the buff a hundred and eighty pounds of sun-dried gun-cotton.

He had pushed the mustang without pause all the way up the long slope from the desert, but now that he

5

was at the mouth of the valley he paused, not to rest the horse but to enjoy the pleasant greenness of the pass. Just north of him Mount Cramer stood to the west and the Sugarloaf to the east, and through the gorge between them the rain-winds bellied out towards the desert just as far as the hill John Templar had reached, and no farther. With a stride one crossed from cactus to lodgepole pine.

The sun was down, and out of the deeper shadow between the mountains lights began to sparkle from the town of Last Luck, which was the goal and the outermost boundary of John Templar's present crusade; for when, six months before, he had passed through the little city, with empty pockets and a heart of hope, he had promised himself that he would return the moment he had gathered the price of a hell of a time. So, because he was a man of his word, he now thrust the mustang ahead with an unpleasant touch of the spurs, and, as he rode, all the joys of Last Luck, seen but not tasted on another day, went up like a cloud of fire from his heart to his brain, and sank like a mist of wine from his brain upon his heart.

In vain one stares on the map now for Last Luck, unless it may be something up Alaska way, where men still feel the frontier and, partly by instinct and partly through imitation, find ways and names such as once blossomed on the mountain-desert. Last Luck is gone, now, from the pass between the mountains, and instead there is a town of concrete with an eight-story office building, a city hall, paved streets that glisten

6

like black ice under the rains and the lights, and roaring streams of automobiles that rush down from the pass or sweep smoothly up from the desert. The frontier is gone; the smoke of the railroad rarely is out of sight, and roads surfaced like the floor of a house are dropped down in thousand-mile strips here and there, over mountains, over deserts. Man has become too strong for nature, but on the day of which I speak nature was far too strong for man, unless it was such a man as John Templar.

He, from the head of the one great street of Last Luck, thumbed the lumps of gold dust inside his belt and, with misting eyes and a watering mouth like a desert wolf at the edge of the sheep pen, wondered where he would begin. Food was not in his thoughts, but from lips to soul he was obsessed by a mighty thirst, not bred of the desert, but born of the fire of joy.

Now in Last Luck there were three palaces among hovels, three noble ships for the eyes of the ship-wrecked, three islands of green among the hot sands. The first was Tabor's Rest House, beyond which the men from the desert rarely got; the second was the emporium of Bill Etheredge; and the third was Lucan's Parlors, into which the men from the mountain mines poured down. Those palaces were not of marble, but of tent-cloth and unpainted boards, with trodden floors of earth; but each was rich in music, bar, and dance-hall. John Templar, bound south in poverty, had marked them all down, and John Templar, bound north with gold dust, only wished that all three were rolled together in one glorious pandemonium of joy, noise, and beauty. However, he was in too much haste to make a selection, and, since Tabor's Rest House was nearest, it therefore was best.

He dismounted and threw his reins, but then he hesitated, for it seemed to the great spirit of Templar that it would be a mean and base thing to enter unannounced. Moreover, he was displeased by the sign, for rest was not what he wanted. So he drew two guns and severed the stout cords from which the signboard was hung. Down dropped "Rest House," and, carrying it under his arm, he entered.

Four stalwart bouncers rushed upon him.

"Here boys," said Templar, "hold my hat, because my head's hot."

He threw it to them and surveyed the scene. To the left was the bar from which streams of waiters trotted; to the right was the dance-hall with all the lamps blue-gold through the mist of tobacco smoke; and farther back was the gambling room. All around him flowed a mass of miners, lumbermen, promotion agents, bunco-steerers, pickpockets, thugs, yeggs, counterfeiters and pushers of the queer, cowpunchers, long riders, sowers of the harvest and reapers thereof, all now in the press of Tabor's Rest House with streams of gold running from them.

"Hello, Wilson!" hailed a cheerful voice. "You're Wilson of the Gulch, ain't you?"

"Sure I am," said Templar, "and you're old Jerry Simple of the Hill? Oh, home, sweet, sweet home! I seem to breathe again the crystal air of the mountains. I find myself among the honest children of nature. Lead me Gerald, to the bar!"

Now from that point the memory of John Templar grew not dim, but overbright, as though many searchlights were focused in a crowd upon swirling colors. From time to time those searchlights were snapped out, and clouds of darkness for a moment obscured the vision of the man from the desert. At last a more enduring shadow enveloped him, and from this he emerged with all his body and his reeling head throbbing with aches or stabbed by pains. A great weight oppressed his chest; other burdens crushed his arms and his legs; and now as he looked about him, he was aware of glimmering rows of steel bars in the distance, and of five men sitting on his prostrate form. Others stood in the background.

"Hello, boys," murmured John Templar. "Glad to see you all again."

"He's coming around," said one in answer. "Let him up.

"Get some irons on his wrists first."

"You better hobble him, too."

It was done. With wrists and legs confined, John Templar sat up and found before him a stalwart fellow who poised a great bludgeon and promised heartily that he would dash out the brains of the prisoner at the first hostile move. He was a marked man, yonder of the club, for one eye was greatly swollen, and turning to a dark shade of purple, and a split lip was also puffed and bleeding. Indeed, all the others carried signs of struggle, for there were ripped shirts, and sleeveless coats, and bumps upon face and forehead.

"Looks like a high wind," remarked Templar. "Gimme the makings, somebody."

Out of silence, the makings were given to him, and he made a cigarette.

"Is this a fairy tale," he asked cheerfully, "and am I really being boarded by the government?"

The answer was no answer at all, for a hoarse voice said: "There ain't a mark on him; he ain't flesh; he's iron."

"Far from it, partner," said Templar. "One shake would make me fall apart. Will somebody tell me what's happened?"

"Beginning where?" asked the man of the club.

"Back in Tabor's Rest House."

A shout which was half groan gave him echo.

"You don't have no recollection of Etheredge's place?" asked the man of the club.

"Never been inside it," said Templar.

"In Lucan's Parlors maybe you're a stranger, too?"

"I am. I'll visit 'em when I get out of this!"

His manacles clinked as he gestured towards the bars.

"Will he visit 'em?" asked the man of the club.

"He won't," said a gloomy chorus.

"Because," continued the first speaker, "there is only some small scraps and junk heaps standing where those places was, son. All you done was walk inside of 'em and explode."

"Ah, ah," murmured Templar. "Was anybody hurt?"

"The only able-bodied men left in Last Luck," replied the other, "is them you now are seein', and if all my ribs ain't broke where you hit me, I'm a liar. Boys, we better leave him be; he might have another charge inside of him."

They filed outside the door of the cell and closed it with a clank. The heavy bolt was turned and slid home. A dozen faces stared through the bars at the prisoner.

"Stranger," said the tallest and the broadest of the lot, "would you mind feelin' the point of your jaw, on the button on the right hand side?"

"Well?" said Templar.

"Might there be a swellin' there?"

"No."

"Or a kind of a sore feelin'?" asked the other hopefully.

"Nothing at all, thanks."

"My God," groaned the big man, "that's where I hit him—me! And all I got to say is his bones are steel and he's got a india-rubber cushion instead of a brain. I'm gunna go home!"

He went down the aisle with a swaying stride; the others began to follow, slowly, with awe-stricken faces.

"Wait a minute," called John Templar. "Who's got a drink for a man that hasn't had liquor for a month?"

CHAPTER II

Moving easily, in spite of irons on his hands, and a forty-pound ball which tugged at his ankles as he hopped, John Templar gained the cot at the side of the cell. It was the only article of furniture, and it was of solid iron and bolted against the bars. On this he stretched himself and puffed cigarette smoke at the dimness above him, watching it drive, billow, and dissolve. Bits of the evening begin to rise before him, now, not in a continuous series of images but single flashes among clouds and darkness, and in those glimpses of the truth a maelstrom always was in progress, filled with heaving shoulders, set jaws, glaring eyes.

Little by little he stretched himself so that the pains and the aches were interviewed one by one, as it were; but the chief annoyance was across his skinned knuckles, the backs of his hands, and the long striking muscles which slipped and glided up his arms until they were lost in the masses at his shoulders. He closed his eyes and sighed with content; afterwards he fell into a sound sleep.

Morning brought a sense of many noises to him, but his subconscious mind erected a barrier against disturbance, and still he slept on until a loud jangling of the cell door roused him at last. Then he turned his head and observed a badly frightened negro entering with a tray of food which chattered in his nervous hands.

Behind him walked two guards armed to the teeth, for one carried a Colt in his hand and the other presented a sawed-off shotgun. They entered grimly, their eyes upon the prisoner as upon big game.

"Hello, boys," said Templar. "I won't eat you. What's it all about? And have I got enough to pay the fine?"

"If you got twenty years of life in you," said he of the shotgun, "maybe you can pay up. I dunno."

They backed carefully out of the door; from beyond it the man of the Colt spoke in his turn.

"Any shenannigans, kid, and you get this. We won't stop to ask questions!"

He tapped his gun significantly, and they withdrew, leaving Templar with his sense of satisfaction sadly shattered. However, the fragrance of coffee on the tray roused him, and presently he was cross-legged on the floor and eating with a hearty appetite. He had hardly finished when the guards returned. They demanded from beyond the bars if he would go quietly, at which he assured them that there was no more trouble in him than in a lost lamb. So the revolver expert was padlocked to the arm of Templar and the sawed-off shotgun walked behind him down a corridor with curious faces pressed against the bars on either side. They called cheerful messages to Templar and hoped cordially that he would get less than life. At the end of the passage a door was opened and Templar was pushed into an office where two men sat, one with a badge of office pinned on his shirt, and the other a heavy fellow, dressed like a professional gambler, with a vast cigar unregarded in a corner of his mouth. They looked long and earnestly at the prisoner.

"D'you know who you're talkin' to?" asked the man in the shirt and badge.

"I don't."

"I'm Sheriff and my name's Aiken. This is Tabor."

Mr. Tabor grinned on both sides of the cigar.

"Where you rested a while last night," he explained. "That was my house."

Said Aiken, who appeared a very tired man: "You ought to get life for last night, young feller. What's your name? Well, Templar, we've buried most of the boys that tried to shoot up this town. Some have got one of the houses, but you're the first that ever got through all three."

"Thanks," said the modest Templar. "The fact is that I don't recall the evening very clearly."

"The hand is faster than the eye," chuckled Tabor with amazing good humor. "Cut down to business, Aiken, will you?"

"Now," said the sheriff, "I'll give you the layout. You raised hell, but you raised it in style. Now, son, this town is a three-ringed circus, and I have to watch all the three rings. Suppose that you could take on one of them. Having sort of introduced yourself to the boys last night, I don't think that they'd make much trouble for you. Tabor thinks the same. He'll blot out the past; so will I; you get a clean slate and a fat job keeping order in the Rest House. If that ain't large and kind, call me a coyote and cut off my tail!"

There was no outburst of enthusiasm from Templar, however, and Mr. Tabor said earnestly: "You'd only be on from eleven to three or four. The rest of the day for yourself. Fifty a week, say, for your work."

"Hey," grunted Aiken, "are you refusing?"

"I'd like to think it over," replied Templar. "I've been my own boss for quite a while, you see!"

He was taken back to his cell, where he hardly had finished an after-breakfast cigarette when once more the guards came for him and brought him back to the sheriff's office. The sheriff no longer was there, but a weazened little man with an eye as bright as a bird's was tipped back in a chair, with his heels resting on the edge of the desk.

"Sit down, Templar," he said. "Shut up, you! I'll be responsible for him"—this to a guard who protested— "name of Etheredge," he continued in introduction. "Now, kid, d'you know what you did to me last night? You busted a thousand dollar mirror and that was only a start. But don't kill a bull terrior because he ain't got the manners of a dachshund. I'm a busy man, Templar. Extra busy today because you gave me extra work last night. I cut this short. Tabor's been here, but forget him. He's a piker; got the best position in town, but I sell two drinks to his one and my faro game's the biggest this side of St. Louis. I'm a growing concern; come along and grow with me. You get easy hours, and you get—say seventy-five a week to start. If you keep things quiet, you get boosted. Don't say yes and don't say no. Go back and think it over."

So Templar was escorted back to his cell and the guards lingered at the door.

"Raising hell is kind of a profitable crop," said the man of the shotgun, and Templar was beginning to agree with him. Before noon he had additional cause, for again he was brought to the sheriff's office and there, as he half expected, was Lucan, whose Parlors stood at the northern edge of Last Luck. He was quite different from the other pair, for he was a long, lank Yankee with a whimsical smile and exceedingly straight eyes. He was not as rapid as little Bill Etheredge, but he was terse enough, for after the introduction he explained that he was the man whose games were straight, in that town, and because they were straight the biggest money went over his gaming tables. His profits, he declared, were not so great as those of Tabor or Etheredge, but his margin was honest. However, five times in five months his establishment had been shot up, and he wanted peace.

"If you want peace, you got to prepare for it," said Lucan, "and I reckon you'd be the preparation that I want. The other boys figger the same, but I'll figger just above 'em. Come with me, young man, and you'll have a hundred a week, a nigger to look after you— and a chance to work up. Does it sound to you?"

"Look here," broke in the prisoner. "I came in for a lark, last night, and happened to make a little trouble. Lemme tell you and the rest that I'm not a professional fighting man. I'll tell you something more. I

16

never killed a man in my life, and I hope to God that I never do. I wouldn't have the name of gunfighter for the whole town of Last Luck multiplied by ten. D'you follow that?"

"Perfect," said Lucan in his drawling voice. "You want peace; so do I—most of all in the Parlors. You hate the bullies; they're the ones I want to muzzle. Why can't we agree? Tell me tomorrow what you decide!"

Once again Templar lay on his cot, but now his brain was whirling. Let it be remembered that in those days men had not begun to juggle billions familiarly, and the pay of a cowpuncher was apt to be thirty a month, or less in winter. As a cowpuncher Templar had worked; or he had prospected through months of bitter labor, to come out with a handful of gold. Now he was offered a hundred a week, or four hundred a month, or five thousand a year!

He translated that sum into his knowledge of men and life, and in those days a five thousand dollar salary was pointed out as a fifty thousand dollar salary is pointed out today. So noon came, and in the drowsy period of the early afternoon he wondered if this were not a strange dream into which he had fallen. The coming of the sheriff for a second time brought him to his feet. He said simply to Templar: "Kid, you're made! Come along with me!"

Leading to his office, he paused to unlock the irons. A free man, Templar walked beside him.

"It's the big chief; it's Condon!" said the sheriff in a

voice fairly husky with awe and excitement. "And *he* wants you! My God, you've reached into the fire and picked out the diamond, you lucky devil!"

It seemed that the coming of Condon banished all thought of further jail, further punishment. Templar tried to ask who Condon might be, but Aiken heard the question with a blank eye, as one would listen if asked about the shining sun. Then Templar found himself for the fourth time in the office, and before him a man in riding breeches and boots, a man with a bald head, a brow swelling above the eyes, a very long jaw. He was a pale fellow; even his eyes were the palest gray-blue, and they were fixed upon Templar with the most quiet, grave thoughtfulness. He decided at once that Condon must be either a half-wit or a very wise man; and it seemed obvious from the sheriff's attitude that he was not a half-wit.

He shook hands with Templar and then said to the sheriff: "May I take Mr. Templar out for a drive, Aiken?"

"Certainly, Mr. Condon," said the eager sheriff. "Here, Templar. I'll loan you a coat. Maybe you want to shave, first—"

"We'll start on," suggested Condon, and with Aiken's coat hastily jumped over his shoulders, Templar walked down the steps into the free air, the free, warm sun, and, though he guessed it not, into more "action" than even his athletic soul required.

CHAPTER III

He was conducted to a runabout at which stood as fine a span of chestnuts as ever knocked sparks out of a road. With snorts, with wrinkling haunches and reaching heads they started away; the dust whirred up and tossed into a cloud behind them. So they passed Bill Etheredge's place of amusement, and Lucan's Parlors. Workmen were fitting a new door onto hinges at Etheredge's main entrance, and, at Lucan's several were setting in new lights. Andrew Condon, keeping his span on a trembling rein, glanced aside at his companion with something of a smile, and so they plunged on through the town, swerved from the path of a charging body of riders who were driving out to the mountains bent on liquor and empty pockets, and so rang a loud echo from the bridge across the river. Turning their backs on the sun-brightened face of Mount Cramer, they drove on towards the dark Sugarloaf, the road becoming better as they proceeded, trees rising high and broad about them, with cheerful glimpses of meadows from time to time.

"My land begins here," said Condon, indicating the first great sweep of pines, and after this, the first word he had spoken, he maintained his silence again.

Sensitive like all youngsters to affectation of any kind, Templar wondered if this silence was assumed to impress him, or if it really was the product of a reserved, strong nature. He was not a pessimist, but he was inclined to the first view.

For another half hour they swept on, putting at least seven miles behind them, and then veered with the road under a sweeping silver spruce and came into view of the house. As befitted a region where the wind was often of hurricane force, and where the winter snows could bring temperatures as biting with cold as the summers were savage with heat, the house had been placed low, to secure shelter. The trees walked down the Sugarloaf and from the hills to the edge of what looked like a circular glacial shadow—one of those old lakes which time had filled with a rich detritus and left, finally, as smooth stretches of green, emerald bright in the sweeping darkness of the mountain forest. This was by no means a house so pretentious as Templar had expected from the reputation of wealth and power which, from the sheriff, he supposed surrounded Condon; it was simply a long cabin on a huge scale, surrounded by a half wild garden through which the walks wandered as idly as cow trails. The only indication of great wealth was the extent of this little wilderness of flowers, for it stretched at least a quarter of a mile on either side of the house, until its outer borders of purple and pink and rose and yellow and startling blue curled under the stern black edge of the forest.

The road swept up to the front of the house, and here a man took the span and held their froth stained heads while the master and his guest dismounted. The door opened. They entered a hall which was garnished with heads of deer, mountain lions, sheep, and goats, great branched horns of the elk, and the pronged shovels of moose. That, it seemed to the keen eye of the young man, was the fatal touch. All the rest could have been shot in the vicinity, given a cold winter or a very long climb to the heights; but the moose ranged far north, and instantly Templar suspected that the whole garnishing had been bought at a stroke, mounted at a stroke, fitted thus to the walls. And what meaning have trophies which have not fallen to the gun of the host and his family?

Across the hall they passed into a small room secured by heavy double doors on the one side, and double windows on the other. Andrew Condon closed the windows, closed and locked both the doors, and shoved down the shutter of the fireplace. He did this before he waved Templar to a chair. After that he offered cigars, a pipe, and tailor made cigarettes; but Templar clung religiously to his home made variety of Bull Durham. So they settled down, Templar near the shuttered hearth, and Condon between the window and the corner of the wall, where the light spared his own face and fell on that of the youngster. Templar recognized the maneuver, and again he was touched by displeasure; yet he scorned such tactics, and told himself that he would endure any eye in the world, whether in dark or light.

In the meantime, his irritation grew rapidly. Four words had been spoken by this pale faced, pale eyed man during the course of an eight mile drive, and those four words had been merely, as Templar felt, a gesture of ostentation.

"You feel," said Condon, beginning quietly in the middle of things, "that I've held rather a high hand; and perhaps I have, but I have to be careful with what I say in public."

"Even in a runabout with two fast horses rattling you along?" asked Templar with a faint smile.

"Even in a runabout with two fast horses," answered the other, but he did not smile, adding: "When one cannot be overheard, one can be watched."

All at once the suspicions of Templar faded; he began to feel that his doubts had been childish, and, settling back in his chair, he waited in a less aggressive attitude.

There was nothing warm hearted or kindly in the manner or in the voice of Condon, but at least he was seriously attentive, and it seemed that he talked to this much younger man as to an equal.

"I want to begin by asking you about yourself," he said. "Do you mind?"

"I rather do," replied the other.

"I won't be pressing or too particular, I hope," said Condon. "But—you've been well educated? College?"

Templar hesitated.

"Never mind," replied Condon. "I won't press that point, to begin with. Will you tell me how old you are?"

"Under thirty," replied the cautious youth, and then flushed a little, for Condon smiled suddenly and frankly.

22

"Under thirty—thank you," said Condon. "And what is your business?"

"Travel," answered Templar.

The smile did not appear so broadly, this time, but Templar saw that it had been restrained by an effort.

"Travel," echoed the grave voice of Condon. "That is very well. Your Western accomplishments are what?"

"I don't know just what you mean by that."

"You ride a rope?"

"I ride. With a rope I'm a loss."

"You follow a trail?"

"Not at all. No instinct for it, it seems."

Condon sighed and looked down at the floor. He remained silent for a long time, and at length looked up with a slight start.

"I beg your pardon," he said. "I believe that closes the interview, and I must have you sent back to Last Luck. I understand that you have other positions waiting for you there?"

Templar stood up, very angry indeed; it had been a long trip and not a particularly amusing one.

"I'll get on, then," said he.

"You may as well," said Condon. "But I must recompensate you for your time. Shall we say ten dollars?"

He held out a golden eagle. Again Templar flushed, but this time a dark and dangerous crimson.

"I take pay when I do work," said he. "I'll get on without that, thank you. Good-by, Mr. Condon."

He looked significantly at the door, but the other waved him back to his chair.

"I beg your pardon again," said Condon. "But now that you're here, please let me ask you another question. You are an expert with firearms, I understand?"

"No," answered the other after a moment. "I've seen half a dozen trick artists on the stage who could shoot rings around me."

"On the stage," nodded the other, "but here in the West?"

Templar thought again. There was a streak of stubborn, matter-of-fact honesty in him.

"Here in the West," he said, "I'm only a second-rater. I hear of men who can knock down an antelope at a thousand yards. Well—I can't!"

Condon made no reply. He seemed to wait still.

"I hear of fellows," went on the youth, "who can cut wire at fifty yards, with a Colt. I can't. Not at twenty-five, either."

"At ten?" asked Condon.

"That's different."

"From the hip?"

"Certainly not!"

"You fan your guns, Mr. Templar?"

"Yes."

"Have you had much practice?"

"About fifteen years."

"Ah."

"When my father came back from—" began Templar, and then shut himself off. "I began early, for him," he concluded briefly.

He talked standing, one hand on the back of the chair.
"No doubt you've handled a knife?"

"To whittle sticks. Yes."

"But the clever Mexican art of throwing them, Templar?"

"I don't know a thing about it." He paused. "I don't want to," he added with a decided emphasis.

"Will you sit down?"

Silently Templar took a chair again. He was not happy, and a single deep wrinkle appeared between his eyes.

"You ride well?"

"I'm not a bronc-peeler, exactly, but I can ride."

"You've had training in wrestling?"

"Yes."

"A college trainer?"

"Ye—" he paused; but already he had admitted college, and the thought that the admission had been tricked out of him angered him still more.

"Boxing?"

"I suppose so."

Condon resumed: "You box—you wrestle—you ride well—you use a rifle, though not on antelope at a thousand yards"—again he smiled a little—"and you split a wire at thirty feet with a revolver shot—"

"Now and then," cautioned Templar.

Condon looked at the floor and began to drum his fingertips lightly on the arm of his chair. They were long, pale, square tipped fingers, very hairy down to the first joint.

25

"Mr. Templar—"

"Sir?"

"I live in constant fear of murder; I want a bodyguard; will you consider the post?"

CHAPTER IV

There are several forms in which shock may come to us—with noise and fury, or again softly and quietly, with the lift of an eyebrow and a whisper. So it was with Templar. That very room in which they sat was suddenly altered as though fire had leaped from the soft gray of its thick rug; far more than if yonder quiet man with the bald, glistening head had leaped to his feet and shouted a furious sentence. For there was no doubt of the sincerity of this gentle, matter-of-fact voice.

"I live in constant fear of murder!"

Templar half rose from his chair, and then settled slowly back into it, he set his teeth over an exclamation and then, erect and poised, he waited. At last he could say: "I don't know. Only I want to tell you in the beginning that I'm not a professional gunfighter. I wouldn't be one!"

"Naturally not," answered Condon. "You're bred above such things. I'm not offering to buy you with money. Your salary we'll make an ample one, but above all I hope to tempt you with the excitement. I move in the midst of terrible danger. Will you step in at my side and move in it also?"

Templar could not help smiling.

"It makes an odd invitation, I know," said Condon, "but I believe that I understand you in part. You're not in the West to ride herd or dig gold or cut timber; then you're here, I have to think, to amuse yourself—or hide your head—"

He made the slightest of pauses, but Templar stirred not a whit.

"I take it for granted that you love excitement; your little game of last night I take as an example, if you permit me. I'll go a little further, if you wish. As I said before, I don't want to try to buy you with money, but if I'm alive at the end of thirty days you will receive— let us say five thousand dollars? Your duties will not be, necessarily, to spend every minute with me. We can decide on your post from day to day and from hour to hour. I don't expect to keep you awake all of each twenty-four hours. I simply know that danger soon will jump at me like a snake from a corner, and I hope to have you with me to shoot the snake." He added after an instant—"or snakes!"

Templar sighed.

"I've never seen five thousand rolled together in one heap," he admitted at last.

Condon, as one who has talked himself out, and expressed every idea worth mentioning, relaxed in his chair, filled and lighted a pipe, and began to study the puffs of smoke as they rose towards the ceiling, curling up at the edges. It began to seem to Templar

27

that the silences in this room were like great shadows. So long as voices spoke, the sun was allowed to slide warmly in through the windows, but when sound ended, then cold and darkness overspread the universe, and the sun beyond the house had no more meaning than painted light; the garden was a painted garden; the sky was a flat and meaningless thing.

He said at last: "I'll admit I want to try the thing just because it looks like trouble and a hard nut to crack. But every grain of common sense in me tells me to hold back. Five thousand dollars is no good to a dead man, and that's what I'll be at the end of thirty days, I have an idea."

"You have a chance of pulling through, no doubt," suggested Condon.

He said it so calmly that the other's lips twisted to the side.

"One chance in two?"

"One chance in five," corrected Condon.

"And you? One chance in five?"

"One chance in twenty. It's worth five thousand to me, you see; and I'm not trying to buy you; I'm not trying to buy life."

"My God!" whispered the youngster, for he was so brave that he was not afraid to be frank. He wanted to hear more talk; he yearned to be persuaded; he was trembling with fear and with eagerness, but Condon said not a word. He continued to smoke, systematically, drawing long puffs and watching them on their curling flight to the ceiling, where now a dull white mist was growing, white mist shot with brown. Templar began to watch those rough edged bubbles rising, too, watched them flattening and dissolving, hypnotized by the process. He dragged himself back from the contemplation and forced himself ahead as a good horse forces himself, despite sore shoulders, into the collar.

"Well, let's talk a little."

"If there's any more to say," replied the mild Condon.

Then Templar exploded: "Damn it, Mr. Condon, you can't ask a man to take a one-way ticket!"

"Mind, now! I don't ask you to do anything. I don't persuade you, partly because I think you're young enough to persuade yourself, and partly because I don't want your blood on my head. This is an age of business; I've talked business, and that's all. I haven't invited you to ride in a crusade!"

"I know—" murmured the boy "—I know—only—"

Then he began more crisply: "You have this section of the world under your thumb; you could have the sheriff and a whole posse to watch your house."

"One of the posse would shoot me in the back," answered Condon without hesitation.

"Ah, I see. You're afraid of numbers."

"Like a jury. You only need to buy one good man and true; that hangs the verdict."

"Who is it that's trying to get you?"

"I don't know."

"Then who—but, Mr. Condon, but you have an idea!"

"Not a thought."

"You've always done business with silk gloves, no doubt."

Condon overlooked the irony.

"I've stepped on toes," he admitted with his usual freeness. "Of course I've stepped on toes; no doubt I've broken hearts."

"Men don't murder you because of a broken toe; and broken hearts don't shoot in the dark."

"No—they don't," said Condon. "I've thought of all that."

As if he had not thought of everything! said Templar to himself; for every moment his respect for this man grew until it had swelled to the dimensions of a great awe. He did not like the man a whit better—there was no warming of his heart, that is to say—but Condon seemed increasingly important.

"You're rich. Are you very rich, Mr. Condon?"

"Newspapers say I'm worth twenty millions. I'm not. I'm hardly worth a quarter of that sum. I'm not a financial giant. But I'm rich. Yes," he admitted slowly, "I'm very rich, and if I live for another month I'll be much richer—much!"

It was the very first note of passion that he had allowed to come in. It was all concentrated in the last word, but that word rang with a fervor that opened the eye of Templar's mind and made him see a sudden vision of piled gold, heaped sacks of it, broken open at corners, yielding to the massive strain, pouring out trickles of dust of nuggets.

"Around here," said Templar, "they seem to like you; you wouldn't have many enemies here."

"Hired ones, perhaps," said Condon. "Hired guns shoot just as straight, I think?"

He put that as a question, and something swelled high in young Templar.

"Ah, no!" he cried. "No, by the eternal God—there's a strength in honesty—there's a strength in honest men, you know!"

"Last Luck learned that the other evening," smiled Condon.

"You don't even know how many? I mean, is it a gang? Is it one?"

"I know this, however," answered Condon obliquely.

He leaned and opened a drawer of his desk. From among heaped papers he took out a black case.

"That's not leather," he said. "It's good steel, and I carry cigars in these cases. They're watertight, unnecessarily strong, but I like unnecessary strength. Not for a year—but a century—a thousand years—a deposit in the lap of time—"

Templar began to stare indeed, for this was enthusiasm with just a touch, as he thought, of madness in it—divine madness, perhaps one might say.

"You observe?" said Condon.

He turned the case over and extended it. The reverse side was smashed in and the steel pierced, but only as by a needle point; the black coating being broken away, the bright, pure steel showed and glittered.

31

"I know this, also," said Condon. "This was the first message."

From the same drawer, he took out a fold of paper, unrolled it, and produced a knife with a six-inch blade, tapering, delicate at the point, very heavy at the forte.

"Weight it in your hand."

It was extremely heavy for its size, no doubt because the handle was loaded with lead.

"That came through the window one evening as I was working here at my desk. You see the mark of it?"

He pointed to a deep, narrow slit in the woodwork.

"And there is a little more testimony," went on Condon.

Still from the same drawer he took out a phial which contained very dark green liquid. When it was held in the sun the color became sparkling and beautiful.

"I have a little affection of the heart, nothing very serious; digitalis keeps it in order nicely. This is digitalis, in this bottle. It has an odd, bitter, green taste. Arsenic has a sharp, bitter taste too. And this bottle now is loaded with arsenic. Not the powder, but a delicate, beautiful sublimation of arsenic such as the Italian poisoners used to produce in the golden age of crime. If I took ten drops of this, you see, I should be dead before morning."

He put everything back into the drawer.

"These things happened in the past week," said he.

"God—God—" said the boy, and covered his face with his mighty hands, and shuddered.

"I'll do it!" he exclaimed. "Of course I'll do it!" He

32

reached forward, but Condon shook his head.

"Thank you," he answered. "I'm glad to have you, but we'll be safer if we keep it a business affair. Emotion clouds the eyes."

CHAPTER V

Whatever enthusiasm had boiled up in young John Templar died at once; but all that was iron in him responded to the pressure which this stern man put upon him. He was given liberty at once to go out and examine the environs of the place.

"You don't have to pretend to be casual," said Condon. "Everybody knows about you, and everybody understands that I have you here because I expect trouble. But look over the premises; there's nothing mysterious about danger, and if you know the avenues of approach, you've taken the first step."

So Templar left the room and went out to explore, an understanding having been reached that his horse would be brought from Last Luck if it could be found, and at any rate clothes would be brought out to him. As for guns, Snyder, who was the head of the household and disposer of all affairs domestic, would lead him to the gun room and there he could pick out whatever he wanted.

The frankness of Condon persisted even when he introduced Templar to Snyder.

"Templar is going to help me through the bad time,

Snyder," he said. And he added to Templar: "Snyder knows everything, as far as you and I know it."

There was a significance about this limitation, for certainly Templar's acquaintance with the case was most abbreviated; if Snyder knew no more, little was to be gained by conversation with him.

Snyder was a big, jovial fellow, with shoulders and arms and hands which seemed to promise that he could take care of himself and of his master, also. He took young Templar down the hall and knocked open the door to a room which looked like an armory. There were rifles, shotguns, and revolvers of all calibers, polished and oiled and supported in long racks. There were many drawers, too, neatly labeled with the character of the ammunition which they contained.

These things were examined by Templar with a professional attention, and a fifteen-shot Winchester won his unqualified admiration. It was in perfect trim for immediate use, and he loaded it at once, while Snyder stood critically by. He seemed unable to make up his mind about the newcomer to the household, merely asking: "You'll be sleeping in?"

Templar nodded, and the butler, he thought, allowed a shadow to fall upon his face. When it came to revolvers, however, he found nothing more to his liking than the old guns which he carried with him, at which Snyder said rather grimly: "Yes, old friends are the best." But, in addition, he asked for and received some strong but supple springs which were reposing in a remnant box, and with these he left the gun room.

"You want to see the rest of the place, I suppose?" suggested Snyder.

"In about an hour," answered the new member of the household. "Will you show me my sleeping quarters?"

It was a very small room, hardly eight by ten, in the rear of the "master's" bedroom. Its only air and light came through a little skylight, and there was a cot in a corner, a small bureau and washstand in another.

"Narrow quarters, eh?" asked Snyder.

"For a house, yes; for a ship, a big, roomy, airy cabin," answered Templar, and he turned and looked the butler in the face, for he felt that he perceived a sort of hidden sneer, a buried vein of contempt in the attitude of that official.

Left alone in his room, at last he was reasonably certain that Snyder had walked off up the hall with a brisk, noisy step—and then had slipped back again. He was tempted to spring to the door and cast it open, but he refrained from doing so. He merely moved his chair to a corner which could not be under observation from crack or keyhole; then he started seriously to work, and, laboring like one who has done the same thing often before, he made two powerful but simple spring clips fitted with leather slings. The leather slings fitted over his shoulders, and the springs beneath his arm pits; in them he lodged the Colts, and, after working at them for some time, he had them so that they received the guns only with a good deal of difficulty and adjustment, but to just the right pull they gave up the weapons instantly.

After that, he put on the coat which the sheriff had so kindly loaned him and stood with his face to the wall going through an odd maneuver which consisted in snatching out both weapons and whirling at the same instant with the Colts held on a mark.

His whole hour was consumed in this manner, but, at the end of that time, he left his room and sought Snyder. The latter was waiting, and he took Templar over the entire house. It was simply planned, with a single hall running the length of the building on the second floor and four bedrooms opening on either side of it. One of these was Condon's, and another had a similar antechamber. This, said Snyder, was occupied by Condon's nephew and presumptive heir. Above the second floor was an attic story containing four rooms for servants, of which only three were occupied, for Condon got on with a cook, a man for the cleaning of the rooms, and Snyder. The stable staff, which was larger, bunked and ate with the cowpunchers, who had a separate edifice for their quarters, and a cookhouse. The space not occupied in the attic by rooms was given over to four compartments of irregular size used for storage purposes. On the ground floor was the big entrance hall, dining room and kitchen to the one side, and library, large living room, and the master's den on the other side, which was much larger. Even into the kitchen and through the pantries went Templar. He found the cook a rather gloomy negro, and the house boy was a black, also, who said in a frightened, furtive voice to the butler: "Is anything more gunna happen, Mistah Snyder?"

"How in hell can I tell?" grunted Snyder.

In the library they found a tall young man who looked up over a pair of studious glasses from behind a very large book. He was the nephew, Munroe Lister. He greeted the newcomer with a semi-puzzled and semi-absent air, and fastened his attention, finally, on the rifle which Templar carried during his trip around the place. To the front door Snyder escorted the new guest and there paused.

"You can see the rest of the layout for yourself," he pointed out, and indicated the buildings to the rear of the dwelling house.

So Templar walked towards them, certain that the odd butler was grinning behind him; but he disdained flashing a glance over his shoulder.

He made a rapid tour. The barn was huge, and there were additional sheds containing surplus supplies of hay for the feedyards during the worst part of the winter; for winter, when it came through the pass, came thick and white and might bury every vestige of grass under a yard of snow, heavily crusted on top. To the side of the yards was a big bunkhouse into which he stepped and found a lounging cowpuncher with a leg bandaged and lying on the table before him.

"Come in an rest your feet," he invited.

But Templar merely nodded and waved; he walked slowly around the room and inspected an array of eleven apparently inhabited bunks; there was room for eight more men.

"You can't find it?" asked the puncher.

"No," ventured Templar. "I don't think there's a good time aboard this outfit; is there?"

"Nothing but," answered the cheerful puncher. "Good pay, good chuck, northers to keep you busy in the winter and rustlers to wake you up in the summer. Now what more can a poor cowboy ask for?" He added: "Are you catching on, here?"

"Sort of," replied Templar, and with a nod he left the long, narrow cabin and started his tour of the woods, taking a horse which was given to him, without question, at the stable. The lay of the land was not too simple. The woods, for instance, took knowing, for in many places they closed up shoulder to shoulder and turned the afternoon into twilight; and again there were stretches of second growth too dense for a horse to penetrate; even a man on foot would have had his work laid out for him.

He worked up to the first hill top towards the Sugarloaf, and there halted to sweep the landscape. Towards the big mountain, there were half a dozen more sharp ridges, each a little loftier than the other, and then the soaring, unbroken height up which the forest climbed for a distance, but then slid away towards the top and left a naked poll, thumb marked with snow in every furrow. South ran a soft, single line of hills, falling to a plateau which shelved rapidly away, green to its outer edge; and beyond that, a distance below, was the desert, now screened with low dust-fog. Only in one direction was the valley open, and that was towards the pass and Last Luck, where lay the white loops and twistings of the trail over which Condon had driven him.

It looked to Templar like a trap, of which the mouth was left open purposely to attract the unwary, and in the center of the trap—how the simile grew upon him!— was the house of Condon, looking more dangerous than endangered. The waves of color and sunlit beauty which surrounded it could not break through the impression of gloom which he had gathered on first beholding that dark, long dwelling house. All black it seemed inside, with the upper windows glistening in the slant western sun, for the lower ones already were brushed across by the climbing shadow of the evening. At his back, between him and the next ridge, ran a strip of good cow country; and he did not need to ride over it in order to tell that the grass was excellent. No doubt between the ridges, wherever trees did not grow, there was an excellent run for cows, but the wealth of this domain remained unattractive to him. The sun still was strong enough to burn home between his shoulder blades, and yet all at once he sighed for the open spaces and the heat of the desert, where one can see danger for five miles and hear it for two.

He remained at the lookout until he heard the sharp snap of a twig near by. Such sharp sounds continually may be heard in the woods; some small branch, long overladen, finally gives to its burden, say. But the sharpness of this sound was just a little muffled, as though by the enveloping weight of a foot. Suddenly, very surely, he felt that he was being watched.

CHAPTER VI

The mustang he was riding reached for the bit that instant, and he let the animal walk off, never turning his head though he felt eyes boring into the small of his back. Glad, very glad was Templar when the mustang stumbled, shied at a white faced rock, and so put an arm of the woods between him and whatever danger lay in the rear. So sheltered, the rider was on the point of turning back, leaving the horse, and scouting through the trees; but he checked that impulse, for the woods were unknown to him, he was no silent footed expert at woodcraft, and instead of one he might find half a dozen. After all, it might have been nothing, or a hunting wolf, say, or a mountain lion beginning to prowl even before the sun had set. In the high country, the prowlers start early to work.

So he went down the slope, reached the garden, and circled towards the barns in the growing chill of the mountain sunset. Sugarloaf was on fire behind him; Mount Cramer was inky black edged with colored mist in the northwest. And all the windows of the house, as he went on, glittered and glimmered black and evil, watching him, threatening him subtly, scorning him. He thought of the hidden, the scarcely hidden sneer in the voice and the eye of the butler, and he grew less confident with every step his horse took.

He determined to put some questions to Condon about Snyder; but that determination died almost at once. After all, for one thing that he was able to read in the face of a man, Condon doubtless could read three. Thinking, however, brought him no comfort, though he tried to be very methodical like a detective in a book. Logical, like a detective, too. Of course those inspired creatures always did astonishing things in the last chapter, but up to that time they seemed to be using just common sense—and a little flavoring luck, say. Very well, then: Here was Condon threatened. Why? Because he was rich, perhaps. Or because he had wronged someone in his past. Or simply because he stood in the way of a person or persons. Motives—those were easy to find, and Condon was a brightly lighted target for any scoundrel's shot. There was a time limit, too—thirty days—and after that, as it appeared, the danger would be gone. Surely Condon could help a great deal if he would admit what it was that was liable to happen or not happen at the end of thirty days!

But there were the eyes that looked out from the forest; there were eyes that watched from the darkened windows of the house; inside and outside there was danger, and it seemed to Templar that it was focusing on him, rather than on Condon.

As he drew nearer to the house, he saw a buckboard rattling down the trail away from the house, and three people in it.

After he had put up his horse, he went towards the big cabin and found Condon walking up and down in the last western warmth and light. He walked with a

41

light stick, which he whirled, from time to time, and hit a pebble a distance, or neatly cut a petal from a flower. He seemed exceptionally cordial to his newest employee.

He pointed out some of the flowers which interested him, and a patch of grass which, he said, he had brought from the higher table of inner China—a hardy grass which laughed at snows, lived through the most terribly low temperatures. Let him succeed in acclimatizing that grass to Western conditions, and perhaps the high lying lands of the range, now worth nothing, might be turned into a profitable string of pastures. Then he asked what Templar had been doing, and was informed. He had seen the house, the barns, the sheds, the bunkhouse.

"And nothing pleased you?" asked Condon, with that faint smile of his which Templar had disliked from the first.

He chose not to answer, and Condon went on: "I have no news to make you happier. The cook and the other negro have just left for town. Snyder's with them, and he'll try to pick up another pair. You and I must take a cold supper."

"We'll be alone, then—in that?" asked Templar, and hooked his thumb at the darkening house.

"You don't like the prospect?"

"It scares me."

"Well," nodded Condon, "two badly frightened men ought to keep a good lookout."

"Ah, I forgot. There's your nephew!"

42

"He?" Condon nodded without enthusiasm. "He'll be in his books! And with glasses on, you understand?"

"I understand," said Templar, but he didn't understand at all. He simply knew that every moment his task grew more and more unattractive, and he exclaimed out of force of an inward pressure: "Look here—that Snyder—old servant?"

"Eight years."

"Then you trust him, I suppose?"

"He can expect from me," said the other, "a small boost in wages every three or four years, and some sort of pension, no doubt, when I die. Well, it's not hard to overbid that, you know."

"No—if a man's always in the market—if there's not something in human beings beyond the reach of coin—no, I suppose it could be overbid!"

"You're irritated," smiled Condon. "I know your viewpoint. My fault that I haven't better people around me. Warm heart attracts warmth, of course. Large soul attracts large souls. But—"

He left off here and went on whirling his light stick as though it were a sword; a fine flexible wrist, young Templar thought.

We'd better go in," said Condon suddenly. At the door he added: "Perhaps I shouldn't inquire, but I see that you're not wearing your gun belt?"

"However," answered Templar with an equal dryness, "I'm armed."

"Thank you," said the other.

43

"Not at all," said Templar, and, as he hung up his battered hat in the hall, he vowed to himself that he would meet metal with metal, so long as he had to be associated with this man Condon.

They had supper at once, the tall young nephew making himself unexpectedly agreeable and useful, cutting bread, laying the table, and bringing in with Condon's assistance the sliced ham and cold beef from the kitchen.

Naturally, Templar regarded him with interest, and he thought to himself that rarely had he seen such good athletic material as this young fellow furnished. He had wrists which would have made the heart of a rowing coach burst with joy; he had the hips which are needed in the center of a football line, to hold a ton of struggling young humanity in leash; he had the shoulders of a weight thrower. Withal, he was a trifle clumsy, perhaps; he looked to need pulling together with a certain amount of training. But all the material was there, down to a square, blunt, prize fighter's jaw capable of enduring shocks, eyes protected by heavy rims of bony brow, and, above all, a good, straight looking pair of eyes, now that his glasses were off.

He did most of the work in the laying out of the supper and then he fell to with a good appetite at which Templar could not help wondering a little, so that he said to himself that perhaps Condon would have done very well if he had not brought out the fighting man from the town, but simply had relied upon the prowess of this burly young giant.

Some of these thoughts were evidently apparent to Condon, and he said with his usual upsetting frankness: "You're not worried, Munroe? You're not worried to be in the house without the servants, are you?"

Munroe Lister raised his head and smiled, and as he shrugged his shoulders it seemed to Templar that he could not tell which man he was more repelled from, the uncle or the nephew. They were like the house in which they lived—full of shadows.

And Condon went on with even more ugly frankness, masked by a polite air: "You must understand, Templar. Of course if I should catch a bullet in the proper place, everything would go to this lad. Therefore, apprehension may be restrained."

The brutality of this speech was softened, so to speak, by the familiar half smile which Templar already knew so well, but young Lister, his big mouth filled with cold ham and beef, managed a grin and said no more. He took it with an astonishing matter-of-factness, and, with one stroke, Templar marked him off the list of possible helpers in a time of danger. He had not the slightest doubt that the big young fellow would be able to fight like a hero if he were so minded, but also he was certain that he would not be so minded. Obviously there was not a whit of affection lost between him and his uncle, and this made the whole picture of that loveless soul of Condon complete. Even his flesh and blood turned to him only perfunctorily—for his money, never for his affection. The very heart of Templar rose against such a state of

45

affairs. Ay, it might be even worse—perhaps young Lister himself was enlisted on the side of the foemen, striving to cut short his uncle's days! Full of that thought, he had to give his full attention to the table, for suddenly it had become difficult for him to look either of his companions in the face.

After a brief meal, they stacked the dishes in the kitchen sink, threw cold water over them, and retired to the library. The big room oppressed Templar with a sense of shadowy places. He could not arrange himself so that all of the space was under his observation, but he took a corner near the fireplace, where a low fire was burning, and kept his eyes wide open. Condon was exactly opposite him, turning over the pages of a magazine; big young Lister, in the distance, was half lost in the darkness; only a pool of light from a table lamp made a shining white spot of his big book and his muscular hands.

"What carried the negroes away?" asked Templar, and he lowered his voice in spite of himself.

"They," answered Condon simply.

There was no need to ask what he meant.

"If something's to happen," observed Templar, "I should say that now is the time. You observe, Mr. Condon, that you're sitting with your back to a window?"

"A shuttered window."

"Shutters can be opened."

"I don't think that they'll try a gun attack again—I don't think it," said Condon. "The fact is, they're too

46

subtle to limit themselves to such methods; bullets are always apt to miss. Never mind the window, Templar. Shuttered, and the curtain drawn, as well."

Templar shut his eyes, threw the picture of the room on the screen of his mind, and studied it; then looked forth again. Something had altered, but he knew not what. His alarm was growing but he told himself that it was pure funk. Because the foolish negroes had been frightened away, that meant nothing. The time was appropriate for an attack hardly more than before. In any case, the black men never would have been of use in the moment of an assault.

Yet something in the room, somewhere, had changed.

He stared everywhere, could detect no change, and then thought that he noticed a faint sound of breathing. He listened more intently; it was the frightened, quick drawn breath of Condon himself. No longer did he look at the magazine, but instead he gripped the paper with a force that turned his thumbs white, and his eyes were turned on the fireplace. Great staring eyes they were, the pupils dilated, and Templar knew, and turned cold with the knowledge, that his host, for all his iron nerves, his steady ways, his marvelous self-control, his experience of men and affairs, his resolute facing of fact, now sat there before him in his room, before his own fire, a nephew at his back, an armed gunman nearby—and yet in a state of terrible, cold, remorseless fear!

CHAPTER VII

There was a loud, crackling, terribly prolonged noise—the turning of a page of Lister's book!

And Condon moistened his pale lips.

A nervous frenzy jumped up in Templar, like the fear of a child left in the dark; he wanted to rush somewhere, shout, cast open doors and windows, fire a gun, curse—

After all, there were the hardy men of that bunkhouse to be called upon. Ay, but as Condon had said, any one of those fellows might be the hired man ready for the purpose! And yonder Lister, busy with his infernal book, it seemed impossible that he did not feel something of what was electric in the air; in fact, Templar vowed that the smile on the lips of the youth was not drawn from his reading—who smiles when he reads law?—but sprang from the knowledge he possessed of something about to happen in that chamber.

Then another and more dreadful thought went home in Templar's breast like the cold opening of a door. How many nights did Condon sit here in this house, hour by hour in the mortal dread of death so terrible that it mastered his nerves, mastered his intelligence, his resolution, and left him a stone faced image of fear? No wonder that all humanity had been ironed out of his heart; a single such night as this was enough to do the same service for Templar's higher self, he felt!

Then double wonder rushed over Templar, for certainly there must be some more protected situation than this lonely valley among the mountains. No matter what Condon might say about his fear of numbers, it seemed to Templar that no man could possibly have chosen a place *more* open to attack and the approach of subtle enemies than this same house. Here it was, almost surrounded by the dark and secret arms of the forest; the unsearchable mountains lay at hand, into which the criminal could retire at once and be lost to the hunters; and every night this man of millions consented to sit here in the wilderness, so to speak, and endure the most frightful tortures of overstrung nerves!

Then an explanation leaped full born into the brain of Templar. He thrust it away; it came back and shouted to him. He could not away with it. Condon waited in this house, dared death, patiently endured hellish pangs of terror, simply because he *wished* for the coming of the danger which he shuddered at the thought of; he nerved himself to the crisis because from it he hoped to wring some golden event.

Ay, for grant that theory, much else fell into line!

For instance, ten armed men would keep off nearly any assailant, whereas one gunfighter—one Templar, say—might be an efficient help in the time of trouble, but his presence hardly would warn off keen, clever, bold, determined enemies such as were apparently in the lists against his host and employer.

Something squeaked, ever so slightly under the floor, as it seemed to Templar, and the small sound

49

brought from Condon a faint whisper that beat louder than guns on the heart of the fighting man.

"God—help me!"

Only that, through strained lips, as though he strove to fight the murmur back.

And that, somehow, unlocked the half frozen heart of Templar, for his pity for this tortured man became greater than his fear of the mystery. He leaned forward, about to say: "Man, you're killing yourself in this way of living!" and then he saw something from the corner of his eye—not much—just the stir of the fold of one of the long, heavy curtains that covered the windows at the farther end of the room. A draft? Nothing perceptible in the currents of air at this end of the room, but perhaps some finger of wind came through the crack down there. So he told himself, but he knew that he was wrong, and that a human agency had moved that curtain—there, just to the right of the straight line between him and young Lister.

He bowed his head as though contemplating the floor; he thrust his hand inside the breast of his coat; a perfect attitude of reflection and thought, as it seemed, and yet all the while, looking up through the sunburned lashes of his eyes, he could stare straight down the room and study the movement of that curtain while his right hand firmly clutched the butt of a revolver. God bless the ghost of Wild Bill, or whoever it was that invented the spring-clip to hold a gun beneath the arm!

Then that dreadful whisper of poor Condon came to him again:

"Templar—for Christ's sake—watch!"

As if he had eyes in his back, seeing with his raw-edged nerves the same thing which Templar watched with his actual eyes.

The curtain had continued to move, though hardly more quickly, in the estimation of the racing heart, the racing mind of Templar, than the minute hand of a clock. No draught under heaven could move a curtain, slowly, steadily, in just that manner, No, no, a human hand, and at just the height at which a human hand would seize the curtain. He estimated the place with profound attention. The curtain hung in folds, a rich, reddish curtain, worked with some sort of metal threads, a sort of brocade, too absurdly extravagant for furnishing a dwelling in the wilderness. And Templar found time to deduce something else from the fact— there was a vast flaw in the education or in the brain of Condon, a lack of true culture, or a sense of humor.

Ay, but a little patch of those metal threads caught the light of Lister's reading lamp like the face of a tarnished mirror. A little patch about four and a half feet from the floor level, about a foot and a half from the edge of the curtain. If a man takes aim at a button because it lies over the heart, why not at such a choice target as yonder glimmering pattern of brocaded cloth?

The whole curtain suddenly shook, very slightly, and Templar swept out a gun to the full stiff length of his arm and fired, wide eyed, driving home the shot with the will power in his soul, sending it winging on a straight line.

He saw young Lister wince back and throw an arm across his face, while Condon toppled headlong from his chair.

But yonder, stifled a little, there was a gasping scream, such as comes from a sudden intake of breath; then the curtain was ripped from its upper fastenings and Templar saw a man lurch forward with a gun in one hand, steel-bright, and the crumpled curtain swept away to his left. No, he was not running, but falling, and as he fell Templar's gun was spitting long streaks of fire. He sent in two bullets, and he knew where they struck—once in the breast, and once somewhere between the base of the neck and the right shoulder as the dropping body came almost horizontal. Cruel work, but Templar was not tender hearted; terror is what leads to massacres, and Templar was very afraid, indeed.

The hammer-like impact of those last two shots—pounding, smashing, forty-five caliber chunks of lead—drove the falling man a little back. He fell on his left side, crumpled back close under the wall.

And Templar, crouched as he had risen from his chair, now sprang back against the wall, flattened himself against the woodwork, and swept the room with a revolver in either hand.

No, there was nothing more—nothing that showed itself, though he could have sworn that yonder man never came in to make such an attack alone, unsupported.

Lister was saying something, over and over again,

gabbling: "You've killed Uncle Andrew! You've killed Uncle Andrew!"

Condon, in fact, lay face down on the floor, his arms thrown out, never stirring from the position in which he had dropped.

"Damn Uncle Andrew!" snarled Templar, and ran the length of the room.

The fallen man turned softly on his back. He looked up at Templar with wide, bright eyes. "Good kid," he said. "Good kid—" And then the light was turned out behind his eyes, and he was dead.

Lister, by the fireplace, was leaning over his uncle. "Get back from him!" yelled Templar.

Lister sprang clear back against the wall, his mighty shoulders crashing against it.

"Get back," said Templar again, "and never come that near him again, while I'm watching you, you toad. Condon—d'you hear me?"

He waited. If Condon was dead—

No, he turned on the floor, like a prize fighter stirring out of a knockdown. He got to his knees, his feet, and then came staggering down the room. Nerve force, not muscles, was moving him.

"Which one was it?" he was muttering, and then, as he saw, he dropped down beside the fallen man and stared earnestly into his face.

"Larry!" he called. "Larry." Then: "My God, my God, it had to be he!"

CHAPTER VIII

Condon, rising from beside that fallen man, said suddenly to Templar: "We can't touch that body till the sheriff has a look at it; we can't move it until he comes. Munroe, send a puncher in to get the sheriff, or go in yourself. Templar, I'm going to lie there on that couch and sleep—I think—sleep, sleep, sleep!"

He groaned out the words with the voice of a sick man, and then, like one fairly overcome and drugged by exhaustion, he dropped on a couch at the side of the room and covered himself simply by dragging up a rug and pulling it over him to the breast. He lived up to the promise of his words, also, for his eyes closed, and his regular breathing began at once, faintly stertorous from utter weariness.

"He's all out," said the nephew, and sat down on the edge of the table to light a cigarette.

Templar raised a hand to cheek the talking, but Lister waved the caution away: "When he's like that, he'll sleep like the devil. You couldn't wake him with a gun and a drum—"

"Templar!" shouted Condon loudly.

He sat up and stared wildly around him.

"I'm here!"

"That's all right, then. That's all right, then. Only, don't you go away, don't leave the room. Don't leave me alone—don't leave me alone with anybody. I'm—going to—sleep—"

He was off again before he had finished the words, and young Lister observed in his usual half studious, half impersonal way: "Guilty conscience, you'd almost say."

To this, Templar returned no reply, but he began to look about the room. Behind the fallen body of Larry and the pool of blood which had gushed from him, the torn down curtain revealed that the shutters had been furled quietly back. Match-light showed that the hinges were fairly dripping with oil, still; which explained how the maneuver had been executed so noiselessly. Then the window had been treated with liberal quantities of oil, also. From the sill to the top the runways of the sashes had been drenched with lubricant. Then, since there was no draft, no sign of wind on that side of the house, it had not been difficult for Larry to make his entrance. As for his long pause behind the curtain, perhaps it had not been a tithe as long as seemed to Templar, waiting in dread at the farther end of the room.

He made the shutters fast again and turned to regard the dead face once more. Larry was not old; certainly he was not young. He would be somewhere between forty and fifty, with the look that is called "well-preserved," meaning that the years show through an envelope of physical fitness. Of middle height, strong shouldered, narrow waisted, he looked an athlete; and the death smile had a most natural look on him. No doubt he was a good-natured man—so good-natured that he even could give a word of praise to the gunmanship of his slayer as he died.

Templar looked to the rest of the windows and their shutters. He drew back all the curtains, so that the light shone clearly upon them, and in that fashion he could keep every apparent place of ingress under his eye.

Young Lister, during this time, remained seated on the table, calmly looking about him; he was so matter of fact and at ease that Templar was almost surprised that he had not taken to his book again, quietly running through law cases, while a dead man lay unregarded in the corner of the room.

Then Templar came back and took up a final post, his back turned to Condon, and his eyes restlessly traveling over the rest of the room.

"You were told to get the sheriff," he suggested dryly to the youth.

"I'll get him, plenty of time for that. I don't suppose *that* will be running away. You *are* a fighting man, Templar."

The latter shrugged his shoulders under the compliment.

"What I've been waiting to say," went on Lister in the same half genial, half noncommittal voice, "is that you spoke to me a bit roughly a while ago. Now, Templar, you may be poison in a fight, and of course everyone has heard a great many things about you and your doings. At the same time, I have to tell you that I box a wee bit myself, and if you use that voice to me again, we'll have to do something more than talk. I hope that's clear!"

No malice in that speech; simply a calm statement of a fact; and Templar for the first time felt a touch of liking for this big young man. Indeed, he was not so very young—he must actually be a year or so the senior of Templar himself!

So the nephew left the house and Templar was alone in the big place. His nerves were much steadier; nevertheless he could not endure having even a sleeping man at his back, so he shifted to a chair at the head of the couch and waited there a cold and lonely number of hours. Twice he threw wood on the fire and watched it burn down again; the mountain air, damp and chill, slipped into the room imperceptibly, and everywhere, except in a brief radius of the fire, the floor was icy, the air was devitalizing. So he kept his right hand warm and flexible under the cover of his coat. Nothing mattered, so long as he could do that.

There was plenty for him to think about—the last touch of quiet manliness in the nephew, for instance—and then there was the collapse of Condon under the strain of that terrible moment. Very interesting, that! You can't draw a man as thin as that in an hour or a day; but for a long time fear had been beating the steel of Condon's nature thin, and at last it had cracked across. Ah, it was very well for him that Larry had not found him alone in the room with his nephew!

However, there was a good deal to be thought about Larry. In the first place, he was probably about to attempt a murder. In the second place, he was about to attack two men, both of them armed, to say nothing of

Templar himself. And no matter how brave Larry might have been or how expert with weapons, it was hard to believe that he would have attempted such great odds unless he looked for help. Perhaps a second man was about to come in through the window—perhaps he had hoped that Munroe Lister would lend a hand—

So Templar sat in that cold room and listened to the dreadfully loud ticking of the big clock in the hall. The sound seemed to draw far away, marching up the stairs; then it promenaded back and forth; then it advanced with loud and regular click of heels straight up to the door of the room where he sat with the sleeping and the dead man. In short, the frightened imagination of Templar was taking control of him, as if he had been a child of six. He jumped up and could have shouted for joy when he heard, in the gravel just before the house, the loud and distinct crunching of the hoofs of horses.

As a key fitted into the front door, he glanced at his watch, and he saw that morning was not far away. Then voices, and the sheriff stood at the door with a file of men behind him. Young Lister closed the rear of the procession as the sheriff entered.

The man of the law paused and looked first of all at the face of the sleeper.

"He's had hell!" he commented softly. Then he went on to examine Larry.

Everything that he did was very perfunctory. He asked Templar to recite his version of the affair, and he made a few notes. Lister already had told the story; Condon would not be troubled.

"Plain as the nose on your face, of course," said the sheriff. "Of course that gent came in here for burglary; didn't know that there was a pet tiger in the house."

He chuckled and tapped Templar on the shoulder.

"You got the gift son," he explained.

Then he had the body carried out to the waiting buckboard, and the party rattled away down the drive.

"You better turn in—I'll hold the fort," said Lister with a sudden touch of kindliness in his voice. "Think of the old man sleeping through all of this trampling and jingling of spurs, and what not! You go up and turn in. You're beat!"

Templar thought that was good a time as any to make his viewpoint clear, so he said: "Thanks. I'll show you my hand. My job is to keep trouble from Condon, but how do I know where trouble's coming from? I don't. So as far as I'm concerned, I got to look on you as a point the wind may blow from. Sorry. But besides, there's the morning beginning, and you haven't closed your eyes. I'll keep this watch to the end!"

To this speech, young Lister made no response beyond a shrug of his big shoulders; then he left the room, and his heavy step went creaking down the upper hall, when Condon opened his eyes.

"You gave away a trick, there," he said with irritation. "Don't do that again, Templar. That was a fool's speech—to let Lister know that you were watching him in that manner. Besides, it undoes—"

He paused, with a click of his teeth; then he sat up briskly on the couch and yawned, stretched himself, straightened his cravat. He began to look steadily at Templar.

"It took something out of you," he commented. "Took enough out, that one night, for you to understand why my nerves were gone. But now I've had a night's sleep and God help the man who thinks that I am today what I was yesterday! Now, you go to bed."

"Where will you be?" asked Templar.

"I'm quite all right, now. Go along."

He followed Templar to the door and there touched his arm.

"I have bigger chances, now," he said quietly and rapidly. "Much, much bigger chances since that fellow is gone. It may be that I'll live the month through, and if it's managed, I tell you that I'll make you a rich man, Templar. Now go to bed and sleep on that!"

Templar followed orders perfectly. When he reached his room, though the little square skylight he saw the heavens turning rose; chill, pure air filled the chamber, and hope began to rise like a fountain in his spirit. Five thousand dollars was a tidy little fortune; at least it was the cutting edge which any sort of hammering could drive through to a goal. So he fell asleep, wrapped in a blanket, and all his dreams were sweet.

CHAPTER IX

There were new faces at the house when Templar got up. Notably there was a new house boy, a mozo with an eager, cheerful face, ready to do anything to please, but cursed with an inability to do anything right. Condon pointed out both features of the new employee's character to Templar, when the latter came down the stairs, and then he suggested that they go together and look over the cook.

"It's a woman," said Condon. "When Snyder got into town, he found that those two infernal niggers had spread such strange reports around Last Luck that nobody wanted to hire out; nobody was broke enough to come to a 'murder house.' They called it that before your work of the evening, my boy. What will they call us today?"

However, Snyder had been able to get this Chinese woman, although she had no recommendation and although she could speak only a few words of pigeon English. He also got the young Mexican mozo, who was in town too short a time to hear any of the gossip.

So, tapping at the rear kitchen door, for he and Templar had been walking in the garden, he cast the door open and asked for some meat scraps to give to his setter.

Then Templar saw a tall girl covered to the chin by a great white apron, with nothing very feminine about her except the slender, round wrists; her bare forearms looked strong enough to swing an axe or bulldog a two-year-old. She was a golden, handsome creature with the truly impassive Oriental face. She brought some scraps in a wooden bowl and lifted her almond eyes as the bowl was taken. She did not exactly look at Templar, but rather at the entire universe of which he happened to be a portion, and he thought there was no more life to her glance than to a pair of painted eyes—badly painted ones, at that. When he went off with Condon he said frankly: "What do you say, Mr. Condon, about that cook?"

"Fine looking thing, eh?" said Condon absently. "I never saw the kitchen looking so clean. She's the northern strain; they're better than your Shanghai, Hong-Kong Chink. If they're dirty, they're filthy. If they're clean, they keep everything white. She's all right."

"She's got almost the look of a man," said Templar seriously.

"Stuff!" said Condon. "Don't go about with a pocketful of suspicions. I've gotten so that I can't help being that way. I'll confess, when I saw her, she reminded me of someone. But you see what a fool fear makes of a man! The person she reminded me of was white and never was in China in his life!"

He paused, taking the arm of Templar. He said earnestly: "That man is my fear! That man is my engrossing fear, young friend. That man, before thirty days, will have come and gone. God keep me alive before—and God keep me alive afterwards."

62

Plainly he referred to the man of whom the girl reminded him, and Templar would gladly have asked more, but he felt that questions were useless.

The rest of that day, he made himself more and more at home about the house, and amused himself in the afternoon by chasing away three adventurous news gatherers and smashing the cameras with which they had taken fresh snapshots of the "desperado, John Templar."

The evening was quiet, distinguished only by an excellent dinner which Snyder served in from the kitchen.

"We have a good cook, at last," said Condon. "A good head on your shoulders, Snyder! But how d'you make her understand?"

"Make gestures and signs, sir. And she says: 'Plenty queek!' That's about all that she can say! But she's a female chef, sir!"

Then they sat by the fire, where young Lister was again at his book, and Condon and Templar pleasantly discovered that they had a mutual interest in pinochle. There was only one touch in the evening that seemed at all memorable to Templar, and that was when Condon asked suddenly: "When you opened up with your gun—at the same time that I fainted, like a fool—tell me what my precious nephew did, will you? How did he act?"

Lister raised his big head and blinked behind his glasses.

"Lister winced a little. Only a little. And the bullets

63

were flying inches past his face."

Condon turned in his chair and regarded his nephew without warmth.

"Ay," he said, "that's about the way that he would act. That's about the way!"

One would have thought that he had heard something most unworthy, most defamatory of the character of the youth.

Otherwise, nothing happened, and with the good dinner as a bright spot in his mind, Templar went up the stairs behind his employer, saw the latter shut his door, and himself turned again into his bunk.

There was not a disturbance in the night, and in the beauty of the morning Templar was out again and selecting a horse at the stable. He and Condon had agreed that, while the latter went to Last Luck on necessary business, he should carry on intensive exploration of the surroundings of the house so as to be prepared with a more intimate knowledge of the valley and the hills in case of necessary flight or pursuit.

After breakfast, therefore, he got a lunch of meat sandwiches from the new cook and departed on a high headed chestnut, full of high feed and small work. His arms were aching from the constant pull before he got to noon of the day. By that time he had worked up through the woods, sifting through the trees on a line west of the Sugarloaf until he came to a more open wood on the top of a ridge. Water broke out in a clear little spring from between the roots of a big pine, and he determined to have lunch on the spot. So he loosed the girths of the saddle and sat down with his back to the tree his rifle at his feet, and the lunch in his lap.

He remembered, then, that it is possible to make neat and effective temporary drinking cups of bark, so he went off to fashion one, and came back in time to see a squirrel dash up the trunk of the tree with bread in its mouth.

"Hard times!" grinned Templar, watching the flight of the robber. "No nuts even for honest workers!"

The cup required still more manipulating before he could use it, but he took his time to it, and at last it served well enough. Then, at last, he sat down to his meal and took up a sandwich. A wild chattering broke out above him, and he looked up with a smile. Yonder robber, apparently, protested against any further consumption of this treasure of food. He could see the little creature on a low branch, jumping up and down, then clinging suddenly to a twig, and all at once it dropped through the air. It was the typical fall of a squirrel, the great tail fluffing out and catching the air like a parachute and arms and legs spread out to press further against the air. It landed softly enough, and yet instantly it curled into a knot, and twisted round and round—then sprang up and bolted straight for Templar.

He got to his knees, amazed, almost alarmed. This was squirrels madness, to attack a man in such fashion! However, he was not the form in the eye of the squirrel, which came to the spring and thrust in its head to the eyes. It drank, paused, drank again, and then keeled over suddenly on the lip of the tiny pool. Its legs worked as though it were running on a treadmill. There was one shrill scream of pain and protest, and it was dead.

This was distinctly odd!

He leaned to examine it, and in the stiff bristles of the moustache of the little animal, near its mouth, he saw two or three breadcrumbs lodged—

Horrible, swift suspicion rose in the soul of Templar.

He rolled up the lunch and hurried straight down through the trees until he came to the edge of the open meadow. There he paused, eyeing the distant house gloomily.

The death of a squirrel, after all, was not much to go on. A crow called hoarsely overhead, and half a dozen of the black fellows flapped heavily out of the nearby trees. Here, at last, was another chance to experiment, and therefore he cast two of the remaining sandwiches on the ground and rode to a little distance.

Such an offering could not be overlooked. Back came the little flight of birds, settled, quarreled and screeched in contention over the prize, and presently the sandwiches were gone and the five clumsy birds were stalking about, looking for crumbs, scratching as though they hoped to find another such feast just under the ground.

"There's nothing wrong, and I'm a fool," said Templar to himself, when one of the crows, with a loud cawing, rose from the ground and flew rapidly for the nearest trees; but it lost balance mysteriously and crashed among the branches, dropped to the ground, rose again, and disappeared with another toppling flight over the heads of the pines. The remaining four seemed to have waited for the result of that flight, before they rose in turn, with a great outbreaking of noise, and they flew away. Three darted off in a straight line, but the fourth suddenly curled up in mid-flight, dropped, and struck the ground like a stone, rebounding a little. Templar, like a guilty murderer, rode to examine, and found that the crow was kicking itself slowly around in a circle, already dead, with muscles still faintly reacting. Now it lay still, and he had all the confirmation that even a court of law, per-haps, would want.

Back towards the house he went, then, a savage and avenging spirit, and as he rode he shuddered He had faced hands and knives and guns in his time—but this!

He came smashing up to the rear of the house and threw his reins. The chestnut, not broken to that maneuver, instantly ran off with a squall of pleasure at its freedom, and Templar kicked open the kitchen door and strode inside. The new cook looked up from a kneading board on which she was working at a white heap of dough.

"Here," commanded Templar. "You eat!" And he took out the remaining sandwich. "You take eat—savvy?"

He advanced close, full of gestures, and at last the dull black eyes understood.

"Plenty queek!" said she, and placed the poison instantly between her teeth.

CHAPTER X

No doubt the actions of Templar had not been those of a perfect gentleman before; now, however, he was outrageous. His fingers, hard as supple iron cables, struck the golden hand of the girl from her lips; the bread and meat sklithered away on the floor and disappeared under the stove.

"By God," breathed Templar, "if you didn't do it, who did?"

The cook said nothing. Perhaps all he had said and done was sheer mystery to her, but at any rate, now she remained looking down at her hand, on the back of which a red place was swelling.

Templar grew terribly humble.

"Sorry," he said. "Frightfully sorry. Bread poisoned, you understand? Food poisoned. Kill pretty quick. Savvy? I—damn it! Don't you know anything?"

"No savvy," said the cook, and her black leaden eyes paused on his and waited.

"If you didn't do it, who did?" asked Templar, and threw out his hands in a wide gesture.

He went first of all to recover the remains of the sandwich, now dirt stained beneath the stove. He wrapped this first in a paper and went into the pantry, where he found Snyder polishing silver. The butler did not rise, but merely nodded familiarly at Templar.

"Snyder," said the youth, "did you give the cook a hand fixing my sandwiches this morning?"

"That's her job, not mine," said Snyder.

"You didn't touch them?"

"Why should I?"

"I'm asking you a question, will you answer?"

Snyder rose slowly to his feet, an impressive form of wrath.

"You—" he began, and then paused to formulate his speech.

"Templar, when Mr. Condon's around, I gotta talk small to you. I gotta serve you at the table. But outside of that, I want to tell you that I'm as good a man as you are, or maybe a damn sight better. You and your guns, they don't bother me. And if you ever was to pull a gun on me—why, I'd make you eat it. Now don't you come swelling up big around me again. Get out of this here pantry!"

Templar left.

He was surprised at himself, and yet there had been something very impressive about the indignation and the pride of the butler. Besides, what could he prove? And if Snyder were scoundrel enough to poison food, then he certainly was also clever enough to conceal the fact that he had done so. If he had poisoned the bread or the meat of that lunch, he would be the last one to admit that he had handled it at all. Even if they could get the word of the cook against him, how could she support herself against him, she with her paltry half dozen words of the language!

Instead, he went straight on into the garden, and walked up and down there, seeing, as he passed the library, the intent face of big Lister, bent over one of his eternal books. Condon came back in his whirling runabout inside the next half hour, and he received the tale of his guard with a grave and quiet attention.

"It's the Chinese woman," he declared. "Snyder—I don't know, of course, but I don't think that he would do it. As for her—"

"She's out of the question," declared Templar. "She had it in her mouth, I tell you; I had to move fast to knock it away from her lips!"

At that moment, they saw her carry a basket of wash into the back yard, where she hung it out on drying lines, singing all the while with a not unpleasant voice, but using a strange tune which seemed little related to music to the listeners.

"She's forgot me manhandling her," said Templar impulsively. "By God, Mr. Condon, that poor girl—makes my heart turn over for her! Working here like a dog—strange country—strange language—no friends—"

He was recalled from this speech and this emotion by the cold eye of Condon, fixed steadily upon him.

"We'd better have none of that," suggested Condon, and Templar flushed.

"She's only a poor damned Chink," he defended himself.

"After all," replied Condon, "I don't think that women have any nationality—primarily!"

He told of the obsequies of Larry. They had been short and simple. Condon himself had bought the

70

coffin of rough pine boards, had hired the men to dig the grave, had written the inscription to be placed on the headboard: "Here lies Lawrence Harmon, who died suddenly in this city."

Condon smiled as he quoted.

"You knew his name?" asked Templar.

"There was a letter in his pocket," said Condon, but he looked Templar in the eye in rather an odd manner, as though wondering all that might be passing in the mind of the younger man.

"I don't mind the other things," said Templar at last, "but poison, that beats me, I admit!"

"We'll send the woman in immediately. We might file a charge against her, and the sheriff would jail her for a month or so."

"Let her stay; I'll keep an eye on her," urged Templar.

"How?"

"I'll find a way."

He found a way and a most simple one.

Beyond his chamber were two vacant rooms, and one of these stood over the kitchen. A knot had worked loose in the upper layer of floor boards, and, when he drew it out, he found that he was staring down through a capacious crack in the secondary level of flooring. In this manner, he was able to survey only a small amount of the kitchen, to be sure, but above all he could look into the mirror. For just opposite the door there was a mirror of some size. It was set into the wall, for this room, originally, had been intended as a dining hall, and after being used for that purpose it had been altered for a kitchen. The mirror remained, and, staring down into it, he could see what it reflected. It showed him a part of the door, now open except for the screen, and beyond the screen there was a faint vista of trees and sky, and one shoulder of the barn in the distance. The central portion of the mirror gave the watcher, from his angle, the stove and all that passed before the stove, and the right hand section of the mirror reflected the sink. Now, for the purposes of Templar, that mirror could not have been placed more providentially.

Lying comfortably at full length at his place of espial, he could watch every movement of that new cook, whether at the sink, washing pans, or at the stove, cooking. She was at this moment putting into the oven a pan filled with little round tubes of paste, stuffed with chopped chicken and pork; and the mouth of the observer watered as he looked at it.

Such a cook could not be a poisoner!

Rising, she was seen to inspect the back of her hand, where the iron fingers of the white man had struck her with such unnecessary force; she shrugged her shoulders and went over towards the sink, while Templar found himself tempted to shout out an apology and explanation.

He spent more than an hour spying on the girl, partly because it was, of course, important to learn what he could about her, and partly because he was fascinated by the grace with which she moved, and the strong, active, slender hands. Her speed was her most amazing characteristic. The brown hides of potatoes flew away at the touch of the knife, and glistening, crystal white balls were dropped into the pot for boiling; carrots were scraped and chopped small as by magic. But in all that the watcher was able to observe there was nothing that seemed in the least unlike the actions which one would expect from any able and industrious cook.

He plugged up his spy-hole with a sense of shame. That was a thing he would try no more! There was even a blush on the cheeks of young Templar as he slipped noiselessly back towards his room—softly, softly across the floor of the vacant chamber—then a careful hand on the knob of the door—

He opened it and found himself face to face with Snyder.

The latter did not wince back. Instead, his face turned a dark wine-red with anger.

"Snooping and spying around!" he said savagely. "You got more ferret than man in you!"

It made that terrible right fist of Templar jerk into a knot of iron, but he did not strike. There were enough enemies of gun and knife and poison; the hostility of a foolish butler simply was not worth taking into account.

He heard more of that incident almost at once, for, just before dinner, Condon told him that Snyder had complained of the manner in which Templar slipped around the house, subtle, soft footed, evil of manner.

73

"You trust that man?" asked Templar aggressively.

"I trust no one," snapped Condon, with what might have been a double meaning. "Snyder a little more than others, perhaps."

"Then I'll tell you my opinion. Snyder poisoned that food while the cook was preparing it. Snyder's a bought man, Mr. Condon, and you're not the one who has paid the price for him!"

He hoped to make some impression with this statement, but Condon simply nodded.

"Very likely you're right," he said. "However, we can't discharge everyone. Cooking is a dreary business, Templar, and so is serving. I don't suppose that you'd care to undertake it, would you?"

That ended the argument, and shortly after they went in to the dinner table, Lister trailing in late, as usual, stuffing the last notes he had taken into his pockets. It was rather a more cheerful meal, that evening, though there was one grim innovation. Condon's pet setter sat by his chair, and, before any one was served from any dish, a morsel was given to the dog, and there was a pause of a few moments.

He showed no ill effects of the food, however, and the excellence of the cookery brought even Lister's tongue into play, while he described events of the last Crimson rowing season. He was in the middle of an eight-oared race, with a failing stroke reeling before the coxswain, when there was a heavy knocking at the front door. Snyder hastened to answer the summons, and came back with a slip of paper.

"No one there, sir. Only this."

Condon sprang up, snatched the paper, and unfolded it. What he read made him drop back into his chair again, and there he leaned forward, gripping the edge of the table, his eyes closed as though to shut out a vision.

CHAPTER XI

Condon hung in his place for a moment only. Then he looked straight before him, narrowing his eyes like an engineer who drives his engine through a mist of fog and of weariness, with red danger somewhere ahead, if only it may be seen! At last he stood up and beckoned to Templar, who followed him from the room, his glance being towards Lister, who was calmly finishing off a second helping of the meat balls.

"Are you ready, Templar?" he asked.

"I'm ready," he said.

Condon nodded, and hurried upstairs; what it was Templar should be ready for was not explained, but he took it for granted, readily, that he must be prepared with every ounce of wariness, attention, and fighting spirit. So he employed that moment in looking to his two Colts, and in getting the Winchester from the hall closet where the guns of the moment, so to speak, were kept in hand. A span and the runabout trotted to the front of the house before Condon came down, hurrying on his overcoat and looking straight before him.

"There's no use delaying," he said to Templar. "We'll go right on and face the music—better quick than slow, better soon than late, eh?"

It was clear that he hardly knew what he was saying; it was also clear that he was in the bluest of funks. And yet that was not the word, but rather he was gripped by the most mighty terror against which he fought back bravely, and was able to keep his head up.

He sent the high bred span shooting down the driveway and on one wheel he settled them down the valley road; over their heads the branches of trees brushed, reaching down with many fingers. It was very dark, for the sky was loaded with cloud masses from the south, forced up and congealing to thick rain-mist in the higher air.

"Look at the sky," commanded Condon.

"It's filled with clouds," answered Templar.

"Take the reins; let me see!"

Templar gladly took the reins, for it was pleasant to let his muscles work against the struggling heads of the pair; it was better than thinking and wondering and trying to paint the future out of nothingness.

"It's filled with clouds," echoed Condon, "and I don't think we'll see the moon tonight. What do you think, Templar? Do you think we'll see the moon?"

"I don't think so. Not unless the wind changes to the sou'west."

"Do you think it will change?"

"I don't think so; it hangs steady in the south for a couple of days, usually."

"Now thank God—thank God!" murmured the other. This was in a whisper which was not intended to be audible, but at that moment they had rattled off a hard surface into dust where the hoofs padded softly and the wheels went hushing along. So Templar heard. There were various reasons why a man should be glad that the moon would not show, but, so far as he could see, there was no reason that was honest or good. Ambushers, sneaks, thieves, murderers, cowards and villians of all kinds pray for dark of the moon or clouds in the sky, but honest men love the light. He, Templar, was an honest man, and the joy of his honesty now filled his heart, filled his veins, filled his strong young soul with a stern exultation. The least tip of his finger never had been stained; the least whisper never could be raised against him; and he willingly would die before these things should be. So, strong in his scorn and in his self-satisfaction—for all good people, men and women, are cruel—he sent the span shooting down the road.

Not fast enough for Condon, who snatched the reins with an impatient exclamation: "This isn't a pleasure jaunt, young man. We're trying to get somewhere!" He used the whip; it merely forced the pair to break, and then he sawed at their mouths to bring them back to a trot.

"You haven't the touch for driving," he complained sharply. "You've thrown this pair out of their stride—confound it Templar!"

Templar was silent, as one is silent when a young

child complains; Condon wanted to fly, and horses can't do that, but this pair was panting and heaving and foaming as they drew near to Last Luck.

"I think this is the place," said Condon, and began to draw down the pace. "Now, Templar, listen to me. I'm going down this lane until I'm between the two big trees, there, just in front of that half built new hotel. You see?"

"I see."

"You get out and stand at the head of the horses. Mind you, if they prance and dance a little bit, it won't matter, so long as you keep drifting a little closer. You'll be ready for action every minute. I'm going to be standing there between the two trees. I'll be talking to someone, perhaps more than one. Now look ahead. Compared with the shadows of the trees, it looks fairly light, doesn't it, along the lane. Not moonlight, thank God, but something that *you* could see by. Listen to me, Templar. If there is anything extraordinary, if there is so much as a loud shout, or if I should suddenly drop to the ground, you begin to shoot. D'you hear me?"

"I'll do nothing of the kind," answered Templar, in disgust. "If I see anyone trying to do you harm, I'll stop him if I can. But you can count on me never budging unless that's the case. I'm not a murderer, Condon!"

"You—you—" stammered Condon.

Suddenly he flung out of the runabout and went up the road, his hands in the pockets of his overcoat, his head down. The darkness was so thick that he disappeared almost at once, and then reappeared once more nearer to the trees. The unfinished hotel, with its wall of pale, new sawn boards made a light background against which, as Condon had said, all objects in the road stood in some relief.

Templar got out of the rig and, at the heads of the horses, his left hand holding the reins close to the bits, he strained his eyes ahead. Plainly he saw that Condon was not moving any longer; no other shadow moved out to meet him; there was no sound of a voice. To make sure of that, Templar dropped on one knee, listening. He remained in that posture. If shooting became the order of the night, he would be firing from a steadier rest.

It must have been a quarter of an hour before the other came. It looked a big man, striding out from the shadows under the trees; it was a big man's voice that rolled and boomed softly through the night. Then Condon answered, quick and high, his accents very rapid. It was all Condon after the first moment. When he paused, a few deeply murmured words replied, then Condon was at it again with a decided air of protest and excitement.

During this time, Templar scanned the trees, probed the woods on either side, looked even back under the body of the runabout, lest anyone should be slipping up on him. Finally Condon came back to him, almost on the run.

"Get in! Get in!" exclaimed Condon, and leaped into

the carriage. He was already turning before Templar could spring into his place, and then they whirled out of the lane onto the open highway again.

The return was at a slower pace, the span being whipped to a gallop at first, and then allowed to make their own way, until at last they were merely dog-trotting down the road. Condon was leaning forward, bunched, the reins slack. He spoke only once, and that was as they came back close to the house.

"Templar," he said, "if I could have counted on you—if I could have counted on your straight-shooting gun—if you would have backed me up like a—like a man, tonight the whole business would have finished. You'd be rich tomorrow. I would have made you! I would have made you! You threw it away—you threw me away—threw away the work of my life—put my back against the wall—because you wouldn't shoot a damned—"

His voice trailed into a murmur, but Templar could not make out the words, and he hardly wanted to. They left the rig at the barn and as they walked back towards the house, he said: "I've failed to please you, Mr. Condon. Also, this job has failed to please me. Suppose that we part company? You'll owe me nothing, and I'll jog back into town. My own mustang is in the stable, now."

Condon merely chuckled.

"You think that I'll let you go?" he asked through his teeth. "I have your promise, my lad, and I'll keep you with that, to the last of the thirty days, by God!"

80

That ended the talk; but it filled Templar with the keenest scorn and disgust. He felt that he never had disliked any human being so thoroughly as he disliked this cold-hearted maker of money.

In the hall Condon turned on him again; he was very glad to have lamp light by which to study the older man, and never had he seen such a picture of marble despair.

"There'll be a few days of rest for you," said Condon. "Three, four, maybe five days of rest for you. Take things easily. Relax. Nurse your strength. Have your nerves as strong as steel. There'll be no trouble during that time. Mind you, there won't be so much as an eye-brow raised against us. You hear? After that, hell comes. Get ready for hell, Templar!"

Condon went straight up to bed, but Templar went into the living room and sat by the smoky cheerless fire; the unflagging Lister was still at his books.

"You keep on," said Templar dryly, "and you'll be president before you're thirty."

"Thanks," grinned Lister. "I think so, too!"

And he was deep in his book again, sliding smoothly over the interruption. It occurred to Templar, not for the first time, that if Condon wanted protection he could hardly have asked for stronger, cooler men than this nephew of his and Snyder, the butler. Both, at least, had been willing to challenge him freely and openly and boldly.

Suddenly Lister was at the fireplace. He had come like a shadow.

81

"The old man's in the last ditch, I suppose?" said he. Templar looked up and said nothing.

"And you're sticking with him through everything?" went on Lister.

Templar shrugged his shoulders.

"You poor fool!" said Lister, and went back to his book.

CHAPTER XII

Templar was like a boxer who, in the midst of training for a championship bout, is told by his trainer to relax and put all care out of his mind. How could he relax, knowing that "hell" was coming? How can a sailor relax, when the water to the north is white under the coming storm? And they were like sailors, committed to storms, and now drifting through a spell of calms.

Thinking was no good; the tangle in which he found himself was so complete that he determined to thrust everything to the back of his mind and take what chance brought to him. To employ himself, he again went exploring on the following day, and forced his way far north across two ridges towards the Sugarloaf. On the top of the second ridge he looked down upon a valley dotted with cattle, and on the farther slope a horseman was riding. He swung his glass into action and made out the undoubted form of Condon journeying still north and north with the steadiness of one who has a purpose. He could guess what that purpose was—to ride away from a danger which he could not shake off.

A little warmth of pity rose in the heart of Templar, and all the way back to the house, he brooded over his employer, his force, his cunning, his wealth which undoubtedly was made and not inherited, and this great and powerful machine now threatened with ruin!

Undoubtedly there was evil behind this; the resolute silence which Condon maintained concerning all his secret affairs proved that his hands were not clean, and yet it seemed to Templar that it would be a relief if he could take the whole burden on his own strong shoulders.

Lister had gone to town; Condon was not expected back for lunch, since he had taken some food with him; so Templar ate alone, under the sneer of the big butler. He stirred restlessly under it for a time and at last his anger grew greater than he could control.

"You hate serving me, Snyder," he stated.

"You got an eye for facts," scoffed the butler. "The way you see through things—"

"Let me see your hand," suggested Templar.

Snyder held it out in the form of a fist.

"Look an' admire," he said.

"I admire," nodded Templar.

He reached out and tapped a low, blunt ridge on the back of the hand.

"Broke all the metacarpals, Snyder, eh?"

The butler snatched his hand away.

"And what in hell is that to you?" he asked.

"What round was it in?" asked Templar curiously. "And who was the young fellow that beat you?" The butler was black of face, now.

"What's in your empty head?" he asked with a brutal violence.

"That you're an ex pug, my friend. You broke those bones swinging on a hard jaw, or a stiff set of ribs. Or else you crashed your hand into an elbow. You were a clumsy boxer, Snyder."

"You lie," said Snyder, turning from lurid to crimson.

"I don't lie. A hard fighter, but a bad boxer."

"Young feller," said the big butler, his nostrils flaring, "I never was knocked out in all my days."

"I've known others the same way," remarked Templar. "When they saw it coming, they preferred to foul the other man."

The glance of Snyder jerked aside and rested on a long bladed carving knife as though he yearned to snatch it up; then he retired behind his powerful self assurance, his huge and well disciplined muscles.

"This is yarning," he said. "You guess. You don't know nothing."

"I soon will," lied Templar. "I've sent back your snapshot to a few sporting editors. Maybe they'll recall something."

Snyder, beginning a retort, changed his mind; his lips remained parted and gave him a peculiar, gaping expression. But then, as one who finds the milling too hot, he turned and retreated through the door. He did not return to carry the desert to Templar, but the tall, golden faced cook brought it, her heelless slippers shuffling with a soft whisper on the rug, and hissing on the bare floor.

He watched the long, slender hand holding the dish while he served himself, and then, as she retreated, he sat for a time with his eyes half closed with reflection. Snyder presently reappeared in the doorway.

"Even a damn Chink is too damn good to be serving you," said Snyder.

No doubt it was foolish to badger this dangerous fellow, but Templar could not help baiting the bull.

"Snarl awhile, growl awhile," he advised. "But you're too old to win even with a foul blow, Snyder."

He snapped his fingers and waved them towards the floor, as though a great form were already stretched there.

"I got a set of gloves," panted Snyder. "My God, wouldn't I like to have you standing up to me for just a two minute round? Only a two minute round, kid!"

But Templar laughed and left the room with the butler raging: "A yella dog, too! A damn sneakin' dog!"

It was not, after all, mysterious that Snyder hated him so, for there are men who, like bull terriers, cannot help curling their lips and showing their teeth. He tried to be sorry that he had enraged the man so thoroughly, and yet in his heart of fighting hearts, he was glad. For he told himself that, before this affair was untangled, he would have one good go with Snyder; he would be dodging those burly, half-broken fists, and trying to reach the blunt chin.

He lay on the couch in the living room after lunch, vaguely aware of the clumsy mending of the curtain which Larry had torn down, vaguely aware, too, of the light spot under the wall, where certain stains had been scrubbed away with much soap and boiling water. The stains were gone, so was paint and varnish.

He dozed awhile, wakened with the sound of wheels biting the gravel of the driveway, and found again in his mind the reflection which had come to him when he was being served by the cook.

Through the window he saw that it was young Lister who had returned, humped on the seat, his head thrust forward, the reins dangling from his hands; certainly the boy made no effort to appear graceful. He lived for one thing, it appeared—law.

Then, because the sun was bright and warm, because an eternal shadow lay within the house, Templar sauntered forth and found on the stretch of lawn behind the house, Lister and Snyder in their shirt sleeves, working with Snyder's gloves. It made a good bout, Lister plunging in gallantly, Snyder standing back with professional skill and stopping every rush with machine like straight lefts, or sidestepping in a way that made Lister flounder ridiculously. When Snyder saw the other, he lifted a gloved hand to stop his opponent.

"There's a young gentleman that might want some of this," said he.

"Not at all," answered Templar. "Not at all! You're

much too clever for me, Snyder."

And then he laughed again, mockingly. No one understands true mockery except the young, and the contempt in his voice made Snyder rage again.

"Put 'em on!" he begged. "Mr. Lister, get him to put 'em on. Now, we've heard a good deal about what he can do!"

Lister grinned maliciously.

"He's had a chance to use his eyes," he said. "He won't put 'em on!"

It was as though someone had held old wine at the lips of Templar. He could not resist beyond a certain point. Now his coat was instantly shed.

"I don't want to," he said as he tugged on the tight gloves, working the laces home. "If you were in your prime, Snyder, it might have been a go. Not now. However, I'll make it short."

All this calmly, mockingly, until Snyder came at him like a bull.

"Look out! Give a man warning, Snyder!" called the angry voice of Lister.

But Templar needed no warning. This was his kingdom. Guns were well enough; wrestling had its place; but to stand hand to hand and fight was a God-given joy. He ducked under a smashing hook and sank his left hand in the body of Snyder. Then he stepped back and studied the writhing face of the big fellow. Lister, in an ecstacy, danced around them.

"My God, what a punch! Templar, you're the real thing. Now, Snyder, make a fight of it!"

"I'll kill him," said Snyder, and feinted for an opening.

A ramrod left beat on his forehead and jerked his head back; a short right thumped on his ribs as on a drum. And Snyder backed up, falling into a crouch.

"Mind you," said Templar pleasantly, following, "if you hit low there's no referee except King Colt!"

"You dirty blackguard!" said Snyder through his teeth.

And then he leaped suddenly in with an overhand punch that fanned the cheek of Templar. Had it landed, he knew it would have fanned him into a far country indeed, but he had put his head aside from it and stepped in with a rising right. Solidly the hand went home beneath the jaw and jerked Snyder upright on his toes, his arms swinging wide.

"I could," said Templar through his teeth, that terrible right hand poised again, "but I won't—remembering your age, Snyder!"

The latter was walking backward, as though drunk, his knees sagging, his head rolling.

"Oh, lovely left—oh, beautiful, beautiful right!" cried Munroe Lister. "Templar, for God's sake teach me something, will you? You—you could be the champion! I never saw such a man!"

"He's old," said Templar cruelly. "Tell the brute that when he comes to. And you take the gloves."

He was stripping them off when, glancing over his shoulder, he saw the handsome golden face of the new cook at the kitchen window and a bright smile on her lips; she stepped instantly out of sight.

CHAPTER XIII

Buttoning his coat, regardless of the panting and curses of Snyder, who invited him to continue the bout, Templar fell into much the same reverie which had occupied him at the luncheon table. He started back around the corner of the house, but at the kitchen door he suddenly turned in. Hat in hand, he leaned against the jamb and regarded the cook. Her hands were feathery with flour for she was rolling out a slab of biscuits on the kneading board. She dusted them clean and came to him carrying a glass of water.

"I don't want water. Savvy? Don't want. Carry away. Not wantee. Damn it, I won't drink it—whish!"

At last she seemed to understand that refusal and went away, while Templar sat down in the corner and rested his elbow on the edge of the drain board of the sink.

"I've dropped in to have a little chat, honey," said he. "And to begin with—no, no,! I don't want a glass of milk either. No wantee—no likee—keep away, will you? I've come in for a little chat, you savvy? Talk, talk!"

"Talk, talk?" echoed the girl in musical singsong. Then she raised her large, slant eyes to Templar, to the world beyond Templar.

"No savvy," said she.

"You will pretty soon," he grinned at her. "If not English, what d'you talk? Something, my dear, more than Chinese—if you talk that!"

She dropped him a couple of low bows and returned to her work at the kneading board.

He beckoned to her: "Listen to me! What's your name?"

"Name?" said the girl, pausing, lifting the dull eyes.

"Yes. What you call? Name? Monniker? Isn't that clear? Name!"

"Ah," said she, and she showed a generous row of teeth, wonderfully white, flashing. "I cook. Work plenty hard. Work plenty queek. I cook. I good cook. I ver-r-ry cheep. I cheep cook!"

This speech was delivered with a crease between the eyes, a frown of intellectual effort, after which she waited with her fingers anxiously interlaced and her head canted to one side.

"You are a good cook," he admitted, "and a quick cook. As good a cook as I ever ate after. But what else are you? Who are you? Where born?"

Light struck into the painfully listening eyes.

"I born all same Hong Kong."

"Where born?"

She repeated it. Then he understood the singsong of the name, coming so quickly that it was hardly two syllables—just one breath of music.

"Hong Kong, my foot," said John Templar. "More likely Richmond, Virginia, or Atlanta, Georgia, or New Orleans, all by itself. Let me tell you something, honey. I'm a kind man. You wouldn't think it, after you've watched me whacking that big Snyder, though he had it coming to him. In the meantime, let's toe the line. Let's hew to the line, as a matter of fact. Where were you really born?"

She gave him the wonderful smile again.

"Yes. You savvy? Born Hong Kong, I. Plenty queek! Yes. Thenk you!"

"Plenty queek," he parodied, "but not yesterday. Oh, you're a beauty. You're a lamb. You're a beautiful golden lamb, my dear, but you weren't born yesterday, nor the day before, for that matter."

Her face lighted. She poured a cup of coffee and carried it to him, presenting it with a curtsy, and holding the cup in both hands, with her charming smile behind it.

"I'll drink it to keep you quiet, honey," said Templar. "I don't want any sugar. Thanks. No sugar. Can't you understand?" he shouted. "No wantee sugar! You keep!"

At last she was persuaded to carry the big sugar can away; but her expression was again anxious and hurt. He regarded her with a thoughtful frown.

"If I'm making a mistake," said Templar, "I'm also making an egregious ass of myself. But I don't think I can be making a mistake. Because, look here! Do they follow boxing in Hong Kong? I think not! Are they fans out there? I think not, again! But when you looked out the window, yonder, a moment ago, you'd been taking the show in and having a grand time out of it."

He pointed, and the cook, trotting in her hissing

slipper across the floor, carried back to him a large slab of Tanglefoot Fly Paper which rested on the sill of the indicated window.

"No—damn!" said Templar. "No, no. Take away. Don't want. No wantee!"

She put back the paper in its former place, looking back at him over her shoulder; then she retired to the kneading board and made a little bow to ask permission to resume her work.

He nodded; she began to cut out biscuits with a rounded tin. But after every one, she glanced hurriedly up to him, as though in fear lest he should be making a demand for her to execute.

"Either," said Templar, "you are gilded China wood, or else you are twenty-four carat gold. I think you are gold, you little actress. You understand every word that I'm saying, and after I'm gone, you'll laugh at this monologue of mine. Well, laugh, my dear! You will have earned the right. In the meantime, I continue to do my own thinking. I've had Chinese girls go by me before today. Usually they smelled of opium and cheap tobacco, like their papas. But you honey, were all clean soap and lavender water. Do they take kindly to soap and lavender water in Hong Kong?"

"Hong Kong? You likee?" asked the cook, pausing in the act of slipping the biscuits into a great wide armed black baking iron.

"Sure I like you, Hong Kong," said he. "I like you a lot. And if I had a chance with a scrubbing brush and some soap, I think I could fade you in five minutes to a color that I'd like a lot more."

"No savvy," said the anxious girl.

She passed a hand across her forehead, and then looked at him again, as though the effort in striving to penetrate the unknown language were beginning to tell upon her.

"All right," said he, and stood up. "I've done all the leading in this first round, but I think you win on points, nevertheless. So long, Hong Kong."

He went towards the door; the hissing slippers followed him and he turned to find her behind him, offering the untasted coffee with a wistful eye.

He took it. And as he raised the cup, her eyes followed; she smiled with pleasure as he drank.

"You are a darling, Hong Kong," said he, handing back the cup. "Twenty-four carat golden darling, guaranteed for life, with a Swiss movement."

He returned the cup.

"You likee?" she asked eagerly.

"I like you a lot, Hong Kong," said he. "You make me dizzy, beautiful. D'you like me?"

"Plenty queek," said she, and hurried back to the stove.

He saw her refilling the cup, and then he fled.

But he was smiling as he fled; his face was hot; pleasure bubbled in his heart like new wine in a vat.

"I'll never be a bachelor, by God," said John Templar, and, turning the corner of the house, he ran into Munroe Lister, purple of face, puffing and panting.

"Snyder gave it to me, after you left," said Lister. "I

tried the things you did. But I couldn't get away with them. I've had lessons. I've worked out a lot in the gym. I can knock the boys about, but Snyder makes a child of me, and you paralyzed poor Snyder. You've been in the ring, Templar. Tell me—you've been in the ring?"

His eyes burned with a sort of happy curiosity. All of the sneering and the scorn were gone; he looked simply an open hearted boy, a handsome, good-natured boy. Templar was amazed at him.

"I've never been in the ring," he declared, and then immediately admitted, "but I used to visit training quarters pretty often."

"My God," cried Lister, "what a lovely left you've got; and what a beautiful right. What a poisonous beauty that right hand of yours! I'd give my heart for half of what you have up your sleeve. At that, I suppose you could have hit him harder?"

"No," answered Templar frankly. "I couldn't, possibly. He has a jaw of iron."

"Jaw of iron? Why, man, you know him! That's Kid Snyder! He was in the ring for eight years. Never knocked over, and you had him groggy in two seconds. I never saw anything like it. I never dreamed of anything like it!"

"He's getting old," answered Templar in explanation. "He's slower, and more brittle. He's well over thirty. That counts. Everything over thirty counts double, in years. In the ring, anyway."

"Ay," nodded Lister, "I suppose it does."

94

They walked on silently, looking far ahead at the dim vision of thirty, that corner which is turned towards old age!

"I have to say something," said Lister, as they came to the door. "I talked to you the other night like a fool. I don't want you to take this wrong. I don't mean to say that I'd take from any man—only—"

Templar extended his hand. It was taken in a mighty grasp.

"I want to explain to you, some time; maybe we could have a bit of a chat," said the law student.

"I'd like that a lot. I'll be down around here by the time you've had your tub."

So they separated, and Templar went up to his room.

Instantly he was out of it again and had glided to the vacant chamber above the kitchen, where he lay flat on his stomach and shamelessly removed the knot.

She was opening the oven door; a cloud of smoke and steam rushed out and streamed to the ceiling; then the door was closed, and she passed from his sight beyond the sink.

Immediately afterwards a window closed with a squeak and a jar and Hong Kong came into view in the mirror carrying a broad strip of fly paper. She paused for an instant; her head tilted gracefully back; laughter rippled in the throat of Hong Kong, silent laughter which made her face beautiful.

Templar replaced the knot in the hole in haste. "Lord God," he whispered. "She understood every word!"

CHAPTER XIV

It became the most restless afternoon in the life of Templar.

And presently he found himself in his room going through the clothes which had been bought for him in Last Luck the day before. It had been many, many months since he had thought of such a thing as clothes, but now he was sharply aware that the material was cheap and that he was not fitted in any respect. As for neckware, nothing appeared except staring bandanas.

It was a gloomy John Templar who came down the stairs.

He found Munroe Lister already waiting for him, and walking up and down the veranda restlessly with a bull-dog pipe, such as the college boys of that generation affected. With boyish frankness, Lister plunged straight into the center of his discourse. He made only the following preamble.

"After you stopped, Snyder said he was only fooling—that he was just a little off-balance, leading you in. But I knew better; so did Snyder, and the dog tried to take his beating out of my hide. He pretty well succeeded, at that." Lister chuckled without malice. "What I liked," said Lister in continuation, "was not only what you did but what you didn't do. You had him spread out limp and you could have put that horrible right of yours straight through him.

Well, you didn't. I liked that!"

He paused, and puffed at his pipe, which was nearly out.

"I liked that a lot," he decided again. "Which rounds me up to the point. I've been hard on you since you came here. Now I'll tell you the reason. There's been some sort of trouble in the air—some sort of danger looking Uncle Condon in the face. He got you out as a special guard. I didn't see why. There was Snyder, and I was here too; we're both able-bodied. So you see why I took you rather hard. However, I was a fool. I think I can tell a white man when I see him. You understand? I had to tell you about it."

Templar thanked him; after his glimpse of Hong Kong and her laughter, he had begun to feel a particularly raw young ass, but Lister made him seem gratifyingly older, wiser.

"That's done, and we turn the page," said Templar. "For my part, I don't know a thing. I've been dropped into a pool of darkness. All that I know is what has passed in front of my eyes. Mr. Condon tells me nothing. Absolutely nothing!"

"He's always that way," sympathized Lister. "He's odd. He's very odd. I'll tell you what I know; and it isn't a great deal, either. Fifteen years ago, almost to a day, he hove over the skyline. I'd hardly heard of him before. I was eight, then. He dropped in at our place. We were poor people. My father was a one-horse lawyer with bad lungs. He barely could pull his own weight, and yet he had to tug along my mother and me, as well. You understand? Life was hell. Even when I was six, I'd begun to dread the first of the month. The bills came in then, you understand? I don't want to be unnecessarily frank; just to explain that when this strange uncle came along and took us out of the muck, he seemed to me like a fine edition of an old god. I wanted to worship him and I went on wanting, but I never could. He gave my father one easy year before he died, but, before he died, I was called to his bedside. He sent my mother out. He told me—Well, that he'd paid for everything for me—and for himself. You don't understand. Neither did I. But he gave me a sealed envelope and told me to read it when I was eighteen.

"I did read it. My mother died long before. Mr. Condon brought me up well enough. I could hold up my head with the other boys at school. Yes, and I'm grateful for what he did. Don't doubt that! Only— there was the stuff in that envelope!

"Well, Mr. Condon always wanted to know if I had learned anything from my father. I never would tell him, but it was what made me take up the study of law. I've studied ever since. Maybe you've noticed that I've studied pretty hard!"

He said it through his teeth.

"I've noticed that," said Templar.

"There you are, then," said the boy. "My uncle and I don't get on very well. You've noticed that it's easy to respect him but hard to be fond of him. Everybody notices that. I know that he's an important man. I

98

don't want to see him go down in the trouble that's staring him in the face now. But, Templar, I have an idea of what that trouble may be! I have an idea!"

He started up from his chair.

Then he paused.

"I don't think I'd better say too much," he said. "Because I only have a lot of half formed facts. Not pretty ones—I'll say that much. You're a white man, Templar. I want to be frank. But I have to stick there— just telling you that if I seem an unnatural brute with my attitude toward my uncle—well, I have a reason for it! Now, damn it, I know I've said too much, and yet I also know that I haven't said enough!"

"You've said enough to rub out a lot of wrinkles for me," replied Templar. "That's gain."

With knotted brow, the other continued: "I thought that I'd always sort of float on the edge of this whirlpool—this trouble, you know. Now I don't know. I may be tugged into the middle of it. I may find myself one of these days doing something black as hell—black as hell. I have it in me day after day. And—Templar, let's break this off. I'm going to go for a walk!"

He paused at the head of the steps and whirled about. "I simply wanted to show you that I'm a human being and not a snake."

Then he hurried off, stepping long and swiftly.

So the next and most unexpected knot had been put in the string, leaving Templar with a double complication. Lister turned out a proper young man, full of the right spirit, full of the right frankness and fight; but also full of danger. And the blackness of his brow as he declared that he was apt to be drawn into the center of the vortex before long impressed the other greatly.

Still he had nothing but the most irritating partial information to go on. From the first to the last, hardly anything had been told to him outright, but rather there was an astonishing mass of partial knowledge, hints, dark suggestions. Most of them had come from Condon, before this. Now the shadowy hands were beginning to point to Condon, too.

He felt like some investigator of the dark ages, who pries through the saint and miracle ridden chronicles, striving to get at the truth about earth, unconcerned about the truth of heaven which was exercising most minds in those far off centuries. So Templar was prying ignorantly at a mountain containing he knew not what—a core of terrible explosive power, he had no doubt, and yet dig away he must, or deny his name of man! He could have wished, in fact that Lister had told him nothing, or much more, except that it rehabilitated the youngster in his eyes.

He was still on the veranda, lost in broodings which had begun to turn from Lister and Condon to the cook, when Lister again appeared from the edge of the wood and hastened to the house. He was red, perspiring with effort.

"I forgot to say," he choked, "that for a good many reasons it would be better if you and I pretended not to have any use for each other. If he thought that there was a gradual approach between us, I have to say that it would be very dangerous, old man. Dangerous for me, certainly, and perhaps the finish of you!"

With that, he went back into the house, and Templar heard him exclaiming, just inside the front door: "Hello, Snyder! What you doing here?"

"Getting the dust off the floor," growled Snyder. "Always dirty here. Nobody ever will keep that front door closed!"

But Templar, with a sinking heart, was reasonably sure that Snyder had not been there for the sake of the dust. Quite another business had brought him there, and now Templar remembered that during Lister's talk he had lowered his voice most ineffectively. God had given him more than his share of vocal resonance, and he could not dispense with all of it.

If it were dangerous to let Condon know, Templar shrewdly suspected that both Lister and he were now apt to be within the shadow of that danger.

He went for a stroll as the evening came on. He walked to the edge of the woods and back, several times, and the day gradually darkened. Once he circled behind the house, vaguely hoping that the girl would appear, but she did not.

He had come closer to the barn, however, on this excursion, and therefore he heard the rapid rattling of hoofs, as a rider galloped hard down the valley and drew up with grinding of pebbles at the stable. He could hear the voice of Condon, sharp, clear, precise, ordering the horse to be well rubbed down and walked before it was fed. Then Condon came by him through the dusk.

"That you, Templar, wandering around here so vaguely?"

"It's I."

"Well," said the other, "this is the proper time of day for the training of weak eyes—or ears!"

He laughed in a harsh key, and stepped hastily on towards the house, leaving Templar half offended by the roughness of the man's tone and words, and half wondering at the change in him. This was not the voice of a despairing man; it was the tone of a fighter, ready for battle against any odds—the tone of a man sure of himself.

He went on slowly towards the barn, and there he saw the black horse which Condon had been riding during the afternoon. It was thoroughly done in, its shoulders and neck spotted with foam, sweat running in a stream from its belly.

"Head down, damn near dying," said the man who was working over it. "Man that handles a hoss like this, he don't deserve to own a decent blood-hoss like this one. No, I say that mustangs, and worn out runts, and cast outs, and wuthless pickups, they is good enough for him, and too good! And what for? For a pleasure gallop, maybe. For a little jaunt, eh? And kill a hoss or half kill him for that! You, Mr. Gunfighter Templar, you can go tell him what I said, too!"

CHAPTER XV

At supper it was apparent that Condon had found news, and good news, during the day, for he no longer gave the impression of a man with his back to the wall and no avenue of escape before him. Instead, there was a superior brightness in his eyes, like the eye of a boxer who looks for an opening, ready to strike. Lister noticed the difference, too; the whole supper table was cheered, and only Snyder was more dour than ever as he served the meal. Apparently his sporting instinct did not extend far enough to enable him to take defeat graciously, and, when he stood in the shadow behind his master's chair, he fixed Templar continually with a look of hate.

Condon talked about the lands in his possession which extended to the south across the edge of the plateau; he had looked down on them from the higher northwestern hills, he said, and wondered what that ground would produce if water were led out onto it. That brought on an animated discussion with Lister, who had read a good deal about irrigation and had a boy's love of romantic improvement of estates. Nevertheless, Templar felt that Condon had been lying; it was not possible irrigation that was in his mind, but something else—he had thrown out the topic merely to furnish a ready explanation of his high spirits.

Presently he fixed a glance on Snyder.

"What's happened to you, Snyder?" he asked.

"To me? Nothing, sir!"

"Is it nothing to collect a swollen mouth and a purple patch on the chin in one day? Have you taught Mr. Lister so much that he's beginning to hit through your guard?"

Snyder let his eye wander balefully to Templar, and before he could speak, Condon had read the answer.

"Not my nephew, but Templar, eh? Are you as clever as that, Templar? But Snyder's a professional—or was!"

He seemed extraordinarily interested over the outcome of a mere sparring match; his eye was hungry as he leaned a little forward.

"Snyder's out of training," answered Templar with modesty, "and he's slowed up a little with time. A man can't stay fast forever, you know."

"In your heart—be honest! You think you could have beaten him in his prime!"

Templar was silent; he never boasted, but after all, there is a point where modesty can be overdone, and that was exactly what he thought—that he could have cut the big butler to pieces, even in his ring prime.

"Smashing through Last Luck, that's one thing," observed Condon. "Beating my big man, here, is another. I thought you were invincible, Snyder!"

"We didn't finish," said Snyder, crimson with anger. "I was hit a little off balance—and Templar, he thought it would be a good idea to stop—"

Lister broke in; "I never saw such a hitting. Like a hammer!"

104

"Besides," said Snyder, "there's such a thing as a lucky punch!"

"Luck is what we all want, pray for, pay for," said Condon.

They talked of other things, but throughout the meal, from time to time, the keen glance of Condon reverted to Templar, and it was clear that something was turning in his brain; he seemed more sinister than ever to Templar because of this upwelling of high spirits. For still no reasons were given, nothing was told except a foolish sham about irrigation. Irrigation, when life and death were knocking at the door!

After supper, since the night was pleasantly warm, they sat on the veranda and watched the stars sifting up over the eastern trees, the eastern mountains, until from the rear of the house a strange melody rose—a woman's voice singing to a jangling accompaniment of some stringed instrument.

"What's that?" asked Condon, stopping short—for he had been walking restlessly up and down, humming to himself.

"It's the new cook, singing—playing her own accompaniment—if you can call it an accompaniment."

"That's right. It's pretty good music for a Chink," said Condon. "I can recollect, now, if you hear the coolies singing—half a hundred of 'em—it don't sound so bad over water."

He paused and listened. As soon as one adjusted one's ears to that odd strain, it was more than pleasant.

Templar listened with held breath.

"She's good—she's clever," said Condon. "Go get her and bring her along, someone. You, Templar, if you please."

Templar went willingly.

He found her sitting on the chopping block in front of the woodshed, and, though he came and stood just in front of her, she finished the long nasal wail she was in the midst of before she ended, and stood up.

"You want?" she asked.

"I want to take you to see the chief," said Templar. "Come along, Hong Kong."

"Hong Kong, you know?" said the girl, gladness in her voice.

Templar leaned above her, standing close.

"You made a grand fool of me, Hong Kong," said he. "But now I know that you understand English as well as I do. Cut out the acting when I'm around you, no matter what you do with the others. I'll tell you another thing, my dear. I ought to let Mr. Condon know how much more his cook understands than he thinks she does. But I won't. At the same time, I'm going to make an agreement with you: You stay here as you please, but you agree that you're not here to make trouble for anyone. If you keep silent, I'll suppose that you mean to make the bargain."

And a little breathless silence followed.

"All right," said he. "You better come along with me, then. Mr. Condon is waiting for you."

"Mister Condon want coffee?" asked the girl.

"Oh, damn it," groaned Templar. "Will you come along? Or are you going to stand me here in the dark and make an ass of me again?"

He took her arm, and, at that, she allowed him to lead her rapidly around the side of the house and to the veranda.

"Here she is," said Templar, and, stepping back, "Soap and lavender," he murmured to himself. "Chinaman my foot!"

Condon had come to the edge of the veranda, and there he paused. He was smoking a cigar, smoking it so rapidly that the glow made his pale, lean face come pulsing out of the darkness and fade away to shadows again as he talked. He spoke, though haltingly, in a tongue which had the singsong of Chinese, and the girl filled in every interval with a smooth and rapid flow.

Like music—like the music of running water was that voice to Templar.

"She's a Chink," he said to himself, bitterly, "damn it, she's a Chink, after all!"

Finally, Condon sent her away and resumed his walking on the veranda. He spoke not a word; neither did Templar nor Lister, for both of them were too overwhelmingly interested in the change in the older man.

At last Condon said: "She's Hong Kong. High blooded little devil, though. Father got his throat cut and friends smuggled her away. She was brought to Mexico, and she was smuggled across the line.

Worked out her pay for the voyage and all as a cook in San Francisco. Her mistress took her south to Phoenix. Broke up housekeeping there. The girl goes adrift. Comes to Last Luck by accident, more than design. And here she is. Now there's a story for you, Lister. Why do you use your spare time reading idiotic stories? Get into life, young man. Rub your elbows with life, and you'll come out with a good deal more excitement than you ever gathered out of a book. Books! Oh, damn books! You can't put the world into them. After all, they're nothing but linen and wood pulp with ink splashed here and there! A set of Shakespeare is not as big as a sapling and an ink-pot."

He enjoyed this speech of his and began to chuckle as he went up and down the veranda again. Sometimes he hummed, and again he paused, as though thoughts leaped into his mind and halted him like presented guns.

"Suppose that she made up that yarn?" suggested Lister unexpectedly.

"Eh? Suppose what? Nonsense! But if she's crooked, let it go. Better have her than another. She's not likely to cut throats at midnight, at least!"

And he began to laugh again, softly; it was plain that he was filled with self-content, he was bursting with it!

Almost immediately after this, he went up to bed and left the two on the veranda, where he flung this casual remark over his shoulder: "Be good boys, now; I don't want you strangling one another. And I half expect that!"

This kind thought kept him chuckling on his way upstairs, and when they heard a door close in the distance, young Lister broke out softly: "What a cad! What a rotter and a cad!"

"Sing a little," whispered Templar in his ear, and Lister, instantly, began to sing a college song—some nonsense about going down the field and winning glory and fighting for dear old Alma Mater, while Templar side-stepped quietly down the veranda and, coming to the front door, jerked the screen open and leaped like lightning into the interior blackness.

There was a gasp before him; then his shoulder struck a heavy body and he lay on the floor writhing and grappling with a powerful and skillful wrestler. Fury gave Templar eyes to see in the dark, as it were. When Lister came running, he found by the light of a match that Templar had a burly man face down on the floor, helpless, his hands worked up into the small of the back.

"Hold that light here—and get out from behind me!" snapped Templar.

Lister did as he was bidden. It was Snyder who raised a convulsed face from the floor and cursed them both.

"Now keep away from me. Lister," said Templar. "And don't get at my back."

"Damn you and your ideas," answered Lister, and slammed back onto the porch.

"Stand up," said Templar, and twisted a wrist of his victim.

Snyder stood up with a lurch and a groan.

"I'll have the carving of your heart one day, for this," he told Templar.

The latter made no answer, but keeping a grip with one hand, he leaned and fumbled on the floor; then he forced the butler before him up the stairs and through his own chamber to the door of Condon's room. The latter came at once—first opened the door a crack, and threw it wide. He was in a dressing gown, with a revolver glittering in his hand.

"This thing has been trailing me around the house," said Templar. "He stands in the dark and listens. Just now I stumbled over him in the hall and he drew this on me. Your orders?"

As he spoke, he dropped from his hand a heavy knife. The point stuck deep in the flooring and the blade hummed wickedly. Condon looked from the knife in the floor to Snyder, and back again.

"He came in at me like a devil—I slipped—he got me down by accident," growled Snyder. "Was I gunna let myself be choked by him? Of course I pulled the knife!"

"Run along, Templar," said Condon. "I'll handle this!"

"I'll run along," answered Templar slowly, "but I want to tell you a little piece that I have in my mind. If this hulk barges around behind me again—he or Lister, either—I'll take no more chances. I'm going to pull a gun on 'em, Condon. I'm getting a little tired; I wouldn't mind a vacation!"

He backed through the door and went softly down the stairs to the veranda, where he found Lister.

To him he said briefly: "I knew Snyder was working dirty politics for your uncle. He was spying in that hall. I heard his shoe creak as he came close to the door."

"Right," whispered Lister. "But is he spying for my uncle or for himself?"

CHAPTER XVI

Snyder himself came down to the veranda a few minutes afterward. He asked for Templar and, when the latter stood up from a chair, he said: "I have to apologize, sir; I took what happened today too hard—a man—he forgets what time does to him—forgets what it means to grow old—hates it—I apologize."

"That's enough," said Templar. "You've been a little hard on me, Snyder. Perhaps I've been a little hard on you. But we'll call this thing square. I've given you your warning. After this, I hope we'll have no trouble."

"I hope so, sir. Mr. Condon would like to speak to you, sir."

Templar went up to his employer's room, and there he found Condon sitting up in bed, smoking the last of his cigar, with a magazine on his knees.

"Don't underline Snyder," said Condon. "I've had it out of him and I dressed him down for it. You broke his heart when you beat him in front of Munroe, today. That's all there is to it. Will you believe me?"

Templar watched him. He believed Condon no more than he had believed in the apology of Snyder. It merely proved to him, finally, that these two were working together, not playing separate games. He no sooner had made up his mind on that point than all of his beliefs were shattered, for Condon beckoned him closer. He moved to the side of the bed, and Condon whispered: "The scoundrel has been spying on me all these days, Templar. But I have reasons for not sending him away. Walk in mortal fear of him, my lad. I have for weeks. But I can't let him go. Don't ask me why!"

Then he added aloud, as though he feared that someone might be listening even to the pauses in that conversation: "I haven't treated you as you deserve, my lad. I intend to begin now, however. By Jove, I don't think I even thanked you for the work you did when Larry came for my scalp. Well, thanks come at the end of the last act. That's the time for them. Now, to begin with, it's foolishness to keep you sleeping at my door, as you have been for the last nights. I've told Snyder to move you into a decent room, the best that we have. I hope that will make some amends."

Templar said good night and left. He found Snyder already moving his belongings from the little antechamber to an apartment down the hall—at the farther end of it, in fact. It was a big, cheerful room looking southeast across the stables and the barns, and

112

the high headed hills beyond. There he was given quarters, and he prepared to turn in at once.

Never was he more thoughtful than on this evening, for it seemed to Templar that the complicated situation was growing momently more and more entangled.

When he was half undressed, he leaned out of his window to breathe more deeply of the pure night air, and try to get the cobwebs from his brain, and, doing so, he heard the voices of Condon and Lister raised high in a fierce contention. Condon was cursing; he could make that out. And Lister seemed to be responding in kind.

A pleasant household!

He went back to his bed, but he could not lie down to sleep. Moths and other small winged insects were darting around the chimney of his lamp, and therefore he blew it out.

Left in darkness he lighted a cigarette, but allowed it to die almost at once, for there is little pleasure in smoking in the night. So, sitting on the side of his bed, he watched the line of the trees and the hills against the southern stars and devoutly wished himself out of this muddling affair. It was dangerous enough to frighten him, yet he had lived for danger, in a way, for a long time; it was rather the confusion that bewildered him and made him feel helpless. He had in his hands ten thousand clues, but he had no possible way of uniting them. The enemies of Condon and the causes of that enmity, the relation between him and his nephew, the peculiar status of Snyder, the coming of

113

the Chinese girl, the attempt by poison on Templar's own life, were all mysteries which he could not probe; therefore he became irritated and sleep left him.

The moon rose; the stars were put out save here and there a specially bright one; and a pale shaft of silver fell through the window, slantwise, into Templar's chamber. Idly he watched the crawling of the light across the fringe of the rug, and saw it glisten on the foot of a small table. Then he went to the window.

As he stepped to it, he thought that he saw a shadow move around the corner of the nearest shed; wood was stored there, he remembered. He would have banished the thought, but, almost at once, as he was in the act of turning away, the shadow appeared again, moving on from the shed towards the line of trees that skirted the meadows to the southeast. It was a figure wearing trousers, but not the trousers of a man. It went with a swift gait, jogging freely forward. Then the width and the flimsiness of the trousers—known by the manner in which they whipped about the ankles of the runner—told him that this was Hong Kong.

He did not stop to think. He was out the window in a moment, and, catching the drain pipe, he lowered himself swiftly to the ground.

Then he struck out in pursuit, turned the shed like a racehorse, and out across the meadow with the wind of his running sharp and cold in his face. If it were she, she was already nearing the edge of the trees. He gained fast, lengthening his stride, but when she entered the shadow of the forest he dropped flat, making sure that, once in cover, she would turn and glance behind her.

She did not enter the trees, however. Instead, he dimly made out her shadow as she moved along the edge of the wood. So he was up again, and, like an eager hound on the trail, he gained the shelter of the trees in turn. Thereafter, he had to go quietly, carefully, for there were ten thousand twigs scattered, and the cracking of one of them underfoot would be a warning to the pursued.

She disappeared around the next tree-corner; when he gained that place she was nowhere to be seen. Yes, for a shadow moved among shadows, deeper, much deeper in the woods—running rapidly away. Templar threw stalking and cunning somewhat to the winds and broke into a run in turn, keeping his attention focused well ahead. Twice he saw the fugitive, and each time the form was closer.

She was following a narrow path among the trees; it presently forked and he headed down the right fork at random when a shift of shadows, a ghostly glimmer, made him spring to the left—and Hong Kong was in his arms.

She had tried a last dodge that failed; then she had striven to writhe from his grasp with an amazing athletic strength. At that, he took her wrists in one hand and held her fast.

"You're coming back to the light, Hong Kong," said he. "I want to have a chat with you."

Without protest she followed. He held her under the

light of the moon and saw she was panting from her run but her eyes were the same dull black as ever, saying nothing.

"Hong Kong," said Templar, "you see that the game's over. You've played a good game and filled out your part well, but luck has been against you twice. Now we'll have some facts. We'll begin with your name, say."

Hong Kong dropped her head to one side and stared wistfully, searching for the meaning of these words.

"Otherwise," said Templar, "you go back with me to Condon, and there you can see for yourself what will happen. He's not a tender-hearted fellow, Hong Kong. He'd think nothing of having the sheriff toss you into jail. As for a charge, he would hardly have to lodge one. The sheriff eats out of Condon's hand. Is that clear?"

"No savvy," said the deep, sweet voice of Hong Kong.

"Then back you go!"

He waved her ahead of him, and slowly she understood. She thrust her arms into her sleeves and preceded him, walking with a step long and free and swift, like the step of a man. And in the moonlight he wondered over her and admired her. By the poise of her head and the carriage of her shoulders he read her strength and her lightness. Such a woman as this, with a pale skin instead of a golden, would have made the mother of a sea-king in an earlier age, or of a fierce, gay Norman.

At the kitchen door he paused with her.

"Now, Hong Kong," he said, "are you going to throw up the bluff and be reasonable?"

She merely waited, and the patience of Templar snapped.

"I could take you into the kitchen and scrub the yellow from your skin," he told her. "By the Lord, I think I will!"

He waved her ahead, and she laid her hand on the knob of the door turned it, stepped before him into the shadows—and jerked the door suddenly into his face. Another inch and the latch would have clicked, but he managed to thrust the door open and sprang inside. The room was white and black with the moon and with the night, and he saw her race for the farther door. One bound brought him up with her, and she swerved aside; his finger tips merely brushed the thin silk of her jacket, and, as he dodged after her, she swept up a silver-bright something from the table and faced him.

It was a massive meat-cleaver, new, with the sharpened edge glistening like a thread of fire in the moonshine, and she held it lightly, with an ample strength. The broad, light sleeve had furled back on her shoulder and in that round and golden arm there was power to drive home the blow.

It had no time to fall. His darting hand caught her wrist; his other arm grappled her close, drawing into the broad shaft of the moonlight the terror and the anger of her face.

"You damned little murderess!" breathed Templar. "You unspeakable devil!"

The cleaver thudded on the floor. In the close fold of his arms all the anger had left her; her head was thrown back, her hands pressed vainly against him, there was only desperate fear in her face.

He was trying to think—what should he do with her? Condon would have a way, but Concho's way was apt to be the way of a heartless devil, and even if she were a very witch for evil—

He could not think. His brain was stumbling, for he was breathing a light, pure scent of lavender that made him think of a garden under the moon. A light tremor was making him quiver—it was the beating of her heart!

He loosed her at once, and she slipped helplessly down in a chair, slumping a little to one side, her head still fallen back, still watching him desperately.

"Steady, steady!" said Templar. "Don't look at me like that. I—I'm not going to throttle you. I'm trying to think what to do!"

The door was open; a cold breeze was stealing from him the warmth that still clung to him where he had held her, and his arms seemed curiously empty.

"I'm trying to think," he muttered again.

Slowly she raised herself, her slender, strong hands gripping the edge of the table—

And then all at once, as at the snapping of the spell, she was herself. She slipped her hands into the alternate sleeves, and her eyes watched him with the same old dark, unfathomable gaze, half child, half woman—and a dash of something else.

It should have cleared his wits but, instead, they floundered more hopelessly than ever, and he stepped back nearer the door.

At that, she rose as if in answer to a signal and walked straight past him. He moved to stop her, but there was no force in his gesture and she went on under the moon straight across the field as she had gone before, as though she had put a spell on him and trusted confidently to its power.

He watched her, without the slightest will to move in pursuit again.

"I'll never see her again," said Templar to himself. "I'll never see her again!"

CHAPTER XVII

He went up the stairs from the rear of the house a step at a time, even pausing now and again. He knew that he could not make himself go after the girl, and yet conscience was fighting a powerful battle in his heart, since duty bade him, for the sake of the safety of Condon to which he was pledged, to follow every suspicion to the death, and surely more suspicion hardly could have been heaped upon one head that he felt for the girl.

Still pausing and moving by starts, he came up to the hall above and was about to turn towards his own door, when he saw another door open farther down the hall—Condon's door.

He flattened himself against the wall.

Out of that door came a slouching, cautious figure, with a ragged felt hat shadowing the face, a ragged coat hanging half way between the hips and the knees. The face he could not see with any clearness, for the hall lamp cast only the most uncertain light. He was only sure of a rather short, dark beard, raggedly pointed.

Two guns slipped smooth as oil into the hands of Templar.

"You there!" he called briskly. "What's your game?" The other crouched almost to the floor, darting a glance up and down the corridor. Then he snatched open the door through which he had just appeared.

"Stand tight!" cried Templar, and fired from both guns.

He had a difficult target, for the door was swinging wide in his line of vision, and the other was darting through it. But, as the guns roared thunderously down the hall, he heard the sharp splitting sound as the door cracked from top to bottom, and with it came a sort of frightened, gasping moan.

Fairly confident that he had tagged the fellow and would soon have him, Templar rushed down the hallway, burst through the broken door to what had once been his own chamber, and crashed against that of Condon.

In no other place could the fugitive have taken

shelter, and a grisly thought came to Templar that perhaps this was the night! Perhaps that room already was empty save for the criminal; and Condon lay dead—

"Condon!"

There was a sort of sleepy snarl from within the room, and then Condon opened the door a trifle.

"Mr. Condon, a man just got into your room."

"The devil!"

"Didn't you see him?"

"I heard two shots. I saw nothing."

"By God," groaned Templar, "this puts the tin hat on the horror! Where else could he have gone?"

He stepped back.

"The skylight?"

He stared upwards at it. A very powerful, athletic man, like himself, could barely have reached that skylight with a running jump, and so gained the roof.

"Nothing came through your room?" snapped Templar.

"Nothing!"

He took a few short, quick steps and, dropping his revolvers into his pockets, he caught the edge of the skylight. But when he strove to pull himself up through it, his shoulders stuck.

He dropped back to the floor with a crash.

"I don't think he could have made that," said Templar. "He didn't look an athlete. I *know* he couldn't have made it. Mr. Condon, he's in your room!"

He made straight for the door, almost as though he

would have forced his way in, but there he paused, for Condon had caught his arm.

"Now, keep out of that room, Templar!" he exclaimed. "You hear me? I'm in earnest!"

"And do you hear me?" raged Templar. "I nicked him. I know that I couldn't have missed him with both shots. I got him and he's left a blood trail somewhere. Condon, while you were getting your eyes open, that man got into your room—and right now he's probably slipping through the window—"

"Will you keep back?" cried Condon, suddenly in a wild rage. "Damn you, will you take your hand away from my door?"

There was a rush of feet down the hallway, and Snyder and Lister tore into the antechamber, filled with questions.

"It's all right," said Condon savagely. "This fool has been seeing ghosts and shooting at them, and now he says that they're lodged in my room. Will you get him away from this door?"

Snyder willingly laid his powerful hand on Templar's shoulder. Lister stood by, agape.

"Condon," said Templar through his teeth, "you've gone rather far with me!"

"I damn the day that I ever brought you to this house," exclaimed Condon. "You've been where you shouldn't be all the while. Of all the damned bunglers and idiots that it's ever been my bad luck to come across, you're the worst and the most stupid."

"All right," said Templar, "that ends our contract

with each other, I suppose?"

"Ends it? I wish that I could rub out the memory of you!" shouted Condon. "Get out of my sight!"

He turned his back, slammed the door of his room, and the three were left alone in the smaller antechamber.

Snyder began to chuckle contentedly.

"Youth will be served," he sneered, and then laughed again. "You'll be served—you poor sap!"

Templar backed up into the hall. His fingers were twitching as they worked at the handles of the guns which he kept in his pockets. Give a bloodhound the taste of blood and it is hard to drag him from the scent. So it was with Templar. He knew, or almost knew, that his quarry had taken covert, and he knew where that covert was, yet he was debarred from the pleasure of making the kill, and every nerve in his body twitched with furious eagerness.

He was almost of a mind to smash down the door of Condon's room by force and go on with his search. But valuable time had passed, now.

What was chiefly worth deciphering was whether or not Condon actually had seen the slouching figure run into his room; or had it been done, really, while the owner of the house was still drugged with sleep.

That appeared most unlikely. For days and days the nerves of Condon had been taut as hair-triggers; two guns had roared close by in his own house; was it not impossible that he should have been anything other than alert and on his feet in half a second?

There was only one other possible answer, and that was that Condon wanted to shield the elfish looking stranger from observation. If so, why?

"I'm well out of the whole damned muddle!" said Templar to himself, but in his heart of hearts he knew that that was not the truth. He wanted to stay with this business until the darkest corners had been flooded with light.

CHAPTER XVIII

Pride might have urged Templar to leave the house at once, under this valley of abuse, but instead, he went back to his room, followed by the sneering laughter of the butler. The hour was late, and pride might go to sleep until the morning.

He went to the window, before turning in, not to look out on the moonlit landscape, but simply to give himself fresh air and a chance to cool down his hot blood. There was something more than landscape to see, however, for at that moment the slender form of Hong Kong came up to the kitchen door and passed inside the house.

Templar sighed, and went to bed.

He woke up later than usual, with him. Ordinarily, the gray of the dawn was enough to open his eyes, but now he slept soundly until a strong yellow beam of light flashed on the wall beside his bed. He was up at once, bathed, dressed, shaved. It promised to be a hot day. From his window, he looked out and saw a mist of dust rising behind the barns, and he heard the shrill squealing of angered horses; the boys were wrangling some new ones, today, and all at once he rejoiced with all his heart that he was through with this house and the strange people in it, and the horror and the mystery which drenched every breath he drew in it. He wanted to be yonder, in the bright, burning sun, sweating, grunting, laboring, using all his muscles and little of his brain, and looking forward to the next meal.

He decided, however, that he would give the brutally insolent Condon an extremely bad time when they met this morning. A contract had been made with him, and it was not his fault that the contract was broken. But even in the honest and fiery sunshine, the conduct of Condon seemed extremely odd, for he was not a fellow to lose his temper; certainly he had reason for valuing Templar, and yet he had gone wild with fury for no good reason. His professional guard had attempted to save him from possible danger at the hands of a stranger in the house, and straightway all this abuse was poured forth.

He made up his pack, took care that nothing was left loose in the room, and went down to breakfast.

There was no breakfast to be had! No cheerful fragrance of coffee, no fumes of frying bacon sifted through the house; and he found young Lister seated in the sun with a book on his knee and a piece of dry bread in one hand, making a miserable meal.

"You're late, too," said Lister. "Everybody's late,

this morning, including the old man."

"What's up?" asked Templar.

"The Chink has gone. They do that, I think. Just slide out and let you stand with an empty hand. It was grand to hear Snyder curse."

He added in a quieter voice: "You're going, I suppose?"

"After I have a yarn with your uncle," grinned Templar. "I feel like making trouble."

Lister nodded.

"He'll patch it up," he said. "Last night—I never saw him act like that before. Like a child, I thought. Why should he have been so keen to keep you out of his room?"

"Nerves," said Templar.

They heard Snyder going up the stairs; they heard his tapping at his master's door, several times repeated. Then: "It's Snyder, sir!"

Again, louder: "Snyder, sir."

After this, the butler descended. He came onto the veranda with an odd look saying: "I knocked, I called; there wasn't any answer. I dunno that I care to knock any louder, sir. Mr. Condon never was a heavy sleeper before, that I know of!"

Lister looked intently at Snyder; then he turned to Templar.

"I've an idea," said Lister, "that maybe we'd better all three go up to that room!"

Up they went, suddenly silent and grave.

"When an exhausted man finally gets well asleep,

126

sometimes it takes a gun to wake him," suggested Templar.

There was no answer from either of the other two.

They knocked loudly. They could hear the echo of the strokes leap and die hollowly within the chamber.

"He hasn't gone out for an early ride?" asked Lister.

"The key's inside the lock," said Snyder. "I'll—I'll go down and ask at the stable, though—"

He hurried away down the hall.

Lister turned and shouted: "Snyder! Come back here! We'll have three present when we open that door!"

Snyder looked a sick man indeed as he came slowly back to them.

"You ain't meaning to smash the door down?" he asked.

"I mean that," said Lister, and, without more words, he produced a Colt and laid the muzzle of it to the lock. There was a crash of metal as the weapon exploded; then a thrust of the shoulder knocked the door open.

First Templar saw the heaped clothes on the bed, and across the pillow a long, wide stain of crimson. That stain reappeared on the gray of the center rug, pointing like an arrow to the corner of the room where the bathroom door stood ajar.

They looked at one another with pale faces.

"We'll go there together," said Lister huskily, and so they marched shoulder to shoulder to the bathroom door.

Inside it, beside the tub, lay the body, and Lister with a deep cry hurried forward and took the fallen man by the shoulders. He raised him, then let the form fall again and staggered back against the wall.

"His face—Templar—it's—it's gone!"

It was almost literally true. With brutal force, the dead man had been clubbed again and again. Only the long, lean, pale jaw thrust forth undamaged.

"We need the sheriff," said Templar. "I'll go get him."

"Let Snyder go," urged Lister. "Stay here with me. Snyder, ride like the devil."

And Snyder, as though already he had felt a spur, was gone at once. It left the two staring oddly at each other.

"We'd better go down at once," said Lister. "Better stay out of the room until the sheriff gets here—nothing should be touched."

They went down to the veranda and sat in the sun, smoking, silent, until Templar murmured: "I know one thing, I think. It was not the sneaking devil that I saw in the hall, that slid back into Condon's room."

"How do you know that?" asked the other sharply.

"I know it by several things—instinct, chiefly. I tell you, Lister, that poor cringing sneak never would have had the courage to do any murder, except by poison. I never saw such a worm of a man, and I only had one flash at him. He never could have—done that."

"I know who did it," said Lister suddenly. "And

you're right. It wasn't the man you thought got into my uncle's room. It was the cook, old man!"

Templar gripped the edge of his chair.

"You had the same idea?" asked Lister eagerly.

"Good God, no! Hong Kong? A woman do such a thing?"

"A woman, but a Chink. When they run amok, they're devils. And she had the strength, I tell you. Did you ever take a look at her forearm?"

Templar said nothing, for he was thinking of that silent moment of the evening before, and how the massive cleaver had been whirled lightly up in her grasp. There was the mystery of her identity, the odd night journey into the forest, her disappearance this morning.

"You're wrong," said Templar. "I know that you're wrong!"

"When we find that woman," said Lister, "we'll have the murderer!" He added: "I don't pretend ever to have been fond of him. But it doesn't seem possible that he's gone, Templar. I tell you, it doesn't seem possible that the machine has finished its work."

Templar said nothing at all. He was thinking of another ugly possibility. There was no good feeling between the nephew and the uncle. That very night he had overheard voices raised in a hot quarrel, and there was something cold and dangerous in this young man. Rouse him past a certain point, and might not anything result?

He put that possibility far back in his mind.

The girl, Lister—perhaps the big, brutal Snyder. Lister spoke as though he had been reading the mind of his companion.

"I thought that Snyder acted in a queer way," he said. "He didn't want to enter the room alone. He seemed to make up his mind right away that something was wrong. You remember that he turned back down the hall?"

Three possibilities, crossing out the furtive man of the beard, who made a fourth, and suddenly Templar said, helplessly: "Murder will out! I hope that old maxim proves true, but I have my doubt!"

They waited drearily. Two hours should have brought the sheriff; but three hours passed and there was no sign of him. They called a man from the stables and sent him in flying; it was after noon when the cavalcade finally arrived. It was the sheriff and four men behind him, and he came onto the veranda with a calm air, as of a man who approaches a thing long forseen. He merely said: "It happened, then?"

"It happened," said Templar.

Said the sheriff on the stairs going up: "That's what comes of going outside the law. I warned Condon. 'You stick to the officers of the law. The regular officers,' I says to him. 'We'll take care of you.' But he had to go his own way. A lot of big men, they're that way. Because they win in business, they got to have their own way in everything."

They entered the room, the sheriff first, walking slowly, humming a tuneless refrain through his teeth.

He turned back from his examination with a dark, dark face.

"Murder wasn't enough," he said savagely. "A knife or a gun wouldn't do. I tell you, there was a whole lifetime of hate went into that murder, young men! I'm gunna stay by this trail till I get the dog that did the thing. I'm gunna stay by it till I've found the man!"

"Snyder couldn't find you?" asked Lister suddenly.

"Not find me? I been in my office all morning. Of course he could have found me."

"Then," said Templar, "suppose you try to get Snyder first; it's plain that he's run for it!"

CHAPTER XIX

Resolutely, as a man shuts the door of a house and closes away what it contains, and forever, so Templar shut himself from the house of Condon and the murder which had been committed there. His resolution was the more violent, because he felt himself tied in many ways—tied to the solution of the mystery, to the puzzled and boyish courage of Munroe Lister, to the golden beauty Hong Kong, and above all tied by a sense of anger and shame because he had failed in the work which had been committed to his hands.

He said good-by to Lister, who plainly wanted him to stay but would not make the request in definite words; then he saddled and mounted his mustang and cantered away while the sheriff and the sheriff's men were still busily employed gathering "clues."

He thought at first of turning his back upon the entire district and not going near even the town; but after all, what he wanted was not distance or loneliness so much as a chance to bathe himself in human society of a kind different from that which he had found at the lonely ranchhouse.

He got into Last Luck at an ideal time, when the working day had ended and the night had not begun— that pleasant gap between the heat of the afternoon and the dimness of twilight when men let their burdens slip, discard their packs, and with a sort of weary good nature, smile even upon enemies.

And he went to Tabor's Rest House.

He could have made himself a center of interest at once; Tabor himself greeted him with a smile on his swarthy face and waded through the thickening crowd towards him.

"You're having a vacation?" he asked.

"Condon's dead," said the other shortly. "And I'm not here looking for a job. I want to creep into a corner and watch the fun. Is that all right?"

"I dunno," answered Tabor, "that we got any corners big enough to hold you, but try your luck."

It was not, after all, a difficult thing to do, for having seen Templar only in action, the crowd of Last Luck hardly recognized him in repose. Slowly he drifted here and there, and as he watched the happy faces come thronging in, and the restless, pleasure-hunting eyes, it seemed to Templar as though waters of Lethe were flowing sweetly through his soul and all the pain, the restless uncertainty of Condon's house was washed from his mind. He did not have to examine these fellows, wondering which was a murderer, which was a thief, which was a gullible fool and which a designing knave; he could stand by and watch, and give no heed.

He even took an odd, passive pleasure in being shouldered and elbowed to one side by men making for the bar. He was driftwood on the verge of the torrent.

Dusk came, the place was more closely filled; liquor began to work with a liberal hand on the occupants of the Rest House; and the more the noise rose and the flame of happiness burned high, the more content was young Templar. He had not tasted a drink. He wanted simply the repose of the observer. From the bar he passed to the dance hall, where the music was just beginning; from the dance hall he went into the gambling rooms and looked on untempted as the reckless hunters of fortune staked their gold; then back through the dance hall, and to the bar again where louder voices were continually rising. One announced that he was the old Colorado in flood, bringing down some pebbles to the sea, and hunting a chance to roar; another declared that the jolly world was only an olive and that he was going to drop it in a glass of Red-eye; and a third punctuated a debate with a bartender by a crash of glass. He had hurled a bottle into the glimmering files that stood empty or filled on the shelf behind the bar, and Templar, mildly amused, came nearer to watch the troublemaker struggling with the same four bull-dog bouncers who had trailed him on his last visit to this place of mirth.

He had a rear view of a mighty man whose shoulders were heaving in effort, and he could not tell whether the bouncers or the stranger were in greater trouble.

The doubt was soon dispelled. One bull-dog went down before the fist and one before the elbow of this magnificent rough-and-tumble fighter, and he finished the argument by picking up bouncer number three and hurling him at the fourth of the quartette.

This display left him master of the field; a circle of admiration had opened around the fight, and in the midst of it stood the victor, flushed, exultant, more than half tipsy, and now shouting: "Ain't there men enough in Last Luck to gimme a fight? Gimme any two of you and I'll tie me left hand behind me. Is there one good lad in the whole of the town?"

So Templar had his chance to see the face of the giant, and he made instantly towards him. Now someone spotted him. And an instant yell went up.

"It's Templar! Fight! Fight! Clear back here and let 'em at it!"

Joyous excitement swept the crowd; poor Tabor was seen vainly striving to break through and restore order; from the distance new spectators were thronging, women and men.

"Lemme see him!" shouted the giant. "Lemme have a chance at him. Clear away, ye scum! Why, it's only a little man!"

This to Templar as he stepped into the open space, and his answer was only: "Danny, you spawn!"

The giant threw up his great arms.

"Johnnie, is it you, me lad. Whisht! If there was only one day in me life, this would be it!"

And they fell into each other's arms.

"Come and likker," urged the big man.

"Danny O'Shay, how long have you been drinking?"

"Two days—two weeks—I dunno—but I ain't worked the moisture back to the roots of me tongue, Johnnie."

"How long since you've eaten food?"

"I'm above eatin'," declared O'Shay. "Likker is faster and likker is enough."

"Come with me," commanded Templar.

"Where?"

"Where I tell you. Come with me."

"Ah, Johnnie," sighed the giant, "I fear you're gunna dry me up."

But he strode gloomily at the side of his friend, and through the entrance to Tabor's Rest House, with Tabor himself breathing deeply with relief.

Down the street they went, with a sprinkling of lesser men at their heels, like boys following a circus. Then they sat in a restaurant long and narrow as the hull of a boat, which had been built in a rift between the general merchandise store and the only bank in Last Luck.

They began a mighty meal, for Templar was a wolfish eater, and he had gone since morning without taste of food, yet he had finished his steaks, his pie, his second cup of coffee and his first cigarette before the monster who faced him shoved back a platter which for the third time had been swept as by fire from end to end.

A fleet footed waiter dashed past with a stack of apple pies on his arm. The giant hand shot out and he scooped the top two from the pile. Seasoned with his fourth cup of coffee, they disappeared down his throat. Then he rolled a cigarette and leaned back in his chair, not with an air of repletion but rather as one who has fallen into a reflective humor.

He was one of those prodigies of manhood referred to in England as twenty stone giants. A two hundred pound athlete could have been carved from him, and there would have remained enough to make a jockey, afterwards. All things about him were gigantic. The ample ring of the coffee cup's handle would not admit the tip of his forefinger. A waist which no ready-made belt would surround was girded with a great, roughly hewn strip of rawhide. His coat had been cut vast beyond belief, and yet it did not allow sufficient play for the enormous piled muscles of his shoulders, so that it gaped at the seams. A battered and tattered giant he looked, and garbed as though he had picked over the off-cast clothes of a city of big men.

He was very blond, and desert-burned to a more excessive sandiness, so that the hair looked almost like the white of an old man's head, and his weathered skin appeared black in contrast.

"Now, me fine bit of shark's leather," said the giant, "me tough old sons, me old chisel-bit and saw-tooth Johnnie, why in hell are you in Last Luck? And why have you got two friends hanging back there in the corner—Don't look!—and keepin' an eye on you like you was a purse of gold on legs?"

CHAPTER XX

Some of the flush of pleasure of this meeting had been dissolved by the last remark; nevertheless, Templar shrugged his shoulders and answered: "I don't care who they are or what they want. Tell me first why you're not back there in the desert making yourself rich?"

"Because I love fun more than money," answered the big man, "and because it was a damn dull job after you'd pulled up stakes. But I'm tellin' you now about the two in the corner."

"How do they look?"

"Like rats at a piece of cheese."

"I mean, describe 'em."

"There's a biggish one with a fighting look and a pair of eyes in his head. He'd catch his fish with a red hot hook, I'm tellin' you. The other is more smallish and I

137

wouldn't have him in the small of me back, brother. A good hand for a knife. He'd cut his way home, if he was lost in a dark night, Johnnie. And now and again the pair of 'em roll their eyes at you. Have you been doin' harm in this town to any man, Johnnie?"

A little round pocket mirror placed at a proper angle showed Templar the two, and he knew at once that they were perfect strangers to him.

"I've never seen either of 'em before," he asserted.

"They've seen you, though," answered Dan O'Shay, "and they'll see you again, if they have their way about it! What do you say to them, me son?"

"Go out with me," suggested Templar. "I can talk as well in the dark—and they can't see as well, I take it!" So they strolled out of the place together.

"We'll stand here at the corner," said Templar, "because I'd like to have another look at those fellows. You've kept your hand in with your guns, Danny?"

"I've worked every day, but I ain't got the poison in me guns that you have in yours, me son."

"A man's head is bigger than a dime," said Templar philosophically. "You may need to use those guns for me."

"I knew it," chuckled the other. "I been knowin' it for days. The call come out to me as clear as the yappin' of a coyote on the edge of the sky, and I knew that there was hell risin' around you somewheres. But was there ever a time when you was catchin' fire? Talk, talk, you little skinny sawed-off stick of dynamite, and lemme know what's been happening."

Quietly and rapidly, his eyes half closed with the effort of memory, Templar told the tale of all that had chanced to him since first he entered Last Luck. They stood not twenty yards from the entrance to the little restaurant, at the corner of the bank, and twice the watchman in his rounds passed, stared at them, and then moved cautiously away again. Last Luck was waking for the night; the lights in front of the Rest House were turned up to full power, and, farther down the street, they could see the glimmer of Etheredge's place. Reduced to facts, the story went in a few minutes, and Templar ended: "Snyder, Lister, the sneaking stranger, or the Chink girl. I'd pick them in that order of probability as having killed Condon."

Far down the street, towards the northern end, guns began to pop, the explosions sounding far and small in the thin mountain air; voices nearby half drowned the shots.

"Maybe one of 'em maybe all four, tied up in the game and working it together," said Danny O'Shay. "Why not walk down to the sheriff's office and see if they're giving out news? I mean, after we've had a look at the two boys in the restaurant. They ought to of come out, by this time!"

They stepped back to the entrance and glanced in. Certainly the pair had not come out by the front way, and yet their table now was empty and the waiter was scooping up the dishes with a great clatter and rattling. The two had slipped out of the rear door, and O'Shay and Templar looked seriously at each other. Then the big hand of O'Shay fell on the shoulder of his friend.

"You've wrote down everybody in the house as a possible murderer." said O'Shay, "and what do you think that they've said to each other about you? Suppose that here's a pair of hired gents to watch you, partner? Come along with me to the sheriff."

"Damn the sheriff," replied Templar. "I'm willing to leave this neck of the woods, Danny. I'm willing to go back to the desert. If you'll march that way, we'll start now!"

The big man simply took his arm and guided him against his will along the street.

"Go where I tell you to go," said he. "I know you. Just now you're tired of the game, but by tomorrow morning you'd have your brain rested and your nerves in order. Then you'd be back on the trail. So come along with me!"

The sheriff's office was not closed in spite of the lateness of the hour. In fact, the office of sheriff in that county was often a lazy job by day, but it never failed to turn up a share of excitement in the hours of darkness.

The sheriff came out to them. He was very glad to see Templar, he said, and he invited him into the inner office at, as he declared, the special wish of young Munroe Lister, who expressed every confidence in him—wanted his assistance and advice. As for giant O'Shay, he must remain outside the office for the time being.

So O'Shay was given a chair in the hall and some old newspapers to read, while Templar walked into the office and there found Lister with a worried face.

The sheriff was the soul of frankness.

"This job will be the breaking of me," he said at once. "The richest man in the county has been murdered, even though he knew that the danger was coming before he was done for. The boys ain't going to keep me in office when things like that can happen off-hand, and I wouldn't run myself for dog-catcher, if I didn't work out this here trail. Up to now, the clues that I got are nothin'. But I would sure ache from pleasure to have a chance to lay hands on the gent that you shot at last night, Templar! There would be a clue and a half."

"Nothing has happened then?" asked Templar.

There was a groan from Munroe Lister. Yes, a great deal had happened. That morning the telegraph wires had been set to work getting in touch with the various known branches of Condon's widespread interests. Startling reports came back to the effect that for the last six months Condon had rapidly been selling out his holdings of every sort and converting his cash account into securities. All of these properties then had been dispatched to the bank at Last Luck, and, only the day before, Condon had driven in from his ranch and totally cleaned out his boxes in the safe, except for one paper, which proved to be his last will and testament. It might be that more would develop later, but at the present moment it appeared that

Munroe Lister was the sole heir of Condon, yet, of the millions belonging to the latter, nothing would descend to the young man except the ranch near Last Luck. Even this was burdened with a mortgage of nearly a hundred thousand dollars which, also, had been raised from the Last Luck bank within the last half year. The remaining value of the place might be perhaps an additional hundred or hundred and fifty thousand dollars, though it could not be realized at once. And of the whole widespread property of the dead man, this one comparatively small bone was all that came into the possession of Lister!

It gave the murder of the millionaire an added significance. As the sheriff put it: "This here is the damnedest, most outstandingest sort of a murder and theft that was ever done in the whole United States. There's near five million dollars that ain't accounted for. Where has it gone? Into the hands of them that killed Condon!"

Why had Condon, then, collected this gigantic fortune in one pool, when he knew that he was in danger constantly?

To that, there was only one possible answer: He had hoped that, if the worst came to the worst, he could flee and take his money with him. Or perhaps he wished to have a gigantic sum on hand so that he could buy off his persecuters.

To this pool of knowledge, Templar added what he knew, that Condon had also delayed his flight from his ranchhouse because something made him keenly eager to stay there, as he had put it, during thirty days. He told of the arrival of the note at the supper table; he told also of his trip with Condon to the verge of Last Luck and the interview with the man of the deep voice. The sheriff and Lister listened fascinated to this last recital, and Lister, with an exclamation, sprang to his feet.

"Find that man and you have the murderer!" he cried.

"And what of Snyder?" asked Templar. "Has he been found?"

"He hasn't been found," replied the sheriff, "but he's gunna be within about five minutes. He's gunna be found, because he's gunna come in here. Lister—we might as well show the whole thing to our partner, here?"

Lister nodded, and the sheriff placed in the hand of Templar a folded sheet of paper, within which he found written:

"Dear Sheriff,
If you'll promise me that I come off skin-free, I can lead you to the murderer and to the plunder. It's a risky business and I can't work at it alone. I got the most dangerous man in the world on my hands, but with your help, maybe we can manage him. If you'll promise me that I won't be held in jail, I'll come in this evening at nine and join you. You'll have to be ready for a ten-mile ride. If you put two lights in your window, it means that you accept.
                                          Snyder.

P. S. You don't want a crowd. Four or five would be the right thing—four or five that don't know how to miss a shot."

"And there," said the sheriff, are the two lights burning in my window. And it's nearly nine."

"I have one suggestion," said Templar. "If I'm to ride in this journey, I'd like to take along the one man in the world that I'm sure of. He's sitting outside now."

"The big man?" frowned the sheriff. "No horse in the world could carry him ten miles."

"He has the horse that can do it," Templar assured them.

And at that moment, a knock on the door announced a newcomer. The sheriff sang out, and Snyder stood before them.

CHAPTER XXI

No man could have presented a more perfect picture of restless guilt than the big butler and ex-prize fighter as he entered, blinked at the lights, and then spotted Lister and Templar. He changed color, shifted feet, cleared his throat, and then jerked his head back with an effort so as to meet the eyes that were upon him.

"Now, Snyder," said the sheriff, "we got your letter here, and it seems that you know something; you promise a lot. There are four of us here. I've seen

Lister shoot; we know about Templar's guns; he has a friend waiting outside; and I'll make the fourth man. Are you ready to ride?"

The butler turned with a scowl of hate upon Templar. "The rest will do—if you think Mr. Lister is man enough. But him—why him?"

He jerked his head towards Templar. The sheriff broke in: "If you don't want our best fighting man, what sort of a job have you on hand?"

"You'll have no luck with him, that's what I mean," said Snyder. "But if you're bound to have him, take him along and be—"

He stopped himself.

"I'm ready to go," said he.

"Will you have something to eat before you start?"

"Food?" cried Snyder, suddenly aflame. "We got something more than food to work for! We got—"

He checked himself again, the muscles of his throat working violently. Whatever it was that he knew, the knowledge was working in him like piled waters behind a dam of uncertain strength.

They went out for horses at once, and Danny O'Shay was introduced to the party. The sheriff and Templar had mustangs; Lister and Snyder were mounted on a pair of Condon's fine-blooded horses; and O'Shay presently appeared on a gigantic black mare of seventeen hands, which bore his bulk with comparative lightness. Every man of the party of five was armed to the teeth with rifles and revolvers, and the sheriff looked them over with satisfaction.

"Snyder," he cautioned their guide, "we're following you blind; we're askin' no questions; but if numbers would make this game safer, I can have half a hundred fighting men with us in two minutes!"

Snyder would have none of that suggestion. He declared that already they were just enough in strength. Any more would be throwing away their advantage.

So they started from Last Luck, and headed straight up the pass. For five miles they went in silence, and then Snyder, in the lead, turned from the road towards the rough country that rolled in the direction of Cramer Mountain. He paused and let the others gather close.

"Gents," he said, "scatter out in single file. Follow me close, the first man, and the others press up on him. The going's bad!"

It was all that he had promised. The way was not marked by any semblance of a path or even a cowtrail, and they wound through sharp rocks, thickets, bits of open woods, down steep sided ravines, and up the cliffs beyond until at last the rising moon helped them and their toiling horses.

At last Snyder checked his horse again. He dismounted and the others followed his example.

"Friends," said Snyder, lowering his voice, "I want to ask you to stop talkin'. Half a mile from here is the most dangerous man in the world, as I take him. I'm going ahead and make sure that he's there. You're to follow along after me. Right over the next hill, you'll see a little valley—a hollow, not a valley. In the middle of that hollow there's a little lean-to, and in that lean-to there's a man with five million dollars. And that makes a million apiece. A million apiece!"

His breathing grew so hard that he was forced to pause.

"He's worse than a fox for smartness," Snyder warned them. "Nobody in the world would ever have thought of the thing that he did! Now he's got the money; he's safe, he thinks, and nobody knows about him, except me. He trusts me, the devil! He thinks that I'm big enough fool to be trusted! He thinks that he has my eyes shut tight; but instead, he's the fool!

"Now mind you! I'm going straight over that hill, and when I get past the ridge, I'll march down the valley and go for the hut. On the way, I'll whistle a couple of times in a queer way. That's the signal.

"I'm going into that shack to talk to him. You four scatter out to the four corners of the hollow. You'll find lots of rocks and bushes, and you can sneak down into the hollow behind them. If you make a noise, if you show yourselves, then I'm a dead man, quick and sure.

"Boys, we have a million apiece to work for. Unless we get it this night, it's gone forever. You keep working up towards the shack. I'll wait for about a half hour, and then I'll walk outside the shack and bring him with me if I can. If he won't come, when I've walked out, you rush the shack. If I bring him out with me, drop him quick, and for God's sake don't miss the first shot."

He added: "A million apiece. And steady, boys, steady!"

The voice of Snyder was thick and shaken with emotion, and it was plain that his mind was so upset that he had forgotten that the total treasure of which he spoke really was the due and the legal property of young Munroe Lister. The gold fever was burning the big man like a flame!

Straight up the hillside, then, he went, and after him marched the others. There was only one thing said, and that was the final caution of the sheriff: "Not a word—not a whisper. Snyder means business. He means five million dollars worth of business!"

So in an utter silence they went to the brow of the hill and they watched Snyder descend into a small vale which was chopped out of the shoulder of a rising mountainside. It was littered with ragged boulders. Stunted trees grew to a meager height, attesting the shallowness of the soil, and through the center of the little valley a stream twisted. There was not enough of it to make more than a moonlit glimmer, now and again, between the steep shadows of its banks, except just at the end of the hollow, where it flattened into a small pool edged with young poplars which stood in a stiff and formal pattern against the brightness of the waters.

Now with the moon sailing higher, and the gilded rocks standing like so many men in armor, and the loftier mountains removed in shadowed dignity, and the breath of the pines abroad, it seemed to Templar a moment of enchantment, and a place for wild deeds. As for the shack, it was so small, crouched as it was under the lee of an enormous boulder which had pitched from the mountain in a former age and half shattered itself on the rock basin beneath, it was so overshadowed and engulfed by this rock that Templar at first did not see the house at all. But afterwards he made it out.

The sheriff did not speak in giving his orders. He merely pointed to each man the direction from which he should work towards the shack, and he himself accepted the most dangerously open post—that route which led up the little creek.

To Templar went the northeast angle of the hollow, and he dropped back behind the rim of the hill in order to make more rapid and unobserved progress towards the post. In this manner he was soon at his place and paused an instant before he began the descent. He had before him a number of shrubs and big stones, capable of sheltering him from the most direct observation; but, better than all this, he had the vast mass of the boulder between him and the shack itself. Of all the routes towards the little house, his was the safest, and he could not help biting his lips at the thought that the wily sheriff had thus, obliquely, made him out the least clever of the lot at trailing.

He went about his task with all the more caution. If ten rifles had been searching for him and regarding every step of his progress, he could not have advanced with a greater deliberation. Every pebble was regarded beforehand or foot or knee was allowed to touch it. Not a stone, however slight, was disturbed by his progress; and all the while the silence grew over the hollow, until he could hear the far off babble of a little cascade, where the brook, unseen in its gorge, broke into music near the shack.

No doubt the place had been built by some hunter who retired here in the winter to fill his traps; now five million dollars, was contained within the small hut!

Even the trained and cultured mind of young Templar had to reach out its arms to embrace such an idea, for millions, as has been said, were not so familiarly on the tip of every tongue in those days. He remembered in his school the son of a "rich" man—and the father had left more than a half million dollars, in dying. Templar had read an obituary notice which referred to "this vast and solid pile of wealth, amassed by the intelligent and honest application of a natural business man." Well, just ten such fortunes would be required, piled one on the other, to equal the huge riches which now lay in that shack before him!

Some Robinson Crusoe with a rich island all his own, and prosperous villages dotted over it, and a neat little seaport, and commodious freighters wending to and fro across the ocean to carry the products—still all of that empire might have been bought and sold for a less sum than five millions.

Then, by inversion, his thoughts turned back to Condon, and, much as he had disliked that man from the first, he now bowed a little to the thought of him.

Genius deserves its tribute, and he paid one to the talents of the rancher at this late and strange hour.

Now he was drawing close to the big boulder; now he was working around the side of it, and, presently, he crouched flat; for there was the door of the shack, yawning before him not ten steps away.

There would be no need for the rifle at his back, at such a distance as this. He thanked God for the bush that grew before him, giving him view of the doorway, but surely shielding him from the observance of anyone who might step into the opening.

He lay on his left side, bade his chilled muscles stop aching, and held a Colt in his right hand, ready for the attack. And, every moment, he was sure that the murmurs within the cabin were growing louder and about to walk out the door. But then again he could not be sure whether they were quiet voices of men talking together, or only the changing murmurs of the creek.

One thing was certain. The half hour had elapsed, and so had another half hour beyond the appointed time!

CHAPTER XXII

Now, while he waited, he took note of something that stirred at the side of a bush just opposite the door of the shack; he had his gun poised instantly, and saw the head and shoulders of a man emerge, thrusting snakelike close along the ground. A great head, a vast

151

spread of shoulders—O'Shay!

And all sense of the strangeness of that cold vigil, and the whispering stream, and the deadly white of the moon left Templar, so great was his admiration of the skill of this monster in working himself towards the shack. Past the bush, he went towards a flat-topped rock which certainly seemed not half big enough to mask the approach of such a monster. But then Templar could remember hunting days in the desert, and how huge O'Shay, on foot, could stalk anything that lived in the desert. He could come softly in point blank range of a coyote, and even the immortal nerves of a lofer wolf were not hair-trigger enough to detect his shadow-like coming. He could slip up behind a horse in a pasture, shifting from side to side, always on the blind spot when the animal lifted its head, and so toss a lariat, at last, over the head of the mustang before it even knew that it was in danger of capture; and twice Templar had seen him stalk within tagging distance of a grizzly.

So he went on now, moving without a breath of noise, until he was recumbent behind the rock. Here he paused only an instant, then he went on again, actually crossing an area which possessed no shelter whatever!

With half an eye on the progress of his old friend, Templar bent the rest of his attention on the yawning darkness of the cabin door, striving to penetrate into its black heart, and if so much as half a shape appeared there, he vowed that he would fire.

Nothing showed, and now the big man, close under the wall of the hut, rose to his knees, to his feet, and began to edge towards the door. He reached it, but, after that, he remained motionless, or at least craning his neck so gradually that Templar could not make out any shift in his position. When he finally did stir, it was to step boldly forth against the interior blackness, and then into that dark pit he disappeared.

Templar could wait no longer, but, pitching to his feet, he ran forward, regardless of the noise which he made, and so lurched into the cabin.

He could not make out anything within the shack, but the voice of O'Shay boomed suddenly to him from a corner.

"Let's have a light here, and steady your nerves when you scratch the match," said O'Shay.

The match was lighted, and Templar, shielding the flame with his hand, poured a flickering yellow shaft on a most horrible picture of a man who lay bunched against the corner wall, his head and shoulders cramped up, the rest of his body stretched forth on the floor. As to his face, it was not recognizable as being more than human; all identity had been smashed out of it by a series of terrible blows that had beaten in the forehead, and all the countenance above the mouth.

"Condon was killed by the same hand!" said Templar, his voice shaken with horror. "The same devil did both jobs, Danny!"

Now other hasty footfalls came to the door, and the sheriff and Lister entered the room; some pine splin-

153

ters were kindled to make a light, and by that wind-tossed flame they made their examination. The sheriff and Lister ran out instantly to make a circle around the shack, hoping to find the murderer in flight, nearby, while O'Shay and Templar remained to study the shack and the dead man.

"Search him," urged O'Shay.

"Search a dead man?" cried Templar. "No, no! Let him alone, Dan!"

"He's a crook; and a low crook," insisted O'Shay, "don't deserve decent treatment. Go through him. We don't know anything about him. Let's try to learn."

"Man, the murderer is putting miles between him and us," said Templar, in a nervous fury of eagerness.

"Kid," responded the giant, "he's miles away already. And I'd rather hunt lions in their cages than that man through the hills by candlelight. Hold the stuff!"

With large, dexterous fingers, he went through the pockets of Snyder. For Snyder it unquestionably was; if there had been a doubt as to his clothes, there was a large purple-black spot at the side of his chin, and Templar knew how it had been put there.

The loot was handed back to Templar, who received with unwilling hands an old pocketbook of imitation leather containing some frayed envelopes, a big gold watch of really fine quality, two pencils whittled to a narrow, femininely long point, each point covered with a tin cap, two pocket handkerchiefs, a knife with three blades, one broken, a package of matches, a box of Turkish cigarettes, a small roll of twine and, oddly enough, part of a stick of sealing wax.

"Let's see it," demanded the giant.

He probed hastily through this collection, even opened the letters and glanced at the contents, while Templar protested in disgust.

"Is nothing sacred to you, big boy?" he asked.

"Justice is," replied O'Shay savagely and, somehow, Templar could find nothing more to say. He even jerked off the boots of dead Snyder and lifted out their inner soles, while Templar stood by, biting his lips.

"We'll get something," said O'Shay, as though in answer to an unspoken question. "Steady, old son. Steady!"

And with that, he actually seized on the closely furled hands of the big butler and opened out the limp fingers. From one of these he picked a round wad of paper. He carried it at once to the flame of the pine splinters, which he freshened, until it was a comfortable light.

Then he pried at the little round wad until it gave way, and then unrumpled into a long, thin, time-yellowed strip of newsprint.

He began to cluck and nod his head. "It's as good as a cold drink after a day's march in the desert, kid," he declared. "We got it!"

He read aloud, making pauses, sometimes stopping and looking aside, so profound were his reflections. And this was what he read:

"The three robbers of the M. O. & St. Q. train of

last Wednesday, who took away a little more than a hundred thousand dollars in Federal banknotes and were captured on the following Saturday, were today identified.

"United States Marshal Felix Crampton identified two, who are found to have had criminal records. The first was Lawrence Harmon, already convicted twice for highway robbery and twice tried for assault with intent to kill, and the second was Roy McArdle, said to have been one of the Allister gang, and already in prison for the charge of manslaughter.

"The third of the captured men was identified purely by chance. One of the jailors, on seeing the third captive, declared that it must be Charles Crane, a young and well-known merchant of his home town. When confronted by his fellow-townsman, Crane at once admitted his identity and showed great emotion, begging that the news might be kept from his family.

"The fourth member of the party of robbers is still at large, and, since none of the loot has been found on the persons of the other three, it is presumed that all of the plunder was borne off by the fourth man. The bulk of it is sufficient to weight him down and make his capture almost certain. It should follow within a few days. When last reported, he was making for the higher hills and his horse was said to be failing.

"Marshal Crampton has set out on the trail; he

and his posse are much admired for their clever work in working out the trail of the three who were captured."

This reading was finished by O'Shay with a certain amount of relish, and he remarked: "We've made a start!"

"A start for what?" asked Templar with an impatient irritation. "Account of an old train robbery. What has that to do with the murder of Condon, the theft of five millions, and the brutal killing of Snyder, here?"

"Oh, maybe nothing in the world," answered O'Shay. "But remember that we found this here account in the hand of Snyder. Now suppose that him that did the killing was one of these old train robbers? Suppose that Snyder was another of 'em. Suppose, say, that he was the fourth fellow, that carried the loot away. I don't know. I'm guessing. I'm jumping in the dark, but I think I may be apt to land on something!"

The sheriff and Lister came in, panting. They had combed the district around the shack, but they had found nothing; no one had been started up by their scouting.

"But a man could hide in every ten foot square of the hollow!" groaned the sheriff. "We may have had him almost under our feet!"

He took the loot which had been gathered from the pockets of the dead man and shook his head over it. "There's nothing here!" said he.

The newspaper clipping was handed to him.

"I'll keep this," he sighed. "But nothing'll come of it. God. God, we been near a big thing this evening, boys. I'd give ten years of life to work out this trail!"

"Lemme see your right heels," commanded O'Shay suddenly.

"Are you makin' a game out of this?" asked the sheriff with cold disapproval.

"Do what I say," said O'Shay. "I'm not playin' a game."

They obeyed him.

"All right," he went on. "Now I'll show you the trail of him that did the murder!"

He picked up several of the pine sticks, bunched them firmly, and with that torch he pointed out some imprints on the soil of the earthern floor of the hut. They seemed to have been made by a narrow heel, equipped with a number of strong nails on the outer curve.

Following those imprints, O'Shay came to the door of the shack, then turned to the right, and finally he dropped on his hands and knees and crawled through the narrow opening between the bottom of the rock and the top of the shack, which leaned against it. He went on around the corner of the huge boulder, and then stood up.

"It's pretty clear," said O'Shay. "He waited in here until Templar come down around the side of the rock; then the murderer hit Templar's back trail. He's over yonder, by now!"

CHAPTER XXIII

"Over yonder" consisted of a rough tide of big hills which swept up to a magnificent climax of mountains, crowding down the pass.

"We'll go on, then!" urged Lister. "I'll go back for the horses!"

The sheriff sighed again.

"Son," said he, "where will we go on? Under what straw in that stack is the needle lyin'? And how will we know the needle when we find it? No, no, we got to go back to Last Luck, and pick up what clues we can. It looks like that to me. Big boy, what's your thought?"

So greatly had O'Shay grown in importance since he had worked out the trail!

Now he nodded.

"We take the back trail," said he, "and get to Last Luck. Speakin' personal, this game is sort of amusin' to me, I'm gunna stick with it while my money lasts. But let's go back to Last Luck. The longest way round sometimes is the shortest way home!"

So they started gloomily back, having covered the face of the fallen man; they would send for his body on the following day.

It was a weary trip, and as they went on, without the heart to push their horses, the dawn began in the east, and, as they reached Last Luck, the Western heights were lost in rolling mist and a rising tide of color.

Lister invited all three to come out to his ranch, but when they refused he went in with them to the town, and, while the sheriff went to his home, the others put up at the first hotel they reached—Delaney's ramshackle pile of sheds and huts, grouped together as a single hostelry.

They had to turn in in one room where there was a single cot and two sets of blankets were furled down on the floor. Lister was voted the cot; the others stretched themselves on the floor and instantly were asleep.

By noon, Templar and Lister wakened, to find their gigantic companion gone before them.

"He sleeps no more than a wild cat," said Templar, and he and Lister began to hunt for a bath.

After that, they descended to the street to search for breakfast. Last Luck never wakened until nightfall, and now the heat and the lazy murmurs of the rude town closed over the heads of the pair. Into the same long and narrow restaurant where Templar had dined the night before, they now went for bacon, bread, and coffee, with a large stack of fried potatoes, white, dripping with grease. Lister stared at the food with a gloomy eye.

"If I could get fifty thousand dollars for my interest in the Condon ranch," he said slowly, "I'd chuck all the game and go back East to finish my schooling."

"Don't they know it, man?" snapped Templar. "Isn't that, perhaps, what they figure on?"

Lister thumbed the handle of his coffee cup; his fingers slid on the half washed surface.

"I knew that no good ever would come out of it," said he. "I knew it, and I was right!"

"No good?"

"Out of Condon, I mean. Out of saddling me on him. Yes, something came out of it. I was put through school this far. That's something, I suppose!"

Templar was politely silent, politely interested. And the other said with a quiet outburst of despair: "Neither of them were right. I mean—suppose I tell you the whole thing, Templar?"

"I'd like to know!"

"Take this and read it, then!"

He took out a long wallet, unfolded it, and extracted an envelope, from which he took a sheet of foolscap, covered with close writing.

"Read that," said the student. "Then you can place me in this rotten affair!"

And Templar read:

"My dear son,

"I have put a copy of this in secure hands. In case you should have met with foul play, I wanted to have a second copy ready for action; and my own life is shortened to a few weeks. As I have told you, this is not to be read until you are eighteen. Now that you read it, you are almost a man; at least you have a judgment of your own worth using. I want you to turn all this matter carefully in your mind, and then decide.

161

"You find yourself under the guardianship of your uncle; I doubt if you will have found him a very warm-hearted uncle, but, at any rate, you have been schooled at his expense and you are his legal heir. I wish to explain how this came about.

"Shortly after I married your mother, she asked me to invest her estate for her. The estate consisted of a little over fifty thousand dollars, a fine fortune, and much larger than I expected to have from her. It was too large a sum for me to handle, and therefore I appealed to her brother, Andrew Condon, who was looked up to by the entire family for his business acumen. He was much younger than I, but he had done much more in the world, everyone felt.

"Your uncle, Andrew Condon, advised me to use my own wits on the investments, which only made me more eager for him to take charge of them, and, in a few days, the entire sum was placed in his hands. I had no doubt of his intelligence, and it never occurred to me to question the integrity of my wife's brother.

"After a few weeks, he told me that he had invested the money in Dakota real estate, and gave me some papers which, he said, represented the property. I was sorry that the money had gone into farm lands and I begged him to continue to handle the business, which apparently consisted in a large tract of wheatland.

"At the end of the year, we received nearly four

thousand dollars, and we were very pleased, because this represented an income of nearly eight per cent on the capital. When Andrew afterwards suggested that he be permitted to sell part of the land and invest it in stock, I gave him a free hand.

"I felt that he was a genius. He declared that he would make us rich, and I believed him. I was more willing to believe in him, because my health was failing rapidly.

"After this, the transactions of Andrew with my wife's money became so many and so entangled that I could not follow them easily. I dismissed them from my mind, merely keeping a happy dream that one day we were all to be rich. So it went on for three years, and during that time we received a diminishing income. For the four first years we had, altogether, only nine thousand dollars, which was a very small return, as you may appreciate; but Andrew continually spoke of twists and turns in the business world, temporary depressions, and such things. I still had faith in him until, in the fifth year, there was no income whatever; and when, in the sixth year, there was another blank, I became terribly worried.

"I wanted to learn what Andrew had done. It was impossible to trace his investments in stocks and bonds, but I went back to the Dakota papers, had them examined, and learned, after six months of weary investigation and delay, that we never had owned the land which he pretended was ours!

"What else he had done with the money, I could not guess. No doubt from the first it had gone into his own personal investments. But now I could prove that, from the first, he had misappropriated our funds. It was a criminal offense. Daily my health grew worse. My death might come at any time and leave my family in poverty. I sent for Andrew and told him he must come to see me.

"He put me off. He proved a slippery fellow. With wonderful skill he dodged me with one excuse after another, until finally I threatened to have him arrested.

"Then he came.

"When I confronted him with the facts, he tried for a moment to dodge. Then he confessed everything. He had hoped, he said, to make a great killing; and of course he had failed. He begged me to give him another chance. He had no great amount of money, but he swore that he would help me with the expenses of the coming year. If I would give him a short time, he would place a large sum in my hands.

"I gave him the wanted time. It was three months. And at the end of it, he came to us. He was very ill. He lay in bed at my house for several days, with an ugly cut in his left side. It looked to me like the groove cut by a bullet of large caliber, but he scoffed at the idea, and told me something about falling from a horse onto a sharp rock. At any rate, he had brought with him the sum of twenty thousand dollars in cash and this, he said, was to go to me. I asked him for the rest of the fifty thousand; he declared that he had no more. I was very angry. I pointed out to him that I was a dying man, that, after my death, twenty thousand would never serve to support my wife and my child. My wife was unfitted for work. My son was barely eight years old. Unless he could give me more satisfaction than this, I would have the law on him.

"At that, he made a long and eloquent appeal to me. He was always a clever talker, when he chose to be, and he convinced me that he was not all bad—that he had followed wrong courses because luck always had failed him. Finally, he swore that if he were given more time to make good in the future, he would constitute you, Munroe, his heir, and pay every penny of your expenditures, until you came of legal age or were finished with your schooling.

"I accepted that proposal. I felt that he was unscrupulous, but I also felt that he had enough brains to go on to great things, if he would keep to straight courses. This agreement we made. It was ratified between us.

"He left shortly afterwards. And a few weeks later he wrote to say that he now had the remainder of the fifty thousand dollars, and that he would will-ingly pay it. He presumed that I would be willing to cancel the agreement we had just made.

"I wrote back that, in addition to the fifty thousand dollars, he owed us thirty thousand dollars for interest and compound interest. He replied that he would send me his check for sixty thousand dollars.

"Then, my son, I permitted myself to become unjust. I remembered that I had lived for seven years in a torment on account of Andrew's dishonesty. That worry doubtless shortened my life; perhaps it actually is the death of me. There are an uncertain number of days remaining to me, and I felt that Andrew should be made to pay for his sins.

"At any rate, I wrote back to him that I had placed in secure hands the papers which convicted him of the fraud of the pseudo-farm in Dakota. If he failed to live up to the letter of his agreement with you, I would be certain that justice would overtake him.

"I realize that I am wrong in doing this, in one viewpoint. In another viewpoint, I feel that I am doing only what is right and improving your chance in life. If I am in error, God forgive me. Certainly I am not sinning for my own sake."

CHAPTER XXIV

There was a little more to the document, but it was chiefly concerned with farewells to Munroe Lister

166

from the dying father, and Templar read them through rapidly.

When he looked up, Lister said: "You see how it stood. When I read that letter, I thought at first I'd go to my uncle and tell him that I didn't want to be his heir. He could simply pay me what was due to my mother's estate—that is to say, he could pay me the sixty thousand dollars due at my father's death, plus the interest on that sum for ten years, minus the thousand or so a year that I had cost him. It would have made, in that fashion, about ninety thousand coming to me. Uncle Andrew was very wealthy by that time; ninety thousand would have been nothing for him to pay. But my second thought was that my father's will might be wiser than mine. I decided that I'd go on through college and study law. I had a leaning toward it, anyway. Law would teach me where I stood legally. In the meantime, I'd be getting better sense and a man's judgment. Is that clear?"

Templar nodded.

"Which brings us up to the time when you came to the ranch."

"I'd like to ask a question."

"Ask ten."

"You had a quarrel with him—"

"A hundred. He always hated me and took little pains to conceal his feeling."

"I mean, on the night of his death."

Lister flushed and bit his lip. But he answered, looking his companion in the eye: "I was sick of the infernal gloom and horror and terror on the ranch. I went to Uncle Andrew that night and made my proposition to him. Let him pay over the share of the estate which was honestly coming to me out of my mother's right, and then I would be glad to give up any claim that I had on the rest of his estate. He broke into a passion and swore it was too late for that. He damned me with all his heart and told me frankly that he hated my soul and body. I had to answer back a little. I don't wonder that you heard the racket."

"He said it was too late?"

"Yes. Exactly that."

"It wouldn't have taken him more than a couple of days, at the most, to arrange the thing, would it?"

"I don't see why it should have taken much longer than that."

"It simply proves," observed Templar, "that he expected the crisis that night—or the next, perhaps. How did he have such accurate information from people who were gunning for him? Can you tell me that?"

"I know nothing," sighed Lister. "That was all a nightmare. I'm only gradually shaking it out of my mind. This touch about Snyder last night—well, it freshens the horror for me a good deal. I think I'll get out of this, Templar. I think I'll get out and go East, my nerves are shot to pieces!"

Templar looked down into his coffee. He could understand such weakness, but he could not sympathize with it.

"There's Mr. Bristol of the bank," said Lister suddenly. "If I could make an arrangement for him to take over my interests out here I could go East."

He suited the action to the word, suddenly springing up and bolting towards the door. There he swerved past a gigantic form, and so darted out into the street and ran in pursuit of the banker. Big O'Shay came on and sat down opposite his friend.

"Breakfast?" asked Templar.

"I eat tonight," said the monster. "Today, I'm thinkin'. I'd rather bull-dog two-year-olds all day than think for five minutes, kid. I'd rather break ten feet of quartzite than think for ten minutes. It does me all up and puts me off my feed. And my God, kid, how hard I been thinkin' all the morning! Hey, waiter. Bring me a quart of coffee!"

He leaned his vast head on his equally vast hand and his fleshy brow puckered with fatigue and pain.

"Sick of thinkin', old son. Sick of it, sick of it!"

"Thinking of what?" asked Templar.

"Thinkin' of what!" growled the big man. "Hell, what would I be thinkin' of? Murder, me lad. That's what! Murder—two of 'em—supposed to be done by a sneakin' little sheep-herder! Can you stretch around that, you anaconda, you?"

Templar sat rigid in his chair and waited.

"Sheep-herder!" went on the giant. "I've heard of sheep-walkers stickin' a knife into the back of somebody, or shootin' down a puncher from behind a rock, or burnin' down a house by night, but I never heard of

169

'em goin' into houses and bashin' fightin' men in the face with clubs. Never heard of that, before. Oh, Johnnie, this is a rare job! I'm gunna grind my brains out workin' at it!"

"Will you stop groaning?" asked Templar unsympathetically, "and tell me what you know or what you think you know?"

"I know this!"

From a vest pocket, he extracted a bit of metal and tossed it onto the table. It was a short nail, with a very odd head, wide and thick.

"This is a hell of a lot to know," remarked Templar dryly. "What about it?"

The giant groaned again.

"There's what comes of brains and brainwork," he sighed. "You go mining and blasting away down in the innards of your wits and you dig up gold, and then you go deeper and you dig up diamonds, and rubies and emeralds, and you throw 'em down, and the damn world, it just walks right on across 'em! Look at that nail!" he ended with a commanding roar.

The waiter, bringing the granite pot of coffee, shrank so decidedly that the coffee slushed over his hands, and he put down the pot with a yell of pain.

The big man seized on it, and, without lingering over cups and saucers, he poured half the sugar bowl into the steaming deeps of the pot and emptied in a large part of a can of condensed cream. With the blade of a bread knife he stirred this portion and inhaled its fragrance while he went on, pointing his thick forefinger, as big and as heavy as the barrel of a gun, at Templar: "You that use your wits every day, you that are smart, I tell you what you do, kid. You just skate along over the surface of the ice."

"And you," grinned Templar, "break through, I suppose?"

"I do," said the giant complacently, "and when I come up I got a whale between my teeth. Go on and look at that nail!"

"I'm looking at it. What is it?"

"Ever seen one before?"

Templar studied it again.

Certainly the head was odd. It was of a hard iron, apparently, and the top surface was deeply lined and cut.

"It's a newfangled sort of nail for shoeing a horse?" he asked.

"For shoein' a man," answered the giant.

He paused to swallow half the contents of the coffee dish. Then he wiped his mouth indelicately on the back of his hand.

"Gimme a smoke, kid," said he. "I ain't had a smoke for a week!"

He rolled a cigarette and lighted it. Under the long and heavy draught the paper curled away and blackened down half its length and the tobacco stood out in a fiery red, sparkling corner. As he smoked one, he rolled another. He talked with the burning cigarette in his mouth. Clouds of smoke gushed from his nostrils and curled outwards on the surface of the table; other clouds burst out of his lips as he spoke and boiled away upwards.

"Nail for armin' the heels of a gent," explained the big man. "Same kind of a nail was in the heel of him that murdered Snyder last night. Same kind of a nail *is made* right here in Last Luck by the old nut who does the shoe repairin' here. He's so far behind the times that he still makes his own nails! That there is a hand-made hobnail, kid. You take a long look at it, because you never may see another! And the face on that baby is the face that was on the nails in the heel of the murderer!"

"You couldn't be sure," said Templar. "Man, man, you would have needed a magnifying glass!"

"When I start thinkin', my eyes, they start bulgin'," declared Danny O'Shay, "and my brain, it starts spinnin', and I tell you, I magnify, old son. Oh, I magnify, all right!"

"Will you cut this short and finish?" asked Templar, fairly trembling with excitement.

"Because you want your fun, eh?" said the big man, lolling back in his chair, until it creaked and sagged terribly beneath his weight. "Your nostrils, they begin to fan out like a stallion's, and your eyes light up like a dance hall. You want to go sashayin' right into the heart of things with a Colt bellerin' in each hand and a knife between your teeth and a dynamite bomb tucked into your vest pocket—why, hell, son, you're plumb selfish! You let me tell this my own way!"

Templar closed his eyes and dropped his chin on his

172

fist. To that pale, tense face, therefore, Danny O'Shay finished his tale.

"There's only one shoemaker. I asked him. Sure, he'd put about a ton of those nails into the shoes of gents. 'Narrow, taperin' shoes,' says I. 'Narrow, taperin' heels, like a puncher would wear?'

" 'Cowpuncher?' says he, he glowers at me. 'Are ye daft?' he says. 'Cowpuncher, with them in his heels, to make him misery?

"No, but for lumbermen and miners, and such folk— cowpuncher? Never in this life, my son,' he says.

" 'You've never tapped 'em into an old pair of shoes with high heels?' says I.

" 'Only a second-hand pair, that the poor sheep-herder on the side of the Sugarloaf bought off me.'

" 'You put them in for him?' says I.

" 'He wanted hobs,' says the old boy. 'So I tapped in a half-circle of these on the outside of each heel.'

"And there, Johnnie, is what I been doin', and there's the whale that I've brought up between my teeth!"

"I'd shake hands with you," observed Templar, "if it wasn't that I've a fancy to keep my bones whole! Man, man, we start this minute for the side of the Sugarloaf! We start for him?"

He and Danny O'Shay rushed out of the restaurant and turned swiftly down the street, but at the very first corner Templar stopped with a gasp.

"What is it?" asked O'Shay. "What ghost have you seen?"

173

Templar pointed a rigid arm at a second-story window across the street.

"Hong Kong!" he cried, and leaped away.

CHAPTER XXV

Two cowpunchers, at that moment, were lunging their horses down the side street, racing for the main thoroughfare; and big O'Shay shouted terribly, like Mars, to stop his friend. It was in vain. Into the dust cloud then rushed O'Shay, and, as the mist cleared, he saw that Templar was not lying crumpled in the roadway; in fact, he had disappeared. O'Shay hurried on. Grinning faces watched him.

"You'll be sorry if you *do* catch him," said someone. "That's Templar!"

And the crowd looked at one another and laughed, as they would have laughed if a man had attempted to chase a thunderbolt with his bare hands.

Templar had disappeared, had dodged through the mob, twisted in at a narrow doorway, and gone up a flight of stairs so fast that they hardly had time to creak under him. He jerked open a door—he saw an empty cot, heaped bed clothes, an old carpet bag in the corner. He jerked open another door; empty, too. Another—

"Who in hell are you lookin' for?"

He retreated and tried a fourth and, as he pulled at it, and the lock held, he thought he heard a sound in the room like the stir of a wind far off, whispering among the tree tops, giving good word of an unknown country. Or say it was the rustle of silk?

He pulled again, and the cheap bolt of the lock turned and sagged like nothing under the iron of his strength. He drew that door open and stepped across the threshold.

This room was empty, too!

"I've been a fool," said Templar to himself. "I might have known I never could have caught her!"

He hesitated, of two minds. He might go on and try other rooms, or else he might give the thing up. Last Luck was a tremendous tangle. An elephant could have been hidden in that town, to say nothing of a thing so swift and slender and strong and light as Hong Kong.

He stepped to the window, and looking down on the street, he saw Danny O'Shay standing on the corner, looking every way, his great arms swinging a little clear of his sides, like a man about to try anything that came his way. He smiled a little at the sight of the giant, and his heart was warmed. Women, after all, are small, and slight, and weak; they are treacherous things too. Books tell you that, and so do the young men of the world; no matter for the old ones! But yonder O'Shay, vast, stalwart, true, unshakeable—a man to die with! He would stand there through all the hours of the day waiting for his friend to come back, and after all that waiting, his heart would be as patient and his temper as sweet as that of a mother welcoming home a child.

So Templar was moved, and in that sun-flooded, cheap little room, with its bare, unpainted floor, and its bare, unpainted walls, and the gaping cracks of the board ceiling, he had a great thought that sobered him and made him look up. So our great moments come, in spite of dinginess; two or three in a life of which they compose the lasting wealth. Why should there be more? And if there is only one light, it is enough to show the ship across the dark sea.

He turned back from the window and eyed the empty chamber, and the bag in the corner, and the thick white enamel of dust that gleamed under the cot, and the crooked, twisted heap of clothes upon the bed.

Disgust filled Templar and he stepped for the door when something stopped him like the touch of a hand. He paused and turned his head, and at that moment he looked for all the world like some proud and fierce young stallion who, on the pasture hill, breathes from the wind some message out of the unknown world where the horizon stops.

So Templar stopped, and turned his head, and the light glittered in his eyes, for he had breathed a delicate scent of lavender such as would have been at home in an antique chamber, draped in chaste linens and faded, kowered silks, with threadbare rugs upon the floor.

But here in Last Luck, on the verge of the wilderness and the desert?

He looked wildly about him. When he started on to the door, the fragrance disappeared. When he turned back into the room, he had it again, thin as a thread of silk that glimmers and disappears in the light of day. A thing to guess at rather than to know.

Where could it be?

He reached idly for the bedclothes and pulled them back. And there she lay, cunningly twisted and curved so that she had fitted, as it were, into the very break and wrinkle of those covers!

"You little snake," said Templar thoughtfully. "You could hide yourself in the wrist wrinkles of a man, if you wanted to! Stand up, Hong Kong!"

If she did not understand the words, she understood the signal of his hand, and she slipped from the bed and stood before him, sleeking her black hair until if flashed like polished metal in the sun.

"You come along with me," said he. "The sheriff will like a lot to see your pretty face, Hong Kong. Walk right up and come along!"

She looked down at his hand upon her arm with vague eyes, lacking understanding.

"I'm not going to waste time here, explaining," said Templar. "I know you savvy what I say—"

"No savvy, mister," said the girl.

She looked anxiously up to him.

He took a stronger grip on her arm.

"It won't do," he told her. "You know what I say as well as I do. You've made a saphead of me before, but I don't think that you can do it again. Hong Kong, forward march! We start. Go. Plenty quick—movee!"

He drew her forward a step, but, in making it, all the

strength seemed to pass from her and she slumped to her knees.

Desperate, dark eyes were raised to Templar. "No likee poor Hong Kong?" said she.

"Here, here," said Templar. "That stuff isn't fair. I'm playing a straight game with you, Hong Kong. It's not right to work the bunco game so hard. Now, you stand up and come along with me, or I'll pick you up and carry you!"

And he did what he promised. He could feel the ripple and stir of strength in her. He held her as one would hold a wildcat, knowing that it could waken instantly into a dangerous fighting creature, But Hong Kong slumped helplessly, deep into his arm. She shuddered. She caught him around the neck with weak arms, and into the hollow of his shoulder she began to cry. Such sobs he never had heard. They were not like the crying of any other person he ever had heard. They were rather high pitched, and there was a moaning, thin, melancholy minor strain in the voice of the girl.

"Don't do it, Hong Kong," he gasped. "I can't take you down, like this. I'd be mobbed if I was seen carrying a crying woman, even a Chink. By God, you know it, and it's all a dodge with you! Hong Kong you devil, stop it!"

He plumped her down on the bed. She slumped weakly against the head of the cot, her hands across her face.

"You witch," said Templar, prickles of horror shooting up and down his spine. "Good God, I mustn't be seen here! Hong Kong, it's not real. You're not really crying, and you're only making a fool of me!"

He drew her hands down from her face. Helplessly she sobbed, unresisting, her hands falling loosely, her head dropping upon one shoulder, and the tears streaming down her face.

Templar took his handkerchief and rudely and vigorously scrubbed one cheek. He stared at the cloth. There was no sign of yellow on it.

"By God! By God!" murmured he. "You're a Chink after all; and it's no stain that you're wearing!"

The sobbing grew greater. It began to have a semi-hysterical wail in it.

"Stop, stop!" gasped he.

He raised both hands to hush her, and backed towards the door. But her crying only grew greater. She had pitched forward on the bed, but her face turned to one side, and the unstifled wailing rang and rose through the room.

Templar fled! With cold perspiration dripping on face and neck, he rushed down the hall, tumbled down the stairs, and came to big O'Shay, where the latter still waited on the corner.

"Danny," he urged, "come quick. I got her!"

"You got what?" asked the impassive O'Shay.

"I got the Chink, Hong Kong, the Golden Devil— you hear? Don't stand there like a hulk, but come along, will you?"

Danny O'Shay slowly allowed himself to be urged into motion.

"You found her? Then where is she now?"

"Upstairs, here!"

Up the stairs went O'Shay. In his left hand he carried a revolver ready. In his right hand he carried nothing. That balled fist was better than any gun, in his judgment. Certainly it was better than a crowd.

"How many has she got with her?" gasped O'Shay. "Do we fight to kill, kid? Is it law we got behind us?"

"There's nobody with her," said Templar. "Here we are!" He jerked open the door; the room, now, was empty indeed.

"But it isn't possible," wailed Templar. "I tell you, she was here, helpless, hysterical, crying her heart out!"

"Wait," exclaimed the giant. "She was here— alone—with you?"

"She was. Yes, yes, and now—"

"Then why in hell didn't you bring her down by yourself?"

"She began to cry, Danny. It was terrible. It made me weak. Then suppose that people had seen me. A crying woman—brute of a man—you understand, Danny? But where is she now? I got to find her!"

"What interest you got in her?" asked the big man slowly. "You want to hang her, kid?"

"Hang her?" repeated Templar, aghast.

"Or," went on Danny O'Shay grimly, "are you in love with her?"

"Danny, you blockhead, she's a Chink."

"Chink hell!" said Danny O'Shay. "She's a woman!"

CHAPTER XXVI

"Get me out in the sun," said Templar presently. "I need a lot of heat and bright light. I don't feel too clear in the head, Danny. A Chink! A damn yellow faced Chink—"

"Golden, you used to call her," put in O'Shay.

"She tried to break my head open with a cleaver," said Templar. "And you think that I could—that I could—"

"Sure you could, and that's the reason," said Danny O'Shay. "You don't do no deep thinkin', kid. Surface skatin'. That's you! A Chink! Well, I'm damned."

"You're a crazy man," Templar assured him with heat.

"'I couldn't bring her away because she cried,'" the big man mocked him. "She cried! Hell, Johnnie, of course she cried, because she seen at a glance that you were a soft-headed sap. I never seen such a sap as you, Johnnie. I never seen such a soft-head. Neither did she. But the next time that you want her handled, you call in Papa O'Shay. Me, I'm special hell on Chinks, kid!"

"We'll tell the sheriff," said Templar anxiously. "We'd better do that. He can find her. Let the law take its course, I say."

Danny O'Shay simply grinned, but he led the way with immense strides to the office of the sheriff and to him he told the story of the hobnails and the high-

181

heeled shoes. The sheriff listened with gleaming, joyous eyes.

"You ought to be sheriff," he told O'Shay, with a frank admiration, "and I ought to be your helper—your doggone errand boy. I'll ride out there and get the news about this sheepman. Do I find you boys in Last Luck when I come back?"

They promised to be there, and the sheriff departed on a mustang in a high-winging cloud of dust.

They went back to the hotel for an afternoon nap, and there they found a note from Lister. He bade them good-by, unless by chance he should find them in the town on the next day. He was leaving Last Luck and the West to go East, and he hoped that he never would have to see that nightmare country of the Pass again.

To O'Shay, therefore, Templar told the story of the message of Lister's father and the old tale of trust and treachery connected with Condon.

"All skunks," said O'Shay, and promptly fell asleep and began to snore.

Templar slept in turn; and the heat of the day was ended and the cool of the late afternoon had begun when the sheriff, white with dust from head to foot, came to them. He had news and important news. He had located the shack of the shepherd, and, from an outriding puncher from the Condon place, he had learned something of the man who, it appeared, was the true lonely, strange-minded type of the walker of sheep. He never was known to mingle with other humans except when he trekked to Last Luck, once in six months, for the sake of a few supplies. For the rest, he kept his flocks well.

Where could he be now? With the puncher to assist him, the sheriff hunted over the range, and found the sheep wildly scattered, and no sign of the man."

There was no doubt of what had happened, especially when they discovered half a dozen carcasses of sheep, partly devoured, and the tracks of lofer wolves around them. The shepherd was gone, and the flock was abandoned to the dangers of the mountains!

Careful inquiry was then made by the sheriff, but the puncher knew very little. Only of one thing he was certain, and this was that the shepherd was a sullen, slinking man. Dangerous? Perhaps. At least, one never wanted to trouble a fellow of that type, saying nothing, lurking by himself, glancing only askance at other humans.

"And so," said the sheriff with an air of content, "he done the murder, and we got our job rounded up. Thanks to you, O'Shay! Doggone me, if you ain't a Sherlock Holmes!"

He added that he was going to the cemetery, where Lister was now due to see the burial of his uncle, which had been arranged for that morning. Templar had no wish to go, but big O'Shay insisted. So all three went to the burial ground and saw the coffin borne to the edge of the grave, with Lister standing by gloomily, looking rather worried than grieved. He greeted them absently; plainly his whole thoughts already were turning towards another country where he could be more at home.

Big O'Shay touched his shoulder.

"Lister," he said, "I got a particular favor to ask of you. Would you let me have a last look at Mr. Condon?" Lister stared with an air of disgust.

"It's a horrible sight, O'Shay," said he. "I suppose that you know that? You saw Snyder; but this is even worse!"

"It's me that will do the lookin'," said O'Shay. "I don't ask anybody else to help me."

So he won a reluctant assent, and, approaching the flimsy pine coffin, he took the projecting top boards and by sheer might of hand slowly raised them, the nails shrieking an almost human protest. For a long minute the giant stared down at the horror within. Then he pressed the boards back into place and, with a stone, hammered the nails down. He thanked Lister with a nod, and retired, apparently anxious to be away.

"What was in your head?" asked Templar with some irritation. "It was a poor thing to ask for, and a poor time for the asking, Danny!"

"I'm a detective," replied O'Shay, with some attempt at a smile. "Now, bein' a detective, I ask you if I don't have to see the dead man before I try to find the murderer?"

"What have you learned?"

"Learned nothin'; guessed a lot. Guessin' goes before knowin', but oh God, kid, you dunno how I ache when I see all the thinkin' that I got to do in the

184

next few days. If we're gunna catch the crook, I mean!"

Lister interrupted by coming to say good-by in person. He thanked them for their attempt to help him find the murderer, but now he felt that the task was beyond him; he was leaving. That farewell was briefly ended before the earthen mound was heaped above the grave of Condon, and the two friends went slowly back into the city.

Templar, on the way, broke out: "I agree with Lister. I'm through with it! I want to quit, big boy! There's only one thing."

"I know it."

"You know what?"

"The one thing that you're interested in, now."

"You do?"

"Of course."

"Tell me, then?" challenged Templar.

"It's the doggone golden beauty, the dumb Chink. Hong Kong is what you want to find, and you'd sail across the damn Pacific to reach her. Am I right?"

Templar paused sharply in the street. He faced his friend.

"I tried to tell the sheriff about her this same day," he admitted, "and the words stuck in my throat. I couldn't talk. But—the stuff about the shepherd was a great deal more important, as you'll admit."

"Sure I'll admit it," answered O'Shay. "I mean, it looks more important. You want to chuck this here murder trail, old son, and find Hong Kong?"

185

"Danny, I'm sorry to say that I do! I know what you'll say—a Chink—a yellow Mongol—well, I won't defend myself. But she sticks in my mind like a burr in a woolen jacket. I can't get rid of the thought of her!"

"Why, son," murmured the big man, "there is only one way to get shut of a woman, and that's to see her every mornin' and noon and evenin'. You gotta look at a girl a thousand times before you see what she'll be when she's old. So we'll go and collect this Chink girl for you, kid. We'll give you a chance to sit and look at her as long as you want to."

"God bless you, Danny," said the boy. "We'll go back to the house where I found her today, then?"

"There? Not a mite of it. Lemme tell you. The way that we'll find her will be along this here trail of the murderer. Keep at it, and she'll pop up again!"

"You think she had a part in it?"

"What do I know? I ain't bent myself to thinkin' about her, yet. But I got an idea that she's part of the dish. You have the steak, and then you have the vegetables, and then you have the green trimmin' around the edge of the platter, but it takes everythin' all together to make up the whole dish. Am I right?"

Templar was silent.

"Oh," said the giant, "is she one that wouldn't possibly have nothin' to do with anythin' dangerous and difficult and mean and ornery?"

Templar groaned.

"There's all kinds of hell in her," he admitted. "She

186

scares me to death, Danny!"

"So does any good woman scare me," said O'Shay. "But let's get down to hard cases. She's been in this pie, and she'll show up in the pie again. It's all gettin' fine and stirred up like a Mulligan, son. Here's first a lot of strong men that could be suspected of the killin'. Here's Snyder, and Lister, and Templar, and a Chink girl with a forearm like the forearm of an athlete. But now we begin to reduce out of the dish and the thing that's left is what? A sneakin' no account sheep-herder that just took a couple o' days off and killed Condon in his own house, and then he killed Snyder and slipped through a circle of fightin' men, and he's picked up five million dollars—and away with him! Now, son, how does it begin to look to you?"

"I don't know. I really don't know!"

"I thought you wouldn't. Because you ain't bent your brain to the job. Surface skimmin' is all that you do, me son!"

"And you," asked Templar with a touch of irritation. "What do you make out of this tangle?"

"I ain't at the bottom of it," said O'Shay, "but what I skim off the top is the idea that that sheep-herder never had the brains to think of two murders like them, and he never had the hand to strike the blows. He was rung in; he's the blind. We'll reach behind that blind and find what? The Chink girl, maybe!"

187

CHAPTER XXVII

What could have been done, with the sheriff to help them, they never were to learn; for that same day an ambitious youth came up out of the southwest and presented himself in Last Luck as one desiring to be registered in the hall of fame. A half-breed was his first victim and a negro his second; both wounded. But when he killed a Mexican, murmurs began to arise, and when he started a general fight in the Chase saloon the alarm was sent in to the sheriff. He found one dead and one wounded, and the promising youth gone back toward the desert. So he picked up a few assistants and started on the trail at once.

After all, no matter how many millions attached to Condon, he was only one man; and here were two deaths and several wounded; the case took precedence!

O'Shay was downhearted, for the law, as he pointed out, was a useful thing to have in your pocket.

"Unuseful too, in a way," he admitted, "because a sheriff, he gets too much attention. You and me, kid, we can work more private. The first thing, we'll lay out and watch for your Chink girl."

"If I could have a one-hour serious interview with her," began Templar, when the giant cut him short.

"It ain't her that we want," said he. "It's the trail that she'll lead us onto!"

"Where shall we start to look for her?" asked Templar eagerly.

"Watch the house."

"She must have left that, after the alarm."

"What alarm? D'you think *you* alarmed her? You didn't, son. It takes long and painful thinkin' to alarm a girl like her. She's got brains, and havin' made a fool of you a couple of dozen times, she ain't goin' to worry her head about you and what you do. She slipped you in that house once, and she'll try to slip you again."

Since the Chase saloon faced the house in which Hong Kong had been found, at the window of that saloon they took up their watch. They had their horses in readiness, in the rear yard of the place, and together, or one by one, they regarded the house across the street through the dusty-dimmed window panes of the saloon's one window. The flare of the great gasoline lamp over the saloon entrance was their light.

Joy and noise and the smell of whiskey grew rank in the Chase saloon, but the two maintained their vigil from the corner, one sleeping, and the other taking his turn, until the hand of O'Shay shook his companion out of a profound slumber.

"Wake up!"

"I'm awake, Danny. Stop busting my shoulder."

"Look out!"

"Is it she? Damn it, Danny, that's only an ordinary puncher!"

He stared sleepily at a man about to mount a horse across the street.

"Smallish for a puncher," said the giant. "But lemme

see! Lemme see. Maybe we can tell when he sits into the saddle."

The man across the street at that moment swung lightly into the saddle. O'Shay leaned to look.

"It's a woman," he said softly. "And most likely it's your special woman, kid. Hike for the horses and swing 'em around here in front. I'll watch her out of sight!"

Sleep still partly bewildered Templar, but he obeyed blindly, got the pair, and rushed them to the front of the saloon, where O'Shay mounted his huge black and they started north up the street.

"Headed south," commented O'Shay, "and then come back north in the dust cloud behind a bunch of the boys; but I seen the flash of the white tip of the tail of her hoss through the fog. It's her, and no mistake, and my God, ain't she a cagey one?"

They spurred ahead, after that, until the last lights of Last Luck turned dim; and then the solid black wall of the night stood before them, with a mysterious bordering of trees on either side.

"It's a fool's trail," said Templar. "We never can follow through this sort of starlight!"

"We're just a half-hour from moonrise," answered the other. "That was one trick that she left out. She wanted to make her getaway by dark, but she waited too long. Keep up your heart, son. Remember about the Scottie and the spider, will you?"

"What's that?"

"The seventh try won!"

They voyaged on through the dark with the hoofs of the great black horse ringing louder than anvils when they struck stones in the road.

They left the level and had begun to climb between the trees when the moon, at last, lightened in the east, and presently the familiar pale flood of light was over the mountains.

It was not, however, a night of unbroken brilliance, for swift, high-flying clouds were streaming from the south and beginning to crowd in the throat of the pass. Now and again those rapid shadows skimmed across the road, blotting the trees into thick shadows and putting out the road itself. They had to trust to the horses to follow the right way, at such times.

"It can't be Hong Kong," broke out Templar. "No woman ever would start out alone through the mountains at this time of night. It's not reasonable; ask yourself if it's reasonable, man, will you?"

"A cleaver to split a man's skull—your skull—then you ask if she's got nerve? Remember, kid, there's five million in this pot, and even a woman will play hard for stakes like that!"

And, just as he spoke, they labored to the top of a rise. Clear moonlight exposed the winding road as it dipped into the hollow beyond, and, climbing to the top of the next rise, they clearly saw a rider on a horse the white tip of whose tail flashed like a tin pan in the moon.

"There we are—there we are!" said O'Shay, and pulled his horse into the shadow of a tree until the other rider was out of sight beyond the next crest.

Then they rode hard into the hollow, and into darkness, for the clouds were rushing together above them, and, as they mounted the farther rise, a torrent of rain beat down on them, cold, stinging, and falling wonderfully thick.

They were drenched when they gained the next height, but here the rainfall mercifully ceased, and they entered a long avenue of almost midnight darkness, so great were the trees which fenced it in. However, the wind had not knocked the clouds apart; the moon was shining once more, and the two picked their way onwards by the glimmer of the new pools of rainwater which stood in the road.

At the end of that tunnel, drenched with the fragrance of the wet pines, they came out in the high, broken country of the upper pass, and here again they had sight of the solitary rider.

The silhouette showed high up a slope, and then, as they watched, it came almost to the top of the crest, and twitched aside into shadow, and went out.

"We're seen!" groaned Templar.

"Get in here in the dark!" snapped O'Shay. "On a trail, kid, you're as useful as a left glove on a right hand. Come in here and keep quiet, and start thinkin' if you can—long, deep thinkin', kid, is what you need to do on this here trail!"

"She's seen us, if it is she," repeated Templar, obeying gloomily. "And now she'll be gone like a bird. We'll never find her again!"

"Shut up," said his big companion. "Shut up and wait, will you?"

Templar became silent. The stillness of the night was not broken, at that moment, either by a wind in the trees or the rustling fall of water drops through the leaves. There was only the breathing of the horses, rapidly becoming softer and more regular. Then O'Shay exclaimed triumphantly.

"She's started on again. Look! Look!"

"I see," said Templar. "But what's the call for yapping so loud, I ask you? Is it particularly wonderful? She's started on, well, what of it? Except of course that we're glad to keep in sight?"

As they started up the road in turn, O'Shay muttered: "Young—too young; smart—too smart; no thinkin'—no thinkin'!"

Then he said, in a louder voice: "Why should she duck under the trees?"

"Because—why, I don't know."

"You don't know!" sneered O'Shay. "Was it because she saw us?"

"No, for otherwise she wouldn't have started back into the center of the road again. She would have worked her way over the rise among the trees."

"Young and tender," said O'Shay, "still, you got the makin's of a brain on your shoulders! Well, then, if she didn't see us, what did she see? Sure she seen something or she wouldn't of dodged for cover."

"She saw something? Perhaps so."

"Well, then, son, it was nothin' that was comin' this

way, or she would of waited for it to pass."

"That's obvious."

"Is it? Then ain't it obvious, too, that what she seen was ahead of her, goin' the same direction that the rest of us are travellin'?"

"I suppose that may be true. There's someone else riding this road. That's not very wonderful, is it?"

"You been hand-raised and spoon-fed," declared the giant, "until you can't use your wits none at all. You poor young heir apparent of nothin'. Lemme tell you, then, what it means. This here young and gentle Chink is just nacherally trailin' somebody across the hills!"

"Danny, what could—"

"How do I know? But I'll swear that she's trailin'."

"And what?"

"What are we all trailin'? Him that murdered Condon, him that murdered Snyder, and the little Chink will lead us to him, me boy, as sure as there's a kind God watchin' over us behind that moon!"

CHAPTER XXVIII

They went on with the greatest caution from this point, for no matter how open the country was, they never could be sure at what a safe distance they were following the fugitive, for the clouds repeatedly covered the moon and they were left fumbling in most absolute darkness.

The clouds, also, gathered repeatedly into thick

sheets from which rain descended in great sheets and torrents, and the two drenched detectives went miserably on. Twice Templar observed that no woman, not even Hong Kong, could be persuaded to travel in such miserable weather, but O'Shay always replied complacently that any trip was easy that had five millions at the end of the road.

After several hours, they found the moonlight diminishing, or so it seemed, but this turned out to be the beginning of the day. The hills, in the meantime, grew up large and black out of the east, and the clouds which had remained broken throughout the night, except for moments, gathered together in a canopy of immense thickness which overspread the entire sky. The rain no longer fell in gusts or great masses but by gradual and steady degrees, turning the whole landscape to soft gray which brightened a little as the day came to the full, the east being stricken across with one line of blazing strength just at the horizon. That was the sunrise.

They were through the pass, with the back country pitching and falling wildly before them. The road grew more obscure. At times, crossing sections of hard rock, it almost disappeared altogether, and finally it fell in at the side of a river, newly swelled and infuriated by melting snows. They wound along, now, in a few great sweeps, covering many miles in each semicircle that followed the bendings of the stream, and still, sometimes clearly seen as the rain lifted, or drowned again as the mist closed down, they had repeated sight of the horse with the white tail.

More than that: straining their eyes far ahead, several times they saw two riders far in advance; and these they had no doubt were the pair the solitary rider was keeping under observation.

Without pausing, then, the chase was continued. The pace had grown so slow that the giant O'Shay insisted on resting his horse by jumping to the ground and walking or jogging forward. In this manner he kept up easily, and finally Templar followed the example, for not only did it make them a less conspicuous object on the trail, but it gave the horses repose.

Therefore, when they came out of the rough lands for a time, and the pace quickened to a gallop down a long valley, the two jumped into the saddle and easily kept up. Then more steep grades rose before them. Noon passed. The horses were plodding with nerveless heads hanging down almost to the ground; midafternoon went by. Still the rain alternately fell in sheets or in a fine-grained mist, softly pencilling the air, and still they pressed forward, almost constantly on foot, and marvelling that the others were able to keep at the work.

"They got lighter weights to handle," said O'Shay, "and besides, they're travelling for life or death!"

"And we're just here for fun, is that it?" asked Templar dryly.

"We don't *have* to ride this trail. It's having to do a thing that makes it twice as hard," answered O'Shay.

The way led up a broken path on a steep mountainside, and going over the shoulder of the slope, they came in sight of a big hollow, or head of a valley, filled with the rain-mist which seemed to thicken like steam towards the ground. They could make out nothing of any habitations, but above the mist sheet, barely discernible, the two could see the thin spire of a church. It was an infallible sign of a town, and rather a more pretentious town than one would expect to run into in such a wilderness of mountains.

"They'll stop there and put up, most likely," said O'Shay, "and we ought to stop, too."

"Stop in a town?" asked Templar wearily. "They'd never dare to do that!"

"They dared to kill Snyder, and they dared to kill Condon," replied O'Shay. "Are you gunna be pretty sure that they won't dare to take this here chance, too?"

Templar was by no means sure; they rode down the slope, therefore, and soon they were so thick in the mist that they barely could see each other, though they rode not five steps apart. They could hear the boom of distant water, as they entered the heart of the valley, and presently as the sun burst through the upper clouds and shone faintly through the lower mist of rain, they saw a great cataract dropping in white clouds down the face of the farther mountain, with wet, black trees struggling up the cliff against the downpour. And embraced by that profound rumbling they saw the village emerging from the pale fog, black as the trees, huddled together, and the spire of the

197

church like a rapier pointing above it.

"They'll stop there," said O'Shay, "and maybe we can stop there, too."

At this, Templar protested loudly. They would be throwing away all of their gains on the trail if they continued into a place where the report of their coming would be so apt to reach the ears of the other people in the town.

O'Shay nodded as though he had thought of this before. Then he urged Templar to remain behind in the shelter of the trees while he, O'Shay, went forward to reconnoiter the town. If the object of their pursuit were in the place, then they would make a halt. If not, they would push on through, and for that pursuit it would be well if the horses were brought into as good condition as possible.

People who marked sixteen hours at a stroke were apt to buy new mounts before they pressed on; and the pocketbooks of Templar and O'Shay could not stand such a strain. Templar, accordingly, put the horses in a thicket of great trees where little or no rain dropped down to them, and then he began to rub them down after loosening the girths. He worked for a whole hour, ceaselessly, and had the pleasure of seeing the two animals lifting their heads and beginning to show signs of interest in the green twigs around them before O'Shay returned.

He had news.

He had gone through the village and found a blank, rain-drenched street with everyone indoors, and the windows misted white and blind. He had almost made sure that his quarry were not in the place when he happened to look into a blacksmith shop, attracted by the glow of the forefire, and there he found a dripping horse having its front feet shod; and the tail of that horse was topped with white, now dingy and dripping with moisture.

That was enough for the big man. Further inquiry might reveal him more quickly than it revealed his goal, so he went straight back to his friend.

He had noticed, on his way into the town, a farmhouse not a quarter of a mile from the beginning of the town houses. There was a truck behind the house, and a pasture dotted with cows still farther in the background, so that he took it for granted that the people of the house sold vegetable and milk in the little town. If that were the case, they were certain to be fairly poor people, and in any case they would put up a pair of strangers who were willing to pay their way.

With that arranged in their minds, O'Shay and Templar went back to the road and journeyed on until, as O'Shay had described it, they found the farmhouse. It was set back a little from the road; a few poplars grew before it; there was a front yard of alfalfa which had been newly mowed and left a pale, sick-looking stubble; and the house was a low, ugly structure.

When Templar knocked at the front door, a little old man with a wooden leg opened to him, and looked brightly out, a pipe in one hand, a walking stick in the other.

His house would shelter the strangers, he said; but why not the hotel? It was only a half mile further on, and it was a good place. He could recommend it.

"You can have all the hotels in the mountains," answered Templar, with a pretense of heat. "I've never found one where the bed was clean, or the chuck even fair; and the prices are all made for the rich or the miners, and we're neither one nor the other."

"In that case," said the farmer, "we got roast mutton for tonight and bacon and eggs for breakfast. We got a room with a double bed. And if that'll do you, you're welcome."

To make all business-like, Templar asked the price, but he was told that the woman of the house, now off marketing in the town, would have to answer that question. So Templar returned with all this good news; they put up their horses in a clean barn behind the little house, and then they went into the house. It was perfectly neat and trim, and they were invited to chairs by the kitchen stove, where their clothes were soon steaming and they were warming body and soul with cups of black coffee. They were desert punchers, they said, tired of the heat and the dust of the plains, and ready now for a better and softer way of life, but if the mountains always gave such weather as this, it would be better to be back on the sands.

The old man of the wooden leg listened with interest and a smile.

"Weather ain't much. You make your own weather," he said. "I've seen a spring day that was snow, and black day that was July. You better go up and change your clothes if you got a change, or, anyway, wring them out and try to dry them. Wet clothes makes rheumatism."

He described the way to their chamber, and they went up and found a dormer room that looked onto the back of the house. Below it extended a lower roof, probably that over the kitchen, and the overhang of the roof came low to the ground.

"Stay here and take your time about wringing out your clothes," urged O'Shay. "I'm going out to look around, and I'm not going out the front door."

He did not wait to explain, but instantly clambered out the window, worked slowly and cautiously down over the sloping roof beneath, and shortly afterwards disappeared around the corner of the building.

CHAPTER XXIX

It was a snug little room, and Templar made himself quickly at home in it. It had a flimsy little stove in a corner, and this he filled with wood from the bin in the hall and started a hot fire. Next he stripped off his clothes and wrung them out the window. After that, he arranged his garments on chairs around the stove and soon had them streaming, while he wrapped himself in a blanket from the bed and settled down to a magazine of uncertain age, for the entire front part of it was torn away, and all the edges of the pages turned up, yellow and brittle with time.

The magazine could not interest him long. He threw it aside and began to clean his guns. He had taken down one of them and vainly looked for dirt in it when a bullet split through an upper pane of his window and ripped a noisy furrow across the plaster ceiling.

He dropped from his chair to hands and knees; then he sprang to his window and peered out. What with rain and dusk together, the lamplight inside and the dimness without, he was able to see little; but he did make out a shadowy form scurrying down over the kitchen roof. At that form he took a snapshot; a frightened yell answered him, and the silhouette disappeared over the edge of the roof.

He was half inclined to follow; if his clothes had been on him, he would have done so.

Instead, he retreated to his chair by the stove again, and wondered gravely what could have happened. He stared at the window. It was misted thickly with the steam which had risen from his drying clothes, and certainly no one could have been able to aim with any accuracy from outside the pane at a figure within. Moreover, the shot which had been fired seemed to have come from a distance; certainly from a greater distance than the kitchen roof.

He was dressing in a furious haste when he heard the peg leg of the old man of the house coming up the hall; there was a knock, and he bade his host enter.

It was a low doorway, but the cripple stood easily under it. Time and his bad leg had bowed him until he stood no higher than a child.

"You ain't hurt?" he asked.

"That's where the shot traveled," said Templar, and pointed to the furrow in the plaster of the ceiling, and the scattered white debris which had fallen to the floor. "How could it have happened?"

"When I was a boy," said the other, closing the door behind him, "we used to hear of folks shooting out the windows, but they mostly shot out the front lights. I dunno that it was done for fun!"

"Someone had climbed up on your roof—a smallish man, as near as I could make him out," said Templar. "I'm going down to see if I can spot his tracks!"

"You won't do much good that way," replied the other. "This here rain—it'll wash the sand in and close over tracks, pretty quick. Maybe you got some friends in this town?"

"I've never been here before in my life," answered Templar.

He tugged on his belt, heavy with cartridges, and then began the hasty work of reassembling his Colt which he had taken apart for cleaning. The old man watched with interest.

"You could do it in the dark, I suppose?" he remarked.

"I could," nodded Templar. "Who sleeps in this room ordinarily?"

"Nobody," said the host. He added: "No, that shot was meant for you. And a terrible bad shot it was, too!"

He shook his head. "Somebody's got a broken heart for making a miss as bad as that," he suggested.

"How far off did the first shot sound?" asked Templar. "Were you in the kitchen?"

"I was. It was from the edge of the trees, I should of said."

"The edge of the trees!" exclaimed Templar. "But, man, how could anyone see through that white, misted window from that distance?"

"They couldn't—not nobody!"

"It gets a little thicker," said Templar through his teeth. "And I'm going to have hell started for this!"

He jammed on his hat as he spoke and turned toward the door when the little cripple exclaimed: "Hello! What we got here?"

With his cane, he tapped a piece of paper which lay on the floor just inside the door.

"Who," said the old man, "has been shovin' paper under there?"

He jerked the door wide; the hall was empty beyond it, and dimly lighted by the lamp at the turn.

Templar, in the meantime, had snatched up the paper and unfolded it. He found written inside, in a bold, rapid, and strong hand:

"Templar, leave this trail; there's nothing for you at the end of it. But first get the sheriff when he comes back to town this evening and take him to the Dunbar Hotel. There are two lodged in that hotel. One is a big fellow; the other is rather small.

Both middle-aged. They came into town today. Both of them are railroad robbers. They are freshly out of prison and they should be put back in jail. As for a charge, they have with them a Chinese girl whom they are taking up through the mountains to dispose of in a place where she will bring them a sum of money. If you attack them carelessly, you will have a bloody fight; they both are expert shots; they both are desperate men. Take them by surprise and all will be well.

Your Well-wisher

P. S. You never can solve the riddle."

"It ain't a love letter, I take it," said the old fellow, watching the face of Templar closely.

"It's not," replied Templar, and folded the letter small. "It's not a love letter," he added slowly, thrusting the note into a pocket.

But in the meantime, his brain was reeling. He was certain that no man in this town could know him except by sheerest accident, for the place was far, far from his line of travel in the past, yet here was word from someone who not only knew him, but also knew, as it appeared, the business which had brought him here.

There was a vague flicker of big O'Shay in this note. As far as Templar could recall, he never had seen a specimen of the giant's hand writing, but just such a large, bold, and sweeping hand he would expect from O'Shay. Yet it was impossible that O'Shay's enormous bulk could have approached the door of the room so silently. Most of all, it was perfectly absurd to imagine O'Shay delivering such a message.

Outside of O'Shay, however, he could conceive of no one and the blank impossibility of the whole thing made Templar's brain spin as though he had received a blow.

He went hastily to the window and leaned out, breathing deep.

"Young feller," said the old man, "You've been shook up pretty bad, by something in that note. But you might remember that a bullet already has come through that window."

Templar paid no attention. Such was his mental turmoil that physical danger seemed nothing to him.

"And where might your big friend be?" asked the host, his voice sharpened a little with suspicion.

"He's gone out."

"I didn't hear him."

"Sometimes he moves like a shadow."

There was a soft sound of incredulity from the other, and then he spoke in a different tone.

"Young man," said he, "I wish you luck. I been through some narrow alleys, myself, when I was young. Same time, I don't hanker after bullets and broken windows. Not now that I'm old. You'll pay for that window and that broken ceiling, maybe?"

"I'll pay for it! I'll pay for it, of course," said Templar. "I'll pay for it if I don't go mad," he added, breaking out into mingled wonder and rage.

The old fellow waved to him, as much as to say that from that moment he stepped out of the mystery, and then he hobbled off down the hall. It left Templar with a clearer mind, and he determined that he would no longer try to read between the lines, but simply follow the advice of the writer of the note, no matter what came of it.

From every aspect, however, it was bewildering. For instance, if someone understood that there were two men in the town worthy of being arrested, why did he not take the information himself to the sheriff?

That might be because he did not wish to make an enmity between himself and two dangerous criminals. But still it remained most wonderful that anyone in this mountain town should have known of Templar at all, or knowing of him, should have understood that he was in the place at that moment, or knowing that he was there, should have dreamed however faintly of the work which he was attempting to do.

There was a slight sound outside the window; and the great head and shoulders of O'Shay appeared.

"Go back," said Templar shortly. "It's no good. The old man has been up here and knows that you went out. Go back and come in through the front door. The devil has been popping since you left; hurry!"

O'Shay was not one to ask needless questions. He disappeared, and presently the front door was heard to open, and he mounted the stairs which creaked heavily under his massive weight. He entered the room and flung his wet hat at the stove. It dropped with a squash of wetness to the floor.

"I been seeing things," said O'Shay softly.

"Seeing what?"

"You remember the two thugs who sat in the restaurant back yonder in Last Luck——"

"And watched us? I remember. Are they here, man?"

"Man, they are."

Templar blinked.

"The girl, I'll lay my money," said the big man, "was following the pair of them. And what are they followin'?"

"God knows! Why do you ask me?"

"The five million. That's what they're followin'. Things are beginnin' to thicken up, son! We're meeting old chums on this here trail!"

"And one of them," muttered Templar, "nearly tagged me. There's his mark!"

CHAPTER XXX

O'Shay listened to the story with perfectly calm attention. His interest even appeared to wander from the words of Templar, and he spent a long time standing at the window and looking earnestly up at the furrow which the bullet had made in the ceiling.

"And after that, I got this note, shoved under the door by a ghost," said Templar. "I thought that hall flooring would creak like the devil if even a child walked over it, but someone came up to that door and shoved the note under. The old man saw it, and pointed it out."

"Maybe the old man put it there?"

Templar started violently.

"The old man!" he echoed, and then sat down with violence.

"Why not?"

"My God, man, what can he possibly have to do with us? What can he know about us and our game?"

"He may not know anything, but he may have carried the note. For that matter, he may have written it."

"Are you trying to drive me mad, Danny?"

"Not a mite. But you gotta consider every chance. The trick you throw away in this deal is the trick that loses the game for us. Anyway, we know that we got a friend in the fracas."

"Go on, Danny," said the younger man, hopeless and helpless. "I don't follow your drift, but you go ahead and lemme know what's what!"

"The fellow who fired that shot," remarked the big man, "was a friend."

"A kind friend who used me for a target? Go on, Danny, I admit it's fun to hear you make a fool of yourself for once. But step on and demonstrate, Danny. Prove your point if you can!"

He lay back in a chair with a grin and waited. The fleshy brow of the giant had contracted.

"I got the hunch," he said, "but I still got to do the thinking. Oh God, Johnnie, when once I get out of this job, I'm gunna go off in the desert where I'll never have to think or talk again so long as I live! I tell you, son, nobody would have fired at your shadow behind the window and missed it as bad as that!"

"A revolver can take all sorts of bad twists in your hand," corrected Templar.

"Sure it can, but that ain't a revolver shot."

"You've found it, maybe?"

"No. I haven't found it. But look at the window it broke."

"I see it."

"If you think I'm wrong, you take hold and send another shot through the other pane of the window, me boy."

"What would happen?"

"You would jes' nacherally blow the pane all to bits, Johnnie. But that other bullet, it crisped in through the glass sweet and clean, and only filled it full of cracks."

"There's a two-inch hole where that bullet went through."

"I tell you, if it had been a Colt forty-five, the slug would have bashed every bit of the pane onto the floor."

"Have you any reasons for that?"

"Suppose that you drag a knife slow through soft butter—the butter drags along with the knife, don't it?"

"Naturally."

"But if you whip the knife through quick, no butter sticks to the blade?"

"That's right."

"Now, old son, you get a rifle bullet and it's a smaller caliber than a revolver slug, and it's travellin' three times as fast, and it snakes through things and just bores a clean hole. It chinked a little hole through the glass, bigger than itself, I admit. But that was a rifle shot, and don't you doubt it!"

Templar was silent.

"It proves," went on O'Shay, "that him that fired the shot aimed to fire high."

"Why should he have fired at all?"

"There was a man on the roof outside, wasn't there?"

"There was, of course."

"Well, son, if that rifle bullet hadn't been fired, the man on the roof would of sneaked up to the window and drilled you fair and clean, and that would of been the end of the trail for you, Johnnie me lad!"

"I'm an ass!" exclaimed Templar with irritation. "I should have thought of that!"

"It ain't your fault," responded O'Shay with a grin. "You was sent to school too long; you wasn't raised to think!"

"But now the letter, Danny? What will we do about that?"

"Do what it tells us to do. Him that wrote the letter also fired the shot. You got to follow the advice of folks that have saved your life. They've earned the right to be believed."

"When do we do it?"

211

"Now, son; now!"

"Explain one thing to me. How in the name of everything mysterious and damnable could there be any man in this town who knows us and all about our affairs?"

"I've explained enough for one sittin'," replied O'Shay. "I'm gunna stop thinkin', now, and start in with some action. Because, me son, there ain't any doubt that the two that are named here in the letter are the two that watched us in Last Luck, and the takin' of them ain't to be any party for babies. with their milk teeth. It's gunna be a crust that'll take molars to crunch, Johnnie, and this is the part of the game where you can begin to shine!"

They left the room at once. In the lower hall, they passed their ancient host and he raised a finger at them with a smile.

"Supper's in one hour," he said. "Don't you be late!" They went on through the door.

"The old man begins to give me a chill," confided Templar.

"Old men always do," replied O'Shay. "It's either what they know or what they don't know that gives folks a terrible shock!"

They turned up the street. The rain had diminished into a fine mist through which the nearer windows poured broad, golden shafts, and more distant rays were refracted into many colored atars, scattering like sheaves of brilliant spears. So low rolled the rain clouds that sometimes the roofs were lost in the fog.

"A grand night for murders," suggested O'Shay.

From a man who went by, glimmering in his slicker as though in polished steel, they learned the way to the sheriff's house at the head of the street, and there they entered the screeching garden gate and thumped up the steps of the front porch. A busy woman, red from the kitchen, jerked open the front door and frowned out at them.

"The sheriff's just in and he's restin'," she told them.

"He's got to stop restin' and see us," O'Shay informed her. "You tell him that, will you? We got a couple of birds in hand for him."

She hesitated, as though minded to send them roughly about their business, and then she turned away and retreated, leaving the door open.

"We'll leave the letter out of it," said O'Shay. "It's better out than in; there's too many things that might make him ask questions about us; and the first thing that I found out west of the Mississippi is that the less the law knows about you the better it is for the law—and for you!"

A bull-necked little man, who looked fat and was simply strong, came waddling towards them. He had a pair of spectacles pushed up on his forehead, a newspaper in his hand, and felt slippers on his feet.

"Hello, boys," said he, "are you comin' in?"

"We ain't goin' to drip on your carpet," said O'Shay. "We just got a couple of ex-train robbers down the street in the hotel. Maybe you would like to have a chat with them?"

213

"They've done their stretch, have they?" asked the sheriff.

"They've done it, I suppose."

"How much?"

"Fifteen years."

"Well," said the sheriff, "fifteen years makes a man either hammered steel or brittle cast iron."

"These are steel," responded O'Shay.

"What have you got against 'em?"

"Nothin' worth talkin' about. A shot in the dark, so to speak!"

"Is that so?"

"I ain't here for fun," said O'Shay. "They got a Chink girl along with 'em. Smuggled goods, I suppose."

"A Chink girl—there in the hotel?"

"They got her done up as a puncher. She makes a sort of a man."

"Goddam their hearts!" said the sheriff with heat. "I hate a damn Chink-smuggler worse'n I hate a snake. Boys, you rest your feet a minute in here while I jump into my things!"

He disappeared; they felt the whole house jarring to the shock of his feet as he ran back towards his room.

"There's a fightin' sheriff," said O'Shay with appreciation. "You take the number of counties there is in the West, and the work there is for the sheriffs to do in 'em, and doggone me, kid, if it ain't wonderful where the supply of straight shootin' sheriffs comes from!"

The sheriff returned almost as soon as this speech

214

was ended. He was shrugging a slicker around his shoulders and buckling a gunbelt around his hips at the same time. His hat sagged over one ear.

"A quick change," complimented O'Shay.

"I used to be a fireman," grinned the sheriff, "before I decided to settle down and have a quiet life. Is this gent with you?"

He indicated the silent Templar.

"I'm the general, sheriff," said O'Shay, "and he's my army. You and me can do the thinkin', and he'll do the work for us."

The sheriff merely grunted: "Standing still makes cold feet. Let's get started."

CHAPTER XXXI

They worked down a muddy, narrow alley between the hotel and its adjoining building, and so came into the little gate of a back yard. Above them rose the rear of the hotel which, since it was built on ground sloping sharply from the street, towered high above them. There was first a rock wall, and above this the cellar story, with four stories of the hotel proper rising higher.

It was in the top story of all, seemingly a vast distance as they looked up through the rain-mist, that the room of the two strangers was located.

"Wait here," said the sheriff, "the pair of you, and make sure that nobody manages to get out of that window. You can shoot, I hope?"

"I hope we can," said Danny O'Shay, "but would you mind tellin' me what you'll do yourself, sheriff?"

"Me? What should I do? I'll go around and up the hall and make the arrest, or else drive 'em out through the window."

"There are two of 'em," suggested O'Shay.

"I have two guns," responded the sheriff carelessly.

"Partner," said big O'Shay, "it's happened to me in me life that I've had to mingle with some hard gents, and I've done my share of fightin', but I wouldn't care to be mixed up with the two of those. Besides, you'd never be able to sneak up on 'em."

"Why not?" asked the sheriff.

"Nobody else has a room in that top story. The rest of the rooms are blank there. Maybe it's a reason why the pair picked that number. And the stairs and the halls screech in that doggone hotel like accordions all out of tune."

"They do," admitted the sheriff. "They do, for a fact. But what d'you suggest?"

"You notice that there is two windows to that room?"

"I notice that."

"Two men could climb up there—unless they fell down and broke their necks on the way."

"Humph," said the sheriff. "You boys are kind of bent on takin' chances, ain't you?"

"We got an interest, between you and me," replied O'Shay with apparent frankness. "What I suggest is that you go around to the front entrance and go in there and pick up a couple of loafers that can shoot straight. Then you go up to the top of the stairs on the third story and block the way. Just sit there easy and comfortable, because I got an idea that two gents might come stampedin' down that way."

"Hold on," muttered the sheriff. "You say these two are hard nuts?"

"They are."

"And apt to be watchful?"

"Is a wolf watchful that's had its tail stepped on?"

"I'd like to point out that the pair of you are aiming at climbing up there and getting into a cage where there's a pair of lions. How d'you aim to drive them out?"

"We got to take a chance," said O'Shay.

"It's only two to two."

"It ain't," replied O'Shay. "I'm one, and me boy friend here is five."

The sheriff paused; then he chuckled and patted O'Shay on the shoulder, reaching high for that purpose.

"Go try your trick," said he. "I'll foller orders, and I wish you luck. If I had a few like you in my county, I'd make crime so damn unpopular that the crooks would hunt for hell sooner that this neck of the woods!"

He went off down the alleyway beside the hotel and O'Shay muttered: "There's a man, Johnnie. The best ones are the ones always that'll listen to sense. Can we climb that wall?"

"We can."

"Then here we go!"

He dropped an enormous hand on the shoulder of Templar, and that touch was all the farewell that passed between them; after that, they bent themselves to the serious work of mounting the wall.

For the vast bulk of O'Shay it was hard enough, but Templar, with fingers of steel and muscles like powerful springs, climbed catlike and swift, finding a fingerhold wherever there was a crevice in the masonry. In this manner he came to the level of the cellar story, and from that point the ascent was much easier.

He had the projecting casings of windows to help him, and then a heavy drainage pipe that slanted down the side of the wall from the gutter of the roof above. Up this he went hand over hand, helping himself with his feet where he could, until he came to the second story. There, shifting his hold, his hands fell on a greasy section of the pipe and his right hand lost its hold at once. He swung by the left, only, and even the fingers of that hand seemed slipping. One wild glance he cast downwards, and saw big O'Shay far, far below, making slow progress; then his left hand slipped clear.

A fall meant death, or shattered bones through all his body, but he had marked the outthrusting case of a window just beneath him and hardly three feet down. He reached for it, gripped it hard as he fell past, and, when the full weight of his body jerked down, his fingers slipped only a little.

He hung at the full stretch of his arms, waiting for his heart to stop racing, and his nerves to steady; then he swung himself up again, catlike, sure of his hold at every move. He regained the drain pipe, and, testing every grip before he trusted to it, he reached beyond the oiled surface and climbed past it to the level of the top story windows. There all immediate difficulties ceased.

As though frightened by the weight to which his building had arisen, the architect had here stepped the wall in, and there was a safe ledge more than two feet deep beneath the windows of that floor. Down that ledge he worked toward the lighted squares of the two windows and, when he reached them, he paused and leaned over to see O'Shay.

The latter was invisible, at the first, but at length he was in sight, having gained the first story and paused there as though to breathe.

When Templar had made sure of this, and knew that there were still long moments of waiting before the giant could possibly arrive, he set carefully about investigating the interior of the chamber.

It would not have been so difficult if the windows had been closed, for then he could have ventured to peer through the rain-clouded glass with little danger of being observed from within, but both of the windows were half open in spite of the darkness and the cold damp of the air. It made his task more difficult if he wished to spy on them, but, also, it enabled him to see clearly, if he could see at all.

He crouched to his knees, and slowly ventured a glance around the lower corner of the sill—and found himself looking straight up into the face of Hong Kong! The shock of that sudden meeting almost made him lose his hold, almost made him cry out, but he set his teeth and so kept his nerves steady.

She was simply standing at the window staring out at the gray mist of the night, and the lights of the village, no doubt, as they streaked down the slope of the hill. Then, not daring to stir for fear her glance should fall down on him, he made out a wide sombrero, pushed far back on her head, and the glistening black braid of her pigtail curved over her shoulder.

O'Shay was right. Even then he had time to wonder at the cleverness of the giant, who had seen through so much. He began to feel a vague certainty that, whether he could understand this trail or not, O'Shay would understand, and so bring him on to goal.

There was a sharp exclamation from a man; the girl stepped back from the window. After that, as his ear grew more accustomed to the sound of dripping water, and the hushing of the wind, Templar could make out the noises within the room with a greater clearness. They were both there—at least, he heard two men speaking. They were playing black jack, and the conversation was simply: "Give me another—another—hit me again—that's enough!"

Or the deeper voice would say: "I'll try another—and another—that's enough to break me!"

He pressed a little closer, still; raised his head, and

now he could look slantwise across the room. Hong Kong had retired to a cot at the farther end of the chamber, and there she sat with her chin resting on her fist, and her slant black eyes regarding infinite distance, infinite sorrow.

Between the window and the cot was a small table, and at this the two men sat, their profiles turned to him. Instantly he recognized the pair whom he had seen in the mirror at the Last Luck restaurant.

Now that he could study them more closely, however, he found that there was much to read in their faces. The larger man appeared older than his companion, perhaps because of a white tuft of hair at his temples. He possessed a certain dignity, as well, and it seemed to Templar that this was the sternest face he ever had looked into. A perpetual frown made a cloud between his eyes, but whether it was an expression of mere pain or of determination was hard to tell.

The smaller of the pair was likewise the less attractive. He looked young enough, and yet something about his eyes made Templar guess him to be forty, at least. But his face was perfectly smooth; there was not a wrinkle about the mouth; he had every attribute of youth except warmth. And, in truth, he was as cold as something cut from steel.

Templar remembered what the sheriff had said. Fifteen years in prison made men either brittle or hard as chilled steel, and there was no doubt what it had meant to this pair. Never had he seen two more dangerous men, and most ardently he wished that O'Shay might come quickly to his side.

"Are you tired of it yet?" asked the bigger of the two. "I'll try you again."

"Don't be a fool"

"I know what I'm doing."

They played; the smaller lost.

"You see," said the big fellow, "luck doesn't go with brains, McArdle!"

McArdle! It rang a bell in Templar's memory. Somewhere before he had heard of it—ay, in the newspaper clipping which was found in Snyder's dead hand!

CHAPTER XXXII

He remembered, also, what O'Shay had said: that the trails might begin to run together, and in following one they might be following many.

"Luck goes with what, then?" snapped McArdle.

"With the man who doesn't care to win."

"*You* don't want to win?" demanded the smaller man aggressively.

"What do you think?" asked the other, and smiled faintly and without mirth.

McArdle cast a single upward glance on him and then suddenly busied himself in the shuffling of the cards.

"I dunno—I dunno!" he answered, and began to scowl. It seemed to Templar that the superiority of the larger of the pair was not a mere matter of size.

"We'd better stop," he insisted.

"Why stop, why stop? If I got money to lose, ain't you good enough to take the coin?"

"I don't want your money, McArdle. You know that."

"Oh, you're a damn queer one!" said McArdle, and he shoved back his chair in a sudden disgust.

He began to look out the window, drumming his fingers rapidly on the table; but Templar did not withdraw his head, for he knew that those angry eyes were seeing their own thoughts alone.

The larger man in the room, regardless of his friend's anger, shuffled the cards, and began to lay out a hand of patience.

"Will you listen to me?" said McArdle.

There was no answer.

"Will you listen to me, Crane?" barked McArdle savagely. And he struck the table with his hand so that the cards jumped and became confused in their piles.

Templar had been waiting, straining for the name, as it were, and now that it came it rang a second bell deep in his mind. McArdle—Crane—those were two of the names mentioned in the list which that newspaper clipping contained. There was a third one whose name began with Lawrence—

And then the door shut, as it were; for had not the man he killed at the Condon house been referred to as Larry? They were the gang. They were the three of the gang who, fifteen years before, had committed a rail-

223

road robbery and had been sent to prison for their offense. Now one of the trio was dead. Here sat McArdle and Crane. Crane, Templar remembered, had been the respectable member of a community—a storekeeper, or some such thing!

He was something more than a storekeeper, now. He was what the sheriff had called hammered steel; he was stuff of which sword-blades might be made. Ay, he would surely take an edge!

Crane turned to the girl and pointed first to her and then to the stove. She rose without a word and filled the stove with wood, shook down the ashes, and arranged the drafts. Then she stood with impassive face until the flame began to roar, after which she arranged the drafts again and returned to her cot.

"I'll listen to you, McArdle. What have you to say?"

"Oh, you're polite," sneered McArdle. "Oh, you're damn polite! But I tell you again, it's got to be done!"

Crane pointed to the door, and the girl rose again, but McArdle said: "Aw, let her stay, let her stay. She ain't gunna find out anything new. Hell, Crane, the way you treat her makes me sick. You'd think she didn't know nothing. I tell you, she knows everything. There ain't a thing that she don't know. She—she's a sweetie!" said McArdle, and he turned on the Chinese girl with a grin of such wolfish cruelty and suspicion and hatred that Templar winced in his cold, wet place on the ledge.

He became aware that the wind was rising, that his hands were beginning to swell and get hot, so terrible had been the strain on the tendons as he climbed the wall of the house. Certainly they would not be fitted to do his skill with guns justice, if this affair should turn into a battle.

"Aw, I dunno," went on McArdle. "Maybe you'll run the whole show yourself, but I say, they're poison. They're both poison!"

"The young fellow's a fool," declared Crane. "If you stop to think a little, you'll see that I'm right."

"*He's* a fool?" echoed McArdle. "Then I wish to God that he'd lend me some of his foolishness! If I could shoot like that, I tell you that I'd—"

"You'd be hanged in six months," said Crane, "whereas now you have a chance of living out the year, perhaps!"

The upper lip of McArdle curled; his head sank between his shoulders. He looked half snake about to strike, half wild dog about to leap. But Crane endured this glare with perfect composure and rearranged his stacks of cards for patience with care and attention.

To Templar watching with fascinated care, it appeared that the card-player had his aggressive opponent in his hand at all moments. McArdle might often snarl, but he would never bite.

"The big man is different," went on Crane. "I admit that O'Shay is different!"

And again the bell of recognition was rung for Templar. O'Shay was 'different'; then he, in person, must be the 'young fool.' He bit his lip and flushed. There were few men in this world much more proud than he, and he was only twenty-one. Yet his closest friend, the giant O'Shay in person, had half seriously told him he was incapable of thinking, and here was further confirmation from men who, it appeared, were in the camp of the enemy.

"O'Shay is *damn* different!" agreed McArdle violently. "He's poison. That's what he is!"

"In the first place," said Crane, beginning to play his hand, "I don't think that they have it."

"Maybe they haven't—maybe they haven't. But if they haven't got it, they've got us. Or they soon will, if they keep on our heels. What do they know about us? What started them after us?" exclaimed McArdle, starting up and beginning to pace the room. "What they got in mind?"

"They're bluffing," decided Crane. "They don't know. But they're guessing, and O'Shay is a clever man."

"And a fighting devil," added McArdle.

"McArdle," said Crane.

"Well?"

"As you say, O'Shay is dangerous, but let me tell you that if we ever come to grips, Templar is the man to watch. Oh, watch him carefully if you love your life!"

"You know that much, do you?" asked McArdle, and he moistened his lips. "Well, you got some sense. It was him that killed poor Larry, and he ain't finished, I got a feeling. He ain't finished!"

Sweet are compliments from our foes; Templar

turned a giddy red with his pleasure.

McArdle leaned across the table and planted the point of a forefinger on a card, as though it were an all important one.

"We gotta finish them!" he said.

"You mean murder, McArdle," said Crane, "but you always forget that I'm not a murderer!"

A veritable shudder of rage and hate convulsed McArdle, but then he controlled himself.

"You used to talk business in the pen," he said. "Nothing would ever stop you, you swore!"

"Nothing that's crooked, McArdle," said the other, "but I have a peculiar sympathy for honest men. You don't understand? I can't expect you to understand, I suppose!"

All acid, all biting acid were these words of his, and Templar wondered why the smaller man did not draw one of the weapons which bulged beneath his coat and attack his companion; but the supremacy of Crane was absolute.

"Then if you're gunna let them wander loose behind us," urged McArdle, "let's not waste time here. Let's get out on our horses and ride like hell!"

"Our horses are tired out."

"Kill them off, then, and buy new ones. Or use our legs!"

"There's no such hurry," Crane assured him. "He doesn't know he's followed. He thinks that he can't be followed, because human wits can't penetrate often through such devilishness as his."

"No," said McArdle, much impressed by some thought, "no, you're right. I give you credit for that, you read the book. I never would of dreamed it. Only, old man," he went on, quite subdued by the reflection which his companion had suggested, "we dunno that we're on the right trail. We can't be sure."

"I *am* sure," said Crane. "I worked it out once, and I'm sure again. In the old days, that was where he went in the pinch and that's where he'll go once more to disappear. You'll find that he's in Tolman." He added gravely, "I'm as sure of it as though I saw him there, and the two of us walking in on him, McArdle—"

He spoke like one prophesying, his eyes half shut; and McArdle, staring wildly and hungrily, listened, and stretched out his hands, and seemed to throttle the empty air.

"God, God!" whispered McArdle. "When that day comes!"

"It will come."

"I believe you!" said the smaller man, his breast heaving. "I ain't going to make any more trouble for you. You got the brains. I'm just a pair of hands for you to use. It ain't the money that I want. It ain't that, old timer. It's him! I want him! I want to get at him! I just want to lay hands on him!"

The words came bubbling rapidly from his lips, and he shook with a terrible delight at the thought of the pleasure that was coming to him.

Crane, in the meantime, had risen and held up his hand.

"Go on, say it!" urged McArdle.

"People are slipping up the stairs to the hall on this floor," said Crane in the same quiet voice.

McArdle, gaping, stared at the other; then he whirled on the girl.

"You!" he said.

But Hong Kong, chin on fist, regarded him calmly, dispassionately. There was no more understanding in her eyes than in two small pools of darkness.

"Put out the light," said Crane in the same quiet tone. And then Templar slipped through the window and stood with them in the room.

CHAPTER XXXIII

"Here comes Christmas," said McArdle, turning a sickly yellow-green. "Here comes Papa Santa Claus! If it ain't Mr. Templar himself!"

"Crowd yourselves together," suggested Templar. "Get closer, friends. I want to have you both under one gun. You, Hong Kong," he called to the girl, "stay back there in the corner."

"Ah," said the girl, with a frightened smile, "You know Hong Kong!"

In the hall there was an approaching stir of feet, and Crane, who had kept his poise perfectly at first, glanced wildly towards the door, towards the window, and then fixed his desperate eye on Templar.

"Crane," cautioned the latter, "I don't want to

trouble you. I don't want to threaten. I only have to tell you that I'm watching hard all the time. And—keep away from that lamp!"

For McArdle had attempted a covert backward motion towards the table.

"I have you both in mind," said Templar. "I don't want to shoot, but if I have to, I'll shoot to kill!"

A heavy, panting voice broke in from the window: "Good boy, Johnnie. You got 'em all lined up like little soldiers! Oh, my it's a pretty picture!"

The two participants in the pretty picture looked hopelessly at the window; there was a soft snarl from McArdle, who looked ready to spring, but Crane said quietly: "Not a move, Mac. We'll take what's coming. And first of all, we'll find out what's in the air. You haven't come here to rob us, Templar. Then what's your game with us?"

"Rest," said Templar with a grin. "I think that you need a rest, Mr. Crane. We suggest a long period of repose for you. Regular hours, and not too much exercise. Don't you agree?" O'Shay stood mountainous inside the window.

"Face the wall," said Danny O'Shay. "Line up agin the wall and stick your hands behind your back. No tricks, boys. We dunno you, but we figure that you're poison!"

They turned obediently to the wall, and then the big man secured their wrists behind their backs.

"You haven't met 'em," said Templar. "This is Crane, and this is McArdle, ex-railroad robbers. Have you ever heard of them before?"

230

O'Shay, with the broadest of smiles, patted the shoulders of his prisoners.

"All trails begin to lead to Rome," said he with unexpected erudition. "Open the door, kid, and ask the sheriff in."

The door was opened by Templar, accordingly, and the sheriff stumbled into the room at the head of half a dozen men. He came guns in hand, and those behind him were armed to the teeth, also, so that it was apparent the sheriff was not taking chances in this matter.

He regarded the scene of the holdup with great satisfaction.

"This here," he remarked, "is something that I sure hoped for, but I dunno that I ever expected to see it. I thought there was gunna be some shooting, boys. And doggone me, how I do hate that! But maybe they ain't mavericks at all. They're just poor old broke-down-broncs!"

"You're an officer of the law?" asked Crane politely.

"It looks like it," said the sheriff, grinning as he responded.

"And I am under arrest?"

"It looks like that, too."

"Then I have the right to know what charge is against me."

"The judge'll tell you that, me son."

"I think you had better tell me in the first place," said Crane. "I know the law, sheriff, and I intend to have it."

"Why, for a damn jailbird," said the impolitic sheriff, "you got a free an' easy way of talk!"

"I *am* a jailbird," answered Crane with perfect composure, perfect dignity. "I have served out my time for a crime I did not commit. However, that isn't to the point. Now I'm a free man; and if you attempt to bully me, sheriff, hell will be cold, compared to the heat which I shall raise in this county."

This he said without raising his voice, and his calmness gave his words a certain cutting edge that made the sheriff roll his eyes uncertainly.

"We got a charge against you," he said, mustering his righteous anger again. "We got a charge of smuggling Chinks on you, and we're gonna see that charge through. Where's the—hey, partner, where's the girl?"

"She's here," began Templar, and then checked himself with a start.

She was not there. Hong Kong had vanished down the hall of the hotel, or out the window; either might have been possible in the confusion which had followed the entrance of the sheriff and his corps, when all attention was focused so strictly upon the two arrested men. Templar leaped to the window and glanced down. The rain was falling fast, hanging a solid gray curtain before the light of each room, and the wall looked as dangerous as a cliff; and yet he knew, suddenly, that Hong Kong would have ventured even that danger if the humor moved in her. Or she might have slipped down the creaking boards of the hall and made them soundless under her flying feet.

There was magic in her; of that he was sure.

"Where is she?" asked the sheriff, his anger beginning to rise. "You ain't got the men and let the testimony go, have you?"

"Will you send out your men, and we can talk it all over?" requested Templar.

The sheriff agreeably waved his followers from the room, and the hall outside boomed and screeched under the pounding of their heels.

"Now," said O'Shay, "tell us frankly: Can you hold these men for twenty-four hours without testimony against them?"

"I've done it," the sheriff admitted. "I've done it a good many times with niggers or greasers, or such. But I hate to do it with him!"

He waved his forefinger at Crane.

"He'd know how to make trouble!" he declared.

"You," said O'Shay, turning on Crane and stepping a little nearer, so that the greatness of his bulk might be more imposing at close hand—"you, my friend, have been running a Chink girl up through the country—"

"I deny it," answered Crane.

"In man's clothes," went on O'Shay. "I guess that's a crime sheriff?"

"The person to whom you refer," said Crane, "arrived at the hotel half an hour after us. I think that's enough to settle the talk. The hotel keeper will prove my point for me."

"Cool, calm, an' happy is what he is," said the sheriff. He scratched his head.

233

"I dunno what to do about it," said he. "I think that they're guilty. I want to hold 'em. I *will* hold 'em, if you give me half a handle to grab 'em by!"

"You were shot at through the window," said O'Shay to his friend. "Of course that was the man who tried the trick!"

He pointed to McArdle, and the latter crimsoned with anger.

"That's such a goddam lie," he declared, "that it's got a green beard. I never shot through a window in my life."

"I was shot at through the window of my room at the farm just up the road," declared Templar, "and I think that's the man."

"You do?" grinned the sheriff. "I'm mighty glad to hear it."

"And does that leave me free?" asked Crane, as quiet as ever.

O'Shay added instantly: "We accuse him of conspiracy in tryin' that murder. There's a charge and a half for you!"

"I can prove," said Crane, "that I haven't left this hotel since I first entered it."

"What about it?" asked the anxious sheriff.

"Conspiracy," said O'Shay, seeming to grow hot, "agin the life and liberty of a doggone subject an' citizen of the United States, and if that ain't a charge, damned if I know what is!"

"There isn't the substance of a spider's web in that charge," said Crane, "And I'll prove—"

"The sheriff isn't going to let you stand here and talk all the night through," suggested O'Shay. "Take your medicine like a man, Crane. You know you're as guilty as hell!"

"I know," began Crane—

"It's a good charge—it's a fine charge," declared the sheriff. "And we'll rake in the girl, later. It's as good a charge as I ever heard. You boys march through the door—wait till I tie you together. I got a couple of beds waiting for you in the jail. They'll make you comfortable, and you can talk to the judge next Tuesday, maybe!"

There was a yell of rage from McArdle, but his taller companion said quietly: "We'll have a writ of habeas corpus tomorrow. There is a law in the land, and I know the points of it! Come along. Don't make noise until there's a point to be gained by it."

Under this persuasion, the pair faced toward the door, and the sheriff made a wry face at O'Shay and Templar.

"You've given me a handful," he whispered, "but I'm gunna bluff it through."

"Watch your jail tonight," warned O'Shay. "And good luck, sheriff."

"I'll get your testimony in the morning, when the row begins?"

"Of course," said O'Shay breezily.

So the sheriff disappeared, far from a happy figure. When the door closed on him, Templar turned angrily to his companion.

"We can't wait here till tomorrow to give evidence," said he. "We've got to ride, and we've got to ride this same night. You hear?"

"Old son," grinned O'Shay, "I never figured on staying. Neither does Crane, if he can work through the walls of that jail. Only—if we ain't got him to lead us, I'm wondering just where we'll be riding so fast, Johnnie?"

"Did you ever hear of a place called Tolman?"

"I know it like a book!"

"Then that's where we're heading, because that's where I heard them say that they're going—the pair of them. Tolman is our riding point, old man! That's where *he* is."

"He who?"

"The murderer of Snyder; the murderer of Condon; the crook who has the five million. Danny, let's start!"

CHAPTER XXXIV

Hong Kong was gone; Crane and McArdle were secured in the jail; vaguely they felt that he whom they sought was in Tolman. So they prepared to journey in that direction as fast as they could. O'Shay, far from easy, now, exhibited every sign of worry. For Crane with his calm demeanor had impressed the giant greatly.

He lay, presently, flat on his back on their bed at the house of the one-legged farmer, and in gasps and groans he cursed the steepness of the wall and the slipperiness of the stones. Thrice, he said, he had hung by the tips of his nails.

"If I'd cut my nails yesterday, I'd be dead today," said O'Shay.

Then he turned his attention for a moment to the girl. She had not got out through the door, he was sure. Either she had taken advantage of some hidden door to make her escape or else, while they were busy with the two men, she had deliberately worked through the window and climbed down to the ground through that downpour of rain.

"Or maybe," exclaimed the giant suddenly, "she's lyin' out there now, a heap, all broke to pieces. That's most likely!"

Templar closed his eyes; then he added, as he banished the picture: "She'd never make a mistake. She has no nerves except the ones she puts on like her clothes and takes off again when they don't suit her!"

O'Shay remained for some moments with his eyes shut tight, his great arms thrown out and projecting far beyond either side of the bed. His chest was rising and falling in enormous spasms, and his fingers twitched so that for Templar the prodigious labor of the giant in clambering up the wall was reconstructed.

"Beauty!" said O'Shay suddenly.

"Hello?" asked Templar.

"Her," said the giant.

"Who?"

"The beauty! Oh God, ain't she a blowed-in-the-glass wonder, kid?"

Templar stirred uneasily. It was a subject that he did not like.

"She's got a skin like soap," said the ecstatic giant.

Presently he expanded the pleasant thought. "She's got a skin like yaller laundry soap with the sun shinin' through it."

Templar was still silent.

"My God, my God!" groaned the giant again.

"Are you sick, Danny?"

"I want no kind words out of you," said the big man in his enormous voice, which flooded through the room and set heavy echoes rumbling. "I want nothing but trouble with you, Johnnie. It's you and the like of you that's ruined the world for the real men. You and the like of you!"

Templar shrank into a corner, and there waited with a grin.

"A skinny little runt," went on the giant, pursuing his uncomplimentary description, "with nothin' in his head but trouble, made up of equal parts of gunpowder and hell-fire—you, kid, are the kind that turns the heads of the girls, and leaves no chance for the man-sized men! What have you got to say for yourself? The whites ain't enough, but you got to go gunnin' among the yallers, too. Kid, what I think of your morals, it would be a terrible thing to speak out in public."

"The stand-in that I have with Hong Kong, because

I suppose that's what you mean," answered Templar, "is a wonderful thing, Danny. She's tried to poison me, and she's tried to bash in my head with a cleaver."

"Little playful attentions—love-taps," grinned the giant. "Johnnie, to speak serious, she's a sort of a yaller peril, I'd write her down."

Templar was silent for a moment and then broke out: "Old son, just tell me whether she's white or Chinese!"

"Look at you!" groaned the big man. "Listen at you, too! Does it make a difference whether a horse is a chestnut or a roan, so long as they cover the ground and got a easy gait? And if the insides of a hoss counts more than the outsides, ain't it true of a woman? Ain't she got more insides than outsides? Here you are up agin a doggone immortal soul, and you ask me is she white or yaller! Which you're plumb disgustin' at times, kid!"

"If she's a Chink," said young Templar, his brow creased with intense thought, "she may have murdered Condon—she may even have murdered Snyder! If she's white—of course that's a different matter!"

"Wrong agin," announced O'Shay. "If she's a Chink, as she looks, most likely she's follerin' around on this trail because the poor girl is busting her heart over some man or other. If she's white, she's a doggone dangerous white, able to play a part, sneakin', two-faced, poisonous as hell! You gotta stop dreamin', kid, and try to think. Work your brain harder and your feet less!"

239

Suddenly he said in a changed tone: "Crane—there's a man, kid."

"He is," admitted Templar. "He's all wool."

He added: "And a low trick that we've played on him, Danny. He'll stay in that jail with his work spoiled, whatever it may be!"

O'Shay grunted.

"He'll stay in that jail not half the night, or I'm a liar," said he. "Jails ain't made in this neck of the woods to hold boys like Crane. He'll just sort of melt out of that jail, son, like a hot bullet through a pad of butter."

"Then we ought to hit the trail!" cried Templar.

"Why am I lyin' here and groanin' some of the wrinkles out of my mind?" asked O'Shay. "Why am I stretched out here like a doggone coyote skin dryin' in the sun? So's I can freshen up for a long ride, me boy. Go down and tell the old man to lay out the chuck. We eat, pay, and run for Tolman, and a devil of a trail we got ahead of us!"

They followed that schedule exactly.

The farmer's wife, her eyes small and bright with curiosity, served them on the kitchen table; then they paid for food and lodging and damages and went to their horses, which they found lying down. In five minutes they were pulling up the slippery mud of the main street of the town.

At the sheriff's house they branched to the left and in a moment they were sunk in the wilderness of the mountains. A good road led them, however; the rain had stopped, and patches of stars shone feebly from time to time, so that they pushed steadily on through the tired hours. Very late the moon arose, and, as it stood white and big at the side of a white mountain, O'Shay stopped his horse.

"This is where Crane makes his break," he said. "Whatever it is that he wants in Tolman, he thinks that we're on the way to be there before him, and the rising of this here moon is gunna drive him almost mad, Johnnie. Mind you, in another few minutes, he'll be driving out from the town, and most likely he'll have fresher horses than ours and a better knowledge of the trail."

He chuckled softly.

"What a game! What a game!" murmured the giant, and urged his horse forward again.

Under the moon they could see the ranges clearly enough. They were on a ridge intermediate between two loftier ones both east and west, and O'Shay pointed out that Tolman lay over the eastern summits in a wild hole-in-the-wall country—the ideal place for one to go who wished to skip out of the ken of man for a time.

The sun rose on two very tired travelers and two utterly spent horses as O'Shay turned down into the eastern valley which lay under the great eastern summits.

Horses never could cover the miles of cliffs, ice, and snow which towered there above timberline; so they left the pair at a small shack which they blundered across, where the owner, looking half hermit and half hunter, promised to take good care of the animals until the owners returned.

He offered them breakfast of cold pone and coffee that tasted like black lye. Then they stretched themselves on the floor of the shack and slumbered heavily in their wet clothes for several hours.

After their sleep, they started on, and climbed through half a mile of stunted trees until they came to the wild frontier of timberline where willows and the other indomitable pioneers of the forest maintained a terrible life in the face of wind and cold. Far to right and left they saw the long dark line stretched out, the forest like a shadow beneath, and the barren highlands above. Then they braced themselves for the crossing. It was not a wide range at this point, but they were forced to keep to the most difficult going, because in the hollows between the peaks the snows were buried a hundred feet deep by the last storm; so they made slow progress, their breath growing scant with the thin air, their heads dizzy with altitude and labor.

A head wind, they felt, would have turned them back, but luckily the only currents of air were from the due north and, though the force of it freshened each moment, still it was not until they were over the worst of the divide that the storm came. They had before them a series of long white slopes, tumbling smoothly one into the other; the dark forests began, then, and these dipped into many hollow valleys. Far and wide to the east lay a broken region chopped with many gorges in which the water flashed far off and faintly, like gleams of blue light.

This was the hole-in-the-wall region of which O'Shay had spoken, and Templar appreciated its points and difficulties at once. Even a fool might hide himself here from a thousand wise men, and certainly he on whose trail they journeyed was far from a fool!

"Hell's popping up north," said O'Shay suddenly. "Start moving, boy!"

They hurried on with all their might. To the north they saw a bluish haze which advanced with seeming slowness until they noticed how it trampled out of sight peaks and ranges to the northward; then premonitory gusts began to dash at them and send up great mists and flurries of the dry, newly fallen snow. Every moment those gusts became more frequent; the bluish haze seemed to be lifting in the north; they could see far and wide, and then the cold wash of the storm closed over them and bit them to the bone.

CHAPTER XXXV

They had hardly two hundred yards to make to the timberline beneath, but it seemed to Templar that they must perish before they gained that meager shelter. He was numb below the hips; his legs worked only through a conscious effort, and he had to flex each knee with individual attention. Black spots were dancing before his eyes, and his thoughts whirled in a strange, giddy fashion.

The wind was increasing to a scream; about them rushed a blast filled with snow particles that blazed like streams of white fire with the sun, which shone with such mocking brightness from above. He was aware of O'Shay like a fabulous white monster, beckoning to him, and standing still. He, Templar, struggled with all his might, but his legs went up and down; he could not advance an inch.

O'Shay came back. His breath was a cloud of steam. Something he shouted, and suddenly swung Templar across his shoulder like a log of wood and so went blundering and floundering along through the snow, leaning far to one side against the blast of the storm.

The whiteness vanished before them; they lay now side by side on the verge of the timberline, with a stunted tangle of trees defending them while they dropped their heads and regained their breath.

By the time they had recovered a little they had before them a strange and mighty spectacle, for the wind all this while had been increasing in power, and now it was like a flood that has burst from a lofty dam. In the cold of the northern polar regions, perhaps, that mighty tide of air had its roots, and now it whiplashed across the mountains with a gathering impetus. The vast piles of dry, heaped, accumulated snows had their crusted surfaces worn away and chiseled off, and then whole masses began to be thrown into motion by the gale. By the shoulders and at the heads of the peaks, delicate white streamers began to appear for a flashing instant before they were jerked down. Then wider flags were tossed on the sea of wind, and finally, from the top of every crest, from every minor peak and towering giant, the enormous flags of translucent, crystal snow were blowing, stretching out, tearing off at the edges, and letting loose streamers dart across the sky. The sun played gloriously over it all, showering rainbow colors in masses, and turning the shadows beneath those trembling white flags to a most unearthy purple. Even in silence, it would have been such a scene as makes all the battles of man as nothing, but it was not silent.

Every small ravine whistled like a piercing flute, and through the staggering forest moans and whinings of violins kept growing, while the larger canons, the hollows, the big valleys roared each with a separate note, and through all some special demon of the wind kept striding up and down with footballs that clanged terribly on the heights and boomed like the fall of avalanches in the valleys.

They watched that grand display and then turned to each other with a common thought. Not until they were well below in the shelter of the woods could they speak with any ease, and then Templar asked at once: "Do you think he would be caught in it?"

"I don't know," said the giant. "But if he was—"

His face hardened, but then he shrugged his shoulders.

"There are ways of livin' out storms like that. We're not mountaineers, but Crane probably would know. A fellow like him knows nearly everything," he added with an air of deep respect, "because he's had fifteen years of silence to do all his thinkin' in. Kid, when we rub against him again, we're gain' to lose some skin!"

As they descended, the turmoil behind them grew less and less; finally they came out on the side of a river that stormed down a narrow ravine, filling it with dashings and white lightning in the sun. O'Shay, after a moment's hesitation, turned down the course of the canon, and they made good time until mid-afternoon. Then their companion river emptied into a greater stream; there was a widening valley garbed in black forest on either side, and looking down this valley they saw a small blur of distant houses.

"That's Tolman," said O'Shay. "It gives me a chill, kid, to look at it, because there or somewhere near there we're going to find the end of this here trail, as I think."

Templar thought so as well, but he said nothing, merely narrowing his eyes a little, and they strode on side by side, glad of the easier going wider foot. Before evening in the golden time of the afternoon, they came to Tolman.

Templar was for putting up at some house near the village or else for living in the woods on what game they could shoot, but O'Shay vetoed that suggestion, for, as he said, the people of Tolman were used to strangers who arrived on foot after a long trek and no questions were asked.

Besides, they must now strive to pick up the trail

itself; hitherto they had been toiling simply in a general direction. There was ample chance that the quarry would be warned, if the quarry were really some person other than Crane or McArdle. At any rate, they would have a chance to ensconce themselves before those two travelers arrived, and, if they could watch the two, out of their actions they might be led to the goal.

O'Shay, as usual, prevailed, and they went on into the town. Tolman was a place which, when not actually land-locked, seemed perpetually just recovering from a storm, or immediately after a thaw. Patches of dirty snow lay on the northern sides of houses; the streets were washed by little runlets which had cut through surface dust and gravel to rock beneath, or to hard clay. The roofs were built with a great overhang, like Swiss cottages, and the walls were braced outside with heavy cross-timbers. So that it was plain that even the tall woods which came to the edge of the village were slight protection against the great mountain winds that swept down the valley, like water crowded into a funnel. The weight of those battering winds seemed scarcely taken from Tolman; it seemed still crushed, like a ship dripping and uncertain after a heavy squall.

Its people were oddly in contrast with their town, for they went about the streets singing, they paused to admire half a dozen sleek cows driven home to be milked, they chattered noisily from open doors and windows, and the air was enriched by the fragrance of

247

suppers cooking in every kitchen.

"Down in the desert or up here, they all gotta do the same," philosophized the giant. "All gotta cook the three squares a day; all gotta work for rent and clothes; and between workin' and sleepin' and complainin', how much time we got for livin', kid? Look here at these folks. Live in a kind of hell, but they've all made up their minds that they're gunna close their eyes agin the facts and be cheerful. What're you gunna do, kid? Laugh at 'em for bein' blind, or praise 'em for bein' happy? Why, it looks to us like they was livin' in the middle of winter, but that's what we're all doin'. Livin' in the middle of winter, and tryin' to call it summer to ourselves. It takes a gent from the outside to see the truth!"

They paused to watch a six-horse team pulling a heavy wagon laden with beer barrels; rolling violently over a deep water-rut, the wagon lurched and a barrel staggered, then crashed to the ground.

Instantly a chorus of sympathetic voices warned the driver to slam on his brakes, and a swarm of helpers poured out to assist him in working the barrel back into the wagon. The teamster, short, burly, powerful, a dark man with beetling brows, warned the crowd back with a huge bass voice.

"Keep your hands off for a minute," said he. "It ain't any use melling around like this here. You gotta take time. You gotta think."

Templar grinned at his companion.

"Like you, big boy," said he.

"He's got the look of a worth while citizen," replied O'Shay, unabashed. "If he ain't a thug of an ex-prize fighter like Snyder, he's a pretty good fellow!"

Finally, under the directions of the teamster, several stout men grasped the barrel and heaved it up, but they failed in proper unison of effort, and the barrel slipped suddenly from their hands. They tried again and yet again, always with less and less success, because plainly they had become afraid of getting too closely under the heavy barrel for fear it would fall and crush their feet. The wagoner was beginning to grow profane when O'Shay strode through the puzzled crowd, where every man now was giving advice. Some favored passing two boards under the barrel, so that more persons could lift with an easy purchase, and others were for making an inclined plane so that the barrel might be rolled up to the rest of the load.

O'Shay settled all of these arguments by leaning and grappling both ends of the barrel in his mighty hands. There was a shrill burst of laughter, followed by an equally sudden burst of seriousness. "He means to try."

"He looks near big enough to do it!"

"You fool, no man could lift that, unless he was a horse!" So they commented in murmurs, and the teamster stood by with ironical encouragement.

"Take a good hold, me lad," said he. "Bend your back to it, and get it up. It's all in the knack. Now, heave!"

O'Shay actually raised the barrel to above his knees,

when one end of it slipped down and the barrel crashed back into the mud. A groan of sympathy applauded this great effort.

"Try again," said the teamster, still unmoved. "Nobody else in the world could get that barrel up to the wagon, but maybe you're the man."

O'Shay spat upon his hands, rubbed them together, flexed his knees, and then took a great breath and laid hold again.

This time he went about it more slowly; the barrel rose slowly to his knees. Half squatting, he rested it there for a moment, the vast burden driving his shoes almost ankle deep into the mud; then he rolled it up the inclined plane of his thighs until it was jammed against his stomach. Then one heave of legs, arms, shoulders and body drove the barrel from him and onto the wagon, where it settled with a smash that threatened to knock the bottom from the vehicle.

There was a loud outcry, but all the noise did not match the wonder of the teamster, who laid a hand upon the trembling shoulder of O'Shay and said quietly: "You're a *man*. Come drink with me!"

CHAPTER XXXVI

O'Shay, however, refused to drink until the load was off the wagon, for, as he pointed out, it was growing late. So the wagon was driven up to the side door of the hotel and the barrels were worked off down a shoot into the cellar, Templar lending a strong hand in the work.

O'Shay found a chance to warn him in an undertone: "We're busted punchers lookin' for a job. We lost everything down to our hosses at faro. We walked across the range, not knowin' what lay on this side. We don't want anything to do but ride range. No lumber, no minin'. This here town is full of that sort of work."

When the load was off, the driver insisted on treating; a crowd gathered as they entered the bar-room; and the proprietor himself took the happy occasion to treat all around. He was going to weigh that particular barrel, he declared, and then prepare another just like it, loaded with an equal poundage of stone. Any man who could lift it earned free drinks for the crowd and a bonus besides.

"I seen Jeff Hammond lift seven hundred pounds of junk iron onto a scales," said the host, "but I never seen a man handle a barrel like that, before. But which is heavier, I dunno—the man or the keg!"

They had their beer. The air fairly reeked with friendship and admiration.

It seemed to Templar that nothing could be much more foolish than to advertise themselves so liberally as this, for certainly whether the enemy already was in Tolman or was about to come, he would be sure to hear in detail about the giant and his feat. So forewarned, such a fox never would be seen again!

O'Shay, however, seemed totally without apprehension. He appeared to have relaxed and, sprawled in his chair, he quaffed foaming beer. When someone sat down to beat the jangling piano in a corner of the bar-room, O'Shay arose to bellow forth songs of the desert range in a voice that deafened his hearers.

It began to be a festival. Supper was forgotten. Money and beer flowed freely, for this was not a whiskey town. And Templar, gloomy in a corner, smoked one cigarette after another and fretted. He would not drink; he would not talk. O'Shay, having led brilliantly over the long trail, now was throwing himself away for the sake of some silly liquor.

The hotel keeper, in the meantime, had called on his two rosy cheeked sons to help him. Three men could serve the crowd which drank and sang, and chattered and drank and sang again! The evening wore old, and O'Shay seemed in deep conversation with a graybeard who rose from time to time to sing comic songs of the old frontier. He was growing tipsy. The step of O'Shay also was unsteady. Smoke filled the room; voices blared and bellowed; it began to appear to sober John Templar like the most utter folly.

He walked out from the hotel, therefore, to take a breath of fresh air under the stars. They were all out, bright and clear, with the sky scoured by a brisk wind out of the north which kept the tall pines swaying and nodding and stung the cheeks and the eyes with cold. It was far better out here in spite of the wind and the chill; the roar of the mirth indoors sounded like the sea breaking on a shore, and a most unmusical shore, at that. So he went back toward the light which hung at the entrance to the stable behind the hotel, but, as he turned the corner of the building, a great form rushed at him out of the trees at the rear of the hotel. It was O'Shay, and he was in a high state of excitement.

"Johnnie, me lad," said he, throwing a great arm about the shoulders of his friend, "I think that I have it!"

"You have a head full of beer," said Templar. "Go sleep it off. You've chucked away our best evening and night, Danny. Damned if I'm not sorry that I ever brought you along!"

"And you, son," chuckled the big man, "what have you been doin' while I sat and drank?"

"I've been thinking that even an intelligent man can play the ass, Danny!"

"You've sat in a corner," grinned the giant, "and you've looked like a murder. They began to edge away from you. They began to ask me questions about you. You looked dangerous. I had to tell them, finally, that you was a poor young feller that had married a wife that was too much for you, and that you had run away from home because you was afraid of your woman. But you was tormented because you'd left a baby behind you and thought that maybe you should of stuck it out, after all, and when—"

"Confound you!" groaned Templar. "You immortal liar, Danny!"

"Hush, man, they stopped suspectin' you at once and they begun to sympathize with you. There was one that had tears in his eye when he seen you walk out. 'Gone out into the night, but the night, it won't give him no comfort and no answer. I've tried it. I've had a woman meself!' "

O'Shay laughed uproariously again.

"You're drunk," said Templar in disgust. "Go get a bed and sleep it off!"

"Drunk on beer?" said O'Shay, with abounding good humor. "There ain't that much beer in the world, Johnnie. No, I been talkin' and listenin'. Questions I've asked which it took beer to lead up to, and talk I've heard that had more than beer behind it. I'm as sober as a judge, Johnnie."

"You've talked," nodded Templar. "I heard you talking. You driveled, O'Shay. I was ashamed to be with you."

"You wasn't with me," answered the big man. "You was a thousand miles away in the same barroom. You was mopin', and I was usin' me brains hard and fast."

"On old, half-witted graybeards?" asked Templar. "A fellow with hardly sense enough to know his name?"

"Ay, there you go, there you go!" complained the giant. "Always leapin' before you're lookin'! But I looked first and jumped afterwards, and the result of it was that I think I've crossed a pretty wide stream—"

"Of beer," added the sarcastic Templar.

"I've rung up on the far side, I think," said the big man, "and shall I tell you the way of it?"

"I'll listen to you, Danny, but I know you're wrong, this time!"

"Who's come through Tolman lately? That was what we wanted to find out, I suppose?"

"I suppose that was it."

"Well, kid. In the last two days there's been an old man seein' can he locate a lumber mill up here, but he got discouraged a good deal because he heard that already there was a mill that was put up on the creek north of town; it run big and failed big after a few years, and the place has been standin' idle ever since."

"What in hell have we to do with old men?" asked Templar angrily. "Did an old man murder Condon—or Snyder? Do you want me to infer that?"

"Then," said the other, "there was a man lookin' for a job in the mines; a big brute with a scar on his chin."

"That sounds more promising," said Templar, growing interested.

"And this same morning, pretty early, there was a young gent blew in with a damn tired horse. He talked Spanish, and there was nobody but the old gent inside, there, that could understand him. This here young greaser said that he'd heard there was some good land for grazin' sheep around about Tolman, and he would like to be directed. My old friend told him that if he went south down the valley he'd find some pretty good grass lands, though the winters was all hard—"

"Confound the grasslands!" exclaimed Templar.

"Hold on, son! Now, the old boy saw the young greaser ride south, and then he started north to the hills above the creek to look at his line of traps, and, while he was up there, he happened to look down and he

255

seen a rider come out of the woods and go across the open near the creek towards the old mill. He was interested, because nobody ever goes near the old mill. It's haunted so powerful, kid, that even in the daytime it's got a scare hangin' to it. And he says to himself that it's like a greaser not to believe in the good advice that he receives. It's like a greaser to just turn around and aim for the opposite direction, figurin' that the truth was always covered up by the lyin' gringos. He guessed it was the young greaser, and when he got out his glass and bore down on the mill, he was sure of it. He recognized him plain and clear and easy."

"You think that a greaser could have done this job?" asked Templar. "Perhaps—I don't know."

"I was sort of interested, too, in the way the old boy described that greaser," said O'Shay, "Said he had the look of bein' maybe sixteen or seventeen—"

"No sixteen-year-old ever did that job on Snyder," said Templar with certainty.

"My God, man, will you hear me out, or are you gunna keep kickin' over the traces?"

"I'll hear you out," grumbled Templar, "but the fact is, old boy, though you don't know it, you've been wasting your time in there. You thought you were getting clever, but you were only getting drunk!"

"All right," said O'Shay, "maybe I was. Only listen to me, will you? This greaser had the look of a kid of sixteen or seventeen. Very yaller kind of greaser he was. More yaller than brown."

"I've seen them that way."

"So have I, but shut up and don't interrupt. This here greaser was a fine lookin' kid, straight and skinny. He had a pleasant smile that sort of warmed your heart, and he had very black eyes, made slantwise, unlike the eyes of most folks—"

"My God!" gasped Templar. "D'you mean—"

"What?"

"D'you mean Hong Kong?"

"I dunno. I just thought that we might slide over to the old mill and see what the greaser was so interested in about the haunted house, so to speak! You willing to foller the lead of a drunk man that far?"

Templar struck his knuckles across his forehead.

"You're right, Danny," he exclaimed. "You're always right. Follow you? I'll follow you to the end of the world. Where does the old mill lie?"

"Me old friend told me all about it. Fall in behind and we start now!"

CHAPTER XXXVII

The road to the old mill opened in the middle of Tolman. It crossed a bridge so worn that it staggered a little even under the stride of pedestrians. As for the road itself, it was hardly worthy of that name, for since it was last used by wagons enough time had passed by to allow a sturdy growth of saplings to spring up, and now it was so choked with lodgepole pines that often it was difficult to tell which was the road and which was the forest.

There was no moon, but there was bright, frosty starlight, and the two worked patiently ahead. Danny O'Shay persisted in breaking trail, sweeping a way before his smaller companion.

"You gotta save yourself," he replied to Templar's protest. "You gotta be good to yourself and shoot straight when the time comes, because I hope that we're gunna shoot it out, tonight!"

That thought was not in the mind of Templar, for what haunted him was the thought of Hong Kong in the haunted mill on this dark mountain night. It was not a picture that made him feel pity for her; rather it was one that frightened him, as thinking of her without nerves, without fear, in a situation which would have shaken the strongest of men. Whether there was more imp or woman in her he could not tell. He only knew that she possessed some quality which upset his equilibrium entirely.

Big O'Shay stopped in the midst of his Herculean task of trail-breaking and said, as though Templar had been speaking his thoughts aloud: "Johnnie!"

"Ay, Dan?"

"D'you love her, or d'you just like her company?"

"I don't know," sighed Templar. "Get on, man, get on! God knows what's happening to her now!"

"She speaks Spanish," said the big man, and straight-way plunged on through the second-growth forest of the roadway as though this last remark were greatly pertinent.

It was not, felt Templar. She might readily have spent long enough in Mexico to learn some of the Spanish tongue, an easier tongue to pick up, certainly, than the English. And yet that she was at home in any European dialect made her more strange, more a power and a mystery to him.

They left the jungle of the road and came into a narrow sweep of open meadow. They heard the loud roar of the creek not far away; under the tall heads of the pines the darkness was so steep and thick that at first they could not make out the mill, but presently they traced its outlines, aided by the faint gleam of starshine on windows here and there. It was a huge bulk, that mill and mill-house, or so it seemed in the dark of the night.

They came closer to it, swinging to the left, so that their eyes were more accustomed to the light of this forest-surrounded clearing, they saw the moldering details of the mill well enough. It was sinking into a hopeless ruin. Yonder was a whole wing reduced to wreckage, and, as they came up, they saw where a great bough had fallen and struck through a roof, already, no doubt, rotting and weak. They became more familiar with the noise of the creek, also, which, as a matter of fact, directly opposite the mill, flattened and widened into a considerable pool caused by the remains of the old dam; and this little lake, half artificial and half natural, made the noise subside somewhat. They only heard the more distant roarings of the stream above and below the mill.

It had been a very considerable establishment. Not only was the mill itself large, but there had been the main house of the owner-manager, and then, to the sides of that, were the quarters of the men. These were the two wings which were so rapidly going to pieces, whereas the central structure was more solid and enduring.

Both the wings they skirted around with caution, O'Shay always keeping the lead and stepping with the greatest slowness and care. He paused once to whisper to the younger man: "One creak, kid, may separate us from five millions!" But Templar did not need that inducement to care. He was thinking of something else, which made him more intense than an Indian on the warpath.

From the farther and more ruined wing, they worked down the bank of the stream towards the main residence. Only a thin screen of young trees grew along that bank, and, as they walked, O'Shay held out an arm like a beam and stopped his companion.

"Look on the water!" he whispered.

And, staring between two lofty poplars, Templar saw a little canoe slide out from the farther bank of the lake. It staggered and struggled—clumsily, as he thought—with the main current that boiled in the center of the pool, but, passing at last through this, it shot on smoothly, struck the bank, and presently the single occupant was out and up past the line of trees that edged the water. He did not turn either up or down the bank, but advanced straight to the wall of the house and stood for a long moment opposite a window. After that, he veered to the left, and suddenly disappeared around the corner of the house.

"After him fast!" said O'Shay, and struck ahead with a sweeping stride, but he kept the lead only a moment. There was little woodcraft in Templar, but instinct made him silent of foot, and nature made him swift. He swerved past his clumsier companion and was increasing his gait to a run when he came opposite the window at which the stranger of the night had paused. There Templar halted as though checked by a rope, and flung up an arm to check the big man behind him. He did not need to explain his halt in words. But when they looked in through the window they saw that inside burned a light so cunningly shaded that hardly a ray reached the window, though a strong glow was in the room itself. Whoever the shadowy man of the canoe might be, that light was more engrossingly interesting.

"Go up to the window—carefully, for God's sake—" instructed O'Shay. "Stand there and watch and see what you can, but don't wander. I'm going away. I'll be back here in three minutes!"

He was gone as he spoke, disappearing among the trees beside the water, while Templar, with a little shudder of loneliness, looked after him. He was strongly tempted to remain where he was until the giant returned. He himself had, he felt, no inconsiderable share of courage and the vital spirit, but to face in one moment the mystery of a haunted house, and

261

Hong Kong, and, perhaps, the murderer of Condon and Snyder, made his courage weaken like starch touched with water.

He had to force himself on, lest O'Shay should come back and find that he had not advanced. There was a slight drop of ground between him and the wall of the house, and, half way down it, his foot slipped on a wet spot and he sat down with a sudden shock.

He was on the very verge of springing up and bolting, after that, but he controlled himself, his heart racing wildly. With all his might he listened, and, very distinctly, he heard from within the house something very like the squeak of a chair, pushed suddenly back, or of a rusted hinge of a door yielding to a quick pressure.

Perhaps they had heard the noise made by his fall, and would come out to investigate, silent-footed as ghosts, swift as birds—

Reaching beneath his coat, he touched and gripped hard the handle of a Colt, and that touch gave him sudden strength. It was a kindly, familiar presence, and it enabled him to go on again. He was irritated. Surely O'Shay's one or two minutes already had elapsed!

Now he was close under the window, but, at the bottom of the bank, as he then was, he found the window to be above his head. It required delicately careful work to find a projecting bit of stonework on which he could step and raise himself until he was on the level with the sill of the window, looking cautiously into the chamber.

What he saw, so far as the very dim, uncertain light revealed it, was a big room with paneled walls—the paneling loosened and warped from place by time, moisture, and neglect. The ceiling was very lofty and quite lost in the shadow. There was a huge table, massively built, from which he judged that this had been either a library or the dining room in the extravagant time of the builder of the big mill. There were even a few chairs, or ruins of chairs, remaining. Otherwise, the place had no furniture.

The light—he could not tell whether it was lamp or candle, but he suspected the latter, because of the occasional flicker of the shadows—was placed in one of the chairs, which then was screened behind and above with thin boards and focused a dim radiance towards the farthermost corner of the room where, seated cross-legged on a low stool, he saw a youth in a broad-brimmed sombrero—a youth with a very yellow-brown skin and—

The head was raised, the screen of the broad hat brim tipped high, and he was looking into the familiar face of Hong Kong, as perfectly impassive as ever he had seen it in the past. She was not waiting idly, but from a fold of paper on her lap she took sandwiches and munched them slowly, contently, her dark eyes fixed before her with the dim good-nature of a happy child.

It was more terrible to Templar than if he had seen her in this moldy, dark, silent house cowering with terror. For it made him feel, at a stroke, that either she was a being totally stronger than himself, or else she was of a different order. Oceans lay between their natures, wider than the broad Pacific which fences the Occident from the land of the Chinaman.

Presently, she folded the paper of the sandwiches and laid it aside. With a dainty white handkerchief she wiped her lips and rubbed the tips of her fingers, and, taking out paper and a bag of tobacco, she rolled a cigarette dexterously, lighted it, and began to smoke.

Marvelously strange and beautiful she seemed to Templar, as he watched the manner in which she held the cigarette, Chinese fashion, between thumb and forefinger; and he saw her head sink back to blow each puff in leisurely fashion above her, and her eyes half close with each inhalation. She could not have been more absurdly leisurely if she had been sitting in a secure home, surrounded by friends, power, and boredom.

Nerves? There were no nerves in her, and she was merely a highly complicated machine which, as it chose, could simulate anything and everything. He did not smile as he recalled how she had played with him in the house of Condon, and in that other house in Last Luck. She could play with anyone or anything; no brain, it appeared, could be matched against hers except—and he felt the truth of this with wonder—the quiet force of Crane, whom they had left behind them in the jail. "Long may that jail keep him!" thought young Templar.

The smoke clouds, thin as they were, were enough to quite screen her face in that very faint light, so that he had only separated glimpses of her; and yet it is by glimpses and side glances that we see the deepest into our hearts and the hearts of others.

Templar, clinging to the window, knew then suddenly that the yellow skin made no difference to him, and, no matter what dreadful crimes lay in her past, he loved her! No thrill of happiness passed through his heart when that knowledge came home to him. Rather he set his teeth and closed his eyes—and, closing them, he heard a light, stealthy sound behind him.

He swung instantly back from the window. It was big O'Shay, of course, and yet he must take no chances. So, maintaining his grip on the window sill with his left hand, he swung himself back, getting a safe support for his foot, and wedging himself into the slight corner made by the changed angle of the wall just past the window.

Then, coming swiftly and softly from the trees, he saw a man coming toward him. He steadied himself, his revolver ready at his hip, his nerves suddenly at ease and his heart leaping at the actual presence of danger. On the top of the bank the form hesitated, crouched low, the faint glimmer of steel distinguishable in his hand.

CHAPTER XXXVIII

As a leaf balances and turns swiftly in the wind, so the mind of Templar wavered; he could not be sure that the stranger saw him, and if he were discovered that instant he would die. Whereas with one shot perhaps he would be striking the murderer on whose trail they were working.

It was really an excellent target which the stranger afforded, for, in the background, the shadow of a tree trunk went upward on either side of him, and he was standing against the faint glimmer of the water of the lake. Only for a moment the other remained; then he slipped noiselessly away in the direction from which he had come and, as though to cover his retreat, the wind blew softly from the north and filled the air with whisperings.

Before Templar could shift his position so as to look through the window again, the unmistakeable bulk of O'Shay loomed before him, and the giant came softly down into the lower ground beneath the window. Templar descended to him at once.

"Is there anything inside?" asked O'Shay in the faintest of whispers.

"Hong Kong!" said Templar.

"Ah, ah," murmured the big man. "I thought that we'd find her at the end of the trail. Anyone else?"

"No."

"But there must be someone else!"

"There is, but who, I don't know. A man with a gun was there looking through the window, a second ago. He went back in that direction."

"Could Hong Kong have been the figure in the canoe?"

"Perhaps. What have you there in your hand?"

"Nothin' much, kid. I only have the loot. That's all!"

"The which?"

"The loot, me boy. I went down to the canoe, and there it was, in this satchel, covered over with a tarpaulin. I risked lightin' a couple of matches. It's filled with bank notes and securities, Johnnie. And all of this has to go to Lister! I wouldn't grudge it, if he'd stayed and worked out the trail."

"Damn the money!" said Templar. "What I want is the man! Climb up here and keep watch over what may happen in the room. You'll see Hong Kong in the far corner. I'm going to soft-foot back there and see if I can't come across the fellow of the gun."

"Stay where you are," answered O'Shay. "I'll do the scoutin'. You watch this room, because I got an idea that things will begin to happen here before long. I'll be back in a few minutes. In any case, don't let Hong Kong move!"

He did not wait to argue the point but faded suddenly into the dark, and Templar unwillingly let him go; after all, he could not pretend to rival O'Shay as a scout!

For himself, he quietly regained his post at the window, and there turned and glanced down. Far below, at his feet, was the satchel containing the stolen fortune. The trail had been long, and yet, now that they had such a great reward, it seemed to Templar that all had been smooth and easy. Confidence rose in him, also, that they would be able to complete their work in all ways, and a tingling expectation rose in him, as if the confessed murderer of Condon were about to stand before him. He tried to conjure up a figure from his imagination: no doubt it would prove to be the slinking form of the shepherd; and yet that hardly matched with the ideas which he held about the criminal—strong, subtle, keen, and relentless. How could such a man force himself to live even for a few months as a wild shepherd among the hills?

In the meantime, there was Hong Kong, slowly finishing her cigarette, in all respects the same as he had seen her last, except that there was an alteration in her attitude. Some of the sleepy ease had departed from her.

The reason for that change appeared at once. Templar heard the soft fall of a foot in the room, and into the glow of the light came a man whose face was quite concealed by a slouching felt hat, whose clothes were tattered and worn in the extreme. He approached the girl slowly, and there was a gun ready in his hand, a Colt with a long, blue-shining barrel. He did not pause or speak until he came to the end of the big table and there he halted and sat down on the edge of it, letting one leg swing freely.

"If any of them located me, I knew it would be you,"

he said. "I've been half expecting you, my dear!"

Templar clung tight in his place; his hair was literally lifting on his head, for the voice which he heard, he knew well, and never dreamed that he would hear it again. It was Condon!

"The rest of 'em," went on Condon, "would never have sent their thoughts around the corner, so to speak. But you are different, my child! I only hope," he added with a slight change of tone, "that you haven't come here with too many false hopes. What do you want, to begin with?"

Hong Kong waved her graceful hand. It left a thin circle of smoke hanging in the air.

Then she said: "I come tell you, Mister Clane, plenty queek he here."

The foot of Condon ceased its pendulous movement. "Crane!" he said at last.

Hong Kong began to roll a new cigarette.

"Do you know who Crane is?" asked Condon. "What the devil *do* you know? And who and what are you?"

She paused and regarded him earnestly.

"No savvy," she said at last, and resumed the rolling of the cigarette, which she finished with the utmost nicety. Condon held a match for her, and when the cigarette was withdrawn from the flame, still he kept it close to her face; and always the gun was ready. He studied her until the fire touched his fingers; then he drew back. He resumed his place on the table's edge.

"How you know I here?" he asked in a feeble attempt at pigeon-English.

"No savvy," said the girl.

"Do I understand this damned tangle?" went on Condon. "You've had some dealings with Crane—you hate him—it gives you a certain amount of odd Chinese pleasure just to disappoint him in his search for me? Is that it?"

"No savvy," said the girl, and puffed smoke very slowly at the ceiling.

"What you want, hey?" asked Condon again.

"Want nossing," said the girl, and she stood up.

"Come over here where I can see you," said Condon. "By light—you stand!" he strove to translate himself.

She came at once and stood where the candlelight shone full upon her. Her hands were passed into the opposite sleeves. There was not a vestige of expression in that blank face and Condon, standing just before her, at last shook his head.

It was not Hong Kong that Templar watched, however; it was Condon, on whom he pored with a grim interest. He was exactly as he had been before; not a line of face or expression had altered; only the situation was changed, and by a new light Templar read him. Yonder in the house near Last Luck, with danger overwhelming him, his nerves crumbling, Condon had seemed formidable, in spite of an apparent helplessness. But now that long, pale face seemed to Templar the most dangerous thing in the world. With all his heart he wished that O'Shay were back at his side!

"You beat me; you beat me altogether," said

270

Condon. "I knew you were a clever little snake when you first came to my house, but I was sure, then, that you were one of the crew, I really thought you were a white woman, made up yellow for the part. Damned if I'm certain about you now! Tell me one thing. Did you try to poison Templar?"

"No savvy," said the girl.

"Come, come," said Condon impatiently. "There's no harm in talking a little more frankly. Templar's dead now, you know!"

Now it had seemed to Templar that nothing in the world could touch the imperturable calm of this girl, but Condon had found a magic word. Under the thin screen of the silken sleeves, her arms were caught close to her breast, her lips parted, and the slant eyes grew almost round with terror or with grief. Twice she tried to speak before her lips half stammered, half whispered: "Mister Templar?"

Condon had begun to grin with an ugly self-content.

"Dead," he said. "He and the big man both dead, my child. Caught in storm—plenty big wind—snow—mountains—both dead! And if—"

He stopped, and sprang back until he was almost lost in the shadows, for a whistle rang through the house, not from the outside, but from within the walls.

CHAPTER XXXIX

The Chinese girl remained without moving, as though she still were dazed by the last word she had heard. The interest of that whistle, whether danger or help for Condon, hardly touched Templar, he was so much more absorbed in poring upon the face of the girl, so much deeper in the riddle of her thoughts, for the mildest modesty could not have kept him from seeing that he was something to her as vital in meaning as she to him. He had only that moment for studying her, since then she began to drift slowly back into the shadows.

A man's voice called: "Condon! Condon! D'you hear me?"

No enmity in that voice, at least!

"I hear you," answered Condon.

"I'm McArdle. I've buried the hatchet. Condon, I'm bringing in the proof that I'm on your side!"

"Bring it in, then."

"I got your sacred word of honor?"

"I won't harm you."

There was a sound of stamping feet, panting, the dragging of a heavy body, and, into the pale shaft of light, McArdle appeared dragging the great bulk of O'Shay, which trailed limp and helpless on the floor. A great red gash on his forehead told what had happened, and there was only one question: Did he live or was he dead?

Turned to cold steel, Templar raised two guns, and waited.

"My God, the weight of him!" panted McArdle. "He's an elephant. How are you, Andrew?"

He held out his hand, and Condon, after the slightest hesitation, took it.

"You don't need to have any doubts," grinned McArdle. "I made up my mind to shift from the old track the minute that I could, but it's been a hell of a job to break away from Crane. He's been a leech!"

"Where is he now?"

"Miles and miles back! He can't get here till morning. I shot his horse and left him in the lurch."

"You're a good boy, Mac," said Condon quietly. "You've ripened a lot in the last fifteen years."

"I think we can use each other, chief," suggested McArdle.

"I think we can," said Condon, thoughtful as ever. "Look out, that man is coming to. Tie his hands behind him."

"Tie hell!" said McArdle brutally. "This is the best rope to tie him with."

He shook his revolver as he spoke.

Condon merely smiled.

"Good old Mac," said he. "Still out for the root and branch methods! But I don't want him dead. I want him living—for a few minutes. We have to learn where his partner is."

"The young one is a fool," said McArdle. "There ain't any need to bother about him!"

Grimly Templar smiled to himself, and kept his bead steadily drawn on McArdle's heart.

In the meantime, McArdle rapidly secured the hands of big O'Shay and he had hardly finished that business before the giant groaned and lurched into a sitting position. His head swayed as though he were sick with pain.

"Wipe the blood from his face," commanded Condon.

McArdle obeyed.

"I found him sneaking at the side door, yonder," he explained. "I cracked him on the head. I thought maybe you'd accept him as a ticket."

"O'Shay!" said Condon.

"Well, well, well," said Danny O'Shay, mastering himself and wakening to all that was around him. "Here's the end of the trail, at last!"

"It may be—or the beginning of a new one," replied Condon. "That rests with you, my friend."

"We talk business, then?" said O'Shay cheerfully.

"We talk business, if you want."

"It looks as though I want to," nodded O'Shay, and grinned at the leveled gun in the hand of McArdle.

"Now, O'Shay, it's fairly plain that we have you?"

"Yes, it's fairly plain."

"We'll make a bargain with you for information."

"Go on, then. I thought you had about all the secret information in the world, though."

Condon was pleased enough to allow another smile. "I want to know about Templar," said he. "Where's your young crony?"

"Back in Tolman," answered O'Shay at once. "Back in Tolman, drinkin' beer and bein' a young fool."

"That," said Condon, "is a good lie, but a lie nevertheless."

"Is it? Then you know him better than I do," said O'Shay, and totally unabashed, he looked Condon in the face.

"They'd never stir without each other," suggested McArdle. "You can't get away with that, O'Shay!"

"I done a good deal of stirrin' before he was out of knee pants," said O'Shay. "Why shouldn't I of moved tonight when he was glassy-eyed with beer? The kid is still young enough to play the fool!"

"That same fool," said Condon, "was man enough to kill Larry. I've half an idea that if I'd stayed by the game there at Last Luck, he would have beaten off the lot of you. Nevertheless, I don't think that you're telling me the truth, O'Shay!"

"Whistle for the truth, then," answered O'Shay. "I can't see in the dark."

"All right, then," nodded Condon.

McArdle raised his gun, and Templar pressed his trigger. Only the weight of a hair and the hundredth part of a second saved the life of McArdle then, for Condon said: "Wait a minute, Mac. I want to chin with this fellow a while. By the way, where's that damned Chink girl?"

"Yonder in the shadow."

"I don't see her."

"You don't see her?"

"No. She's gone, Mac. Get out of here on the double and find her for me, will you? She can't have gone far. I'll tell you what—she won't try to run for it. She'll try craft. You'll find her sneaking slowly along in the shadow by the river trees, most likely."

MacArdle instantly was gone.

"Watch O'Shay close!" he cautioned, as he fled through the door.

Condon sat down on the table. The light from the candle now struck him fairly on the face.

"As if I needed a caution about watching you, Danny!" said he, dropping his Colt on his knee.

"No," agreed O'Shay, "that's one thing that I could trust you to do. I always could. You've always watched everybody, Andy. And a damned poor return you've had for it!"

"I've had enough," nodded Condon. "I have a little satchel hereabouts with the harvest in it. Not bad. Enough for me, at the least!"

"Yes, you've got the money. But damned little happiness."

"You mean friends, and such things," replied Condon. "They live no longer than dollars, and friends won't work for you except when the humor strikes them—which is only now and then. Dollars, my lad, work day and night forever!"

"I've heard you say that before, in the old days," answered O'Shay.

"Only tell me," went on Condon, "how you happened to take up with this trail?"

"It was partly accident. The kid is a friend of mine. I wanted to help him out with his little puzzle. And then I had a look at the dead 'Condon' that you left behind you."

"It was near enough to the real thing, I take it?" said Condon eagerly.

"Near enough," admitted O'Shay, "but not quite. I had the thing reduced to the sheep herder as the murderer, and it was too damned much to accept, no matter how logical I made it. I couldn't conceive of a half-witted shepherd killing you—and then Snyder on top of you. So I looked at the corpse, and of course I saw that it wasn't you. With his face bashed in, that way, it made a good imitation. That was all. Did he look much like you before you smashed him up."

"Most astonishingly like!" nodded Condon, "so much so that I could see the similarity through his crop of black whiskers, and if I'd had another day or two I would have worked up that thing so carefully that nobody could have suspected that he wasn't I. Not even you, O'Shay."

"It was a grand idea," sighed O'Shay. "But then, your ideas always were grand. Born a century quicker, you would of been a doggone king or something, old son! Was the old gang pressin' you so hard?"

"I didn't mind the rest so much," said Condon. "But when I had the note from Crane, I was scared. One can't take chances with such a fellow. I got a time limit from him by a good deal of begging. I told him that I'd make good with him and split up evenly on everything. That gave me a little while for plans and, when I rode out the next day, I blundered on that shepherd and saw his resemblance to me at the first glance. Nothing occurred to me at the moment, but on the way home I saw how I might use that resemblance—kill myself, and let the law hunt the shepherd, if ever it got any clues at all; and leave the poor fellow behind me, filling my grave, blinding the eyes of my old gang. And I would have done it all, except for chance!"

"What chance?"

"Snyder, who blundered into my room at the wrong moment, and saw the finish of the shepherd! I made terms with Snyder, then and there. But Snyder didn't trust me; he brought along the gang of you to get me. Well, it was a narrow squeak, that evening, but I paid Snyder his back wages and a bonus, besides!"

He laughed a little, and the laughter jarred with an uncommon harshness on the ear of Templar.

"I want to ask you one thing," said O'Shay. "Who's Hong Kong? Who's the Chink girl?"

"That," said Condon, "beats me. I thought you might know. You were always good at conundrums. But you've got a last one to solve now, Danny. Where are you about to travel? Are you going up or down?"

And he steadied the revolver on the breast of O'Shay for a target.

CHAPTER XL

O'Shay nodded in return.

"That's your way of keepin' your bargain?" he asked.

Condon chuckled.

"Be reasonable, Danny," said he. "You didn't expect me to let you go, did you?"

"No. Not really."

"Outside of Crane, I'd rather have any man in the world loose on my trail than you."

"Now, that's a real compliment, Andy."

"It is, and you're worth it. If I could have had you with me, we would have conquered the world, my boy!"

"Then why didn't you team it with Crane?"

"Because, like you, he's an honest man."

"An honest train robber, you mean?"

"You have a lot of information," murmured Condon, his brow darkening for a moment. "As a matter of fact, I don't mind telling you that he was simply my tool, that day. I had to have a fourth man to bring in the horses at the right time. I got Crane to do it, and so we got away. He had no idea that a train robbery was planned. He found out afterwards!"

And Condon laughed again.

"I rather hate to do this, Danny," he went on. "We've hated each other for so long that it's almost worse than parting with an old friend. However, in spite of your information, I think that we'll have to say good-by."

"Hold up just a minute, man, will you?"

"Are you afraid of it, Danny?" asked the criminal, leaning forward with a devilish eagerness to search the face of his victim. "Are you afraid at last, old son?"

"I'm not afraid, but what difference does a minute or two make to you?"

"Crane is after me. That means that every minute counts. Ah, God, what luck, Danny! What luck! Never a man had a finer, braver, neater scheme than mine, but the hound Snyder had to blunder in on me at the last minute. He passed the tip to Crane—"

"Crane bought the news, eh?"

"Yes, yes! And than on the other hand you, Danny, had to slip into Last Luck and bear down on me with your young trained tiger, Templar. I tell you," went on Condon, his angry impatience rising, "no man ever had more reason to expect that his way would be straight, easy sailing to the finish; and no man was ever more horribly disappointed. And in addition to being driven out of this safe hiding place—God knows how Crane spotted me here!—in addition to that, there's the strange girl, the Chinese. What is she doing in this affair? By heavens, O'Shay, she came here tonight, and I found her waiting for me, as cool as a Chinese idol, smoking cigarettes. All she had to say was that Crane was coming after me! What is she doing in the puzzle? It begins to annoy me, Danny!"

Then his face hardened: "But *you'll* annoy me no more, old boy. I don't mind hearing your last prayer,

280

though—and will that ass of a McArdle be able to find the Chink?"

"I have only one last prayer," said O'Shay, "and that is that Johnny Templar will shoot straight."

"When he finds me? But he'll never find me! What does the poet say? Lay not that flattering unction to your soul! No, son, when I disappear from this place, nobody will ever set eye on Condon again. He's going to disappear and show up ten thousand miles away. Maybe inside of a turban!"

He laughed softly.

"You ain't been followin' my drift," replied O'Shay calmly. "The kid already has found you."

"Found me already? You're getting mysterious, Danny."

"Oh, no," said O'Shay. "It's simple enough. We watched you land in the canoe—that's right. But take hold of yourself. Brace your nerves, Andy. We watched you land. The kid came to examine this window; I went down to the canoe—"

"God in heaven!" whispered Condon, and his gun sagged to his side.

"That's right," grinned O'Shay. "I got all the swag and brought it up for safe keepin', and I found that the kid was watchin' the window. He's there now, Condon. He's watchin' you now, with a gun that can't say no!"

Templar, listening to the last words of O'Shay, knew well what was coming. Thick shadow covered the corner on which his window opened, and therefore he risked nothing but the danger of making a noise by swinging lightly inside. Now he advanced slowly out of the shadow.

"You don't deserve a chance, Condon!" he told the latter. "But I'll give you one."

He stepped closer. Condon, like one stunned by misfortune, had allowed his head to fall forward, so that it thrust out between his shoulders. His mouth sagged open; his eyes seemed hollows of darkness. Templar stepped slowly closer. The gun of Condon hung helplessly, at arm's length.

"It's Templar," he managed to say at last, hoarsely. "It's that devil—that—Templar!"

O'Shay had lurched to his feet. Covering Condon with his gun, Templar cut the cord which secured the great wrists of O'Shay, and the latter yawned and stretched eagerly until his muscles had grown more limber. Then he stepped lightly to Condon and carefully took his weapons from him. There was only the one revolver and a small hunting knife. Still stunned, Condon looked from one of them to the other. He moistened his loose lips.

"Keep a stiff lip," urged O'Shay. "Hanging ain't half bad, compared to what you deserve to get."

A touch of color returned to the face, and of life to the eye of Condon.

"Boys," he said in an unsteady voice, "if you give me up to the law, this money has to go to Lister—the damned ingrate, the cold-blooded scoundrel, Lister! But if you forget about the law, the three of us can

282

split it up—a third for each of us."

"How much will that be?"

"Nearly eight hundred thousand."

"Hold on," said Templar. "Didn't you tell me yourself that you were worth five millions?"

"I was," said Condon savagely, "if I'd had a chance to collect my affairs gradually and turn my estate into gold. But I was hurried, and forced sales are robbery, robbery."

He grew pale with rage as he thought of it, and the anger gave him sudden new strength.

"I've had five millions in my hand," said he, "and the door opened to ten millions in addition. Now I'm bargaining for a chance to have a third of eight hundred thousand for myself."

He writhed.

"Crane always swore he would make me pay. But I never dreamed that he could bring me to this. Boys, you've got me where you want me. You see I offer to pay up straight and fair, with you."

"And what about McArdle's share?" asked O'Shay.

"McArdle? Crane's errand boy? Oh, damn McArdle. A taste of Templar's gun will be enough for him! But now, my friends, you agree?"

"What do you say, Danny?" asked Templar, hating himself for testing the honesty of his old friend; but the voice of O'Shay rang back clear as a bell: "I'll never live on a penny of stolen coin with the blood of God knows how many men behind me. I'll have my reward in the hangin' of you, Andy."

"Tell me," said Condon with a sudden savage curiosity. "Did you follow the Chink girl on this trail, Templar?"

"We followed it part of the way—then we reached Crane and McArdle. It's a long story."

"She's at the bottom of it," nodded Condon. "By God, I could guess at the poison in her from the first day I saw her. It was like—it was like a taste of fate far off, when I saw her. I thought I recognized someone in her face! You, Templar—you lost your head about the Chink?"

"Don't speak of her again," warned O'Shay. "The kid is touchy on that subject, and I don't want you murdered before the law gets you into its lily white hands, Condon!"

He departed and tumbled through the window, returning almost at once with the satchel in his hand; and he flung it down on the table.

"There's my whole life," murmured the captive. "There it is, tossed in the air and coming now on the table with a crash. And all that life work goes to a damned ungrateful brat who will hate my heart, alive or dead! God, God, I thought I was ready for anything, but I'm not ready for this!"

He caught the satchel to him with a sudden reach of his hands. It appeared for an instant as though he actually would attempt to bolt with his treasure; but he mastered that desperate impulse, his wild eyes working rapidly from face to face. They, as if from a distance, looked at him with a curious detachment, for eons and oceans lay between them, standing so close.

"Are you ready to watch him, Danny?" asked Templar. "What do you want to do?"

"McArdle is out searching for Hong Kong. If he finds her—well, I want to be near! I've waited too long already."

He started hastily for the door.

"Wait," said O'Shay. "If he finds her, he'll bring her straight back here."

Templar, his face working, stared towards the door and then turned slowly back.

"I don't like it," he said gloomily. "I don't like it! Danny, I hope to God that everything goes well!"

"Mad about a Chink!" said Condon curiously. "Ay, that's being young—that's being young!"

There was a loud slamming of a door, a sound like the splintering of wood, and then a noise of feet approaching down the hall.

Condon jerked back from the table a step.

Templar, like a swift and silent tiger, was streaking for the door, when Condon's shrill voice called: "Mac! Mac! Look out! O'Shay's loose and Templar's here! Keep your gun on the girl! She's your ticket—"

O'Shay was too far off to act with a hand stroke, but he cast a chair and it bore Condon crashing to the floor.

CHAPTER XLI

McArdle, hurrying down the hall, struck the door at the same moment and knocked it wide; dim as a ghost in the hallway he stood, Hong Kong still struggling as he thrust her forward. She ceased her struggles now and McArdle, seeing Templar on the spring towards him, shouted: "Keep back—you! She'll go first! She'll go first, by God!"

O'Shay, for the moment, was an unthinking madman. As Condon began to drag himself to his feet, the giant seized him and held him by the throat, while his bellowings of fury shook the house.

Templar, however, gun poised, uncertain, backed away. Condon was gasping: "Templar—O'Shay, we'll bargain for her!"

Templar cried suddenly: "Danny, I can't stand it! I can't stand it! Let Condon and the money go. Let Condon be damned. I want to see her safe. Danny, d'you hear?"

The answer of O'Shay was far beyond the power of mere words. Vast were his blasphemies. He strode back and forth, dragging Condon with him. He lifted the murderer in his hands and threatened to dash his brains out on the floor. But finally he released his captive, and Condon staggered back against the table. He took out a handkerchief and wiped the blood from his face.

"You've heard Templar make the proposal,

O'Shay," said he. "The money and I for the girl. Do you agree?"

O'Shay cast his great hands towards the ceiling, as though he would pull down wrath from heaven.

"Oh," groaned O'Shay. "I'd rather be dead than to see such a minute! Let her go, then, McArdle. Let her go, and damnation to the pair of you. Let her go!"

"What sort of security have we got? The minute that he's gone, Templar'll be at me," answered McArdle in heavy doubt.

The voice of Condon was like the scream of a bird. "Let her go! Stand away from her!" shouted Condon. "We'll trust their word. They're square!"

At that, McArdle released her. It seemed as though the Hong Kong Templar had known was dissolved and her strength stolen. At the first step she staggered; Templar reached her and caught her in his arms, while O'Shay was damning the two criminals from the room.

Condon went without a word, slinking close to the wall; and McArdle backed away from the door. It slammed behind the pair; the rapid clatter of their running feet rattled and thundered in the hall, beat hollowly on the outer porch, and then they were gone. The ravings of O'Shay were interrupted by a sharp call from Templar.

"What shall I do, Danny? She's fainted dead! She *is* dead! Danny, Danny, they've killed her!"

"I hope they have!" shouted O'Shay. "Open her dress at the collar—lay her flat on the floor and raise her heels—fan her a bit. You and your damned women would break the heart of any man! And I had Condon! I had Condon! Oh God, I had him in the hollow of me hand!"

Templar with trembling hands was following the advice of the giant, then: "Danny, she's dead! She's dead! I can't hear her heart!"

O'Shay fell on his knees beside the prostrate form and laid his ear on the breast of the girl.

"Ticking like a clock," he announced suddenly. "She'll be awake in a minute. She's most likely awake already, and listening to us yammer. Her? She's a tough bird! And we've chucked Condon for a Chink—"

"Hush, you fool—you fool!" whispered Templar, who finally had unfastened the high collar of the Chinese jacket. "Man, she's as white as snow."

"No, Johnnie," murmured the big man. "You don't mean that! Not white, boy. Not white!"

He snatched off his coat as he spoke and, raising her gently, spread it beneath her. On their knees, on either side of her, they stared at each other, and the long minute went slowly by.

At length her head turned towards O'Shay; her eyes opened, empty of light. Only gradually recognititon came in them, and fear with it.

"Where is he?" she asked faintly.

"It's you, Johnnie," said the giant, and rose to his feet. He went to the window and stared out into the blackness of the night, until he could see the tall trunks of the trees and the dull gleam of the water, like tarnished metal, beyond.

He heard a murmur of voices, the girl's growing higher and higher until it broke in sobs, and Templar's deep and low like a father soothing a child. Then: "I'll be all right, now," said the girl. "Something snapped—the light went out."

"I love you!" answered Templar.

O'Shay leaned out the window, but the night wind did not cool his face.

"I've spoiled everything," said she. "I've turned into a flabby faby at the last minute—I—I'm ashamed!"

"I love you," answered Templar.

She started to speak again; then all voices stopped; and O'Shay leaned still further into the night. At length he started erect.

"Johnnie!" he said. "Do we let the pair of them go free?"

"I don't care where they go," answered the triumphant voice of Templar. "Come here. Danny, come here!"

The giant slowly strode towards them.

"I want you to know her name—by gad, my dear, I don't know your name myself!"

"I'm Elizabeth—Crane—"

"You!" exclaimed the two men in a single voice. "Not the daughter—"

"Yes."

They gaped on one another. Even after so many threads of this strange story had been drawn together, traced from the start, there seemed volumes still to be explained.

She exclaimed quietly: "We knew from his letters in prison that he never would forgive the man who had betrayed him—who had given him over to the law. When he came out, I saw him and begged him to come back to us. But he was like iron. I followed him West. I hoped that I could stop him from doing some desperate thing; I knew that he was the leader, now, of all the men who had been wronged by Mr. Condon."

"How had he wronged the others?" asked O'Shay.

"He let them go to their trial without a penny of help from him. He kept the money from the robbery; they had nothing to pay lawyers, for instance. When I got to the West I saw that I'd have to go with a different name, of course, perhaps a different color. Then I thought of the Chinese disguise. I could talk a little. We'd always had Chinese servants. I could cook, too, in the Chinese way, because our own old cook had taught me how. And that's everything. I wanted to protect Mr. Condon, so that father wouldn't have a terrible crime lodged against him. But if I hadn't been here this night—everything would have been ended happily. Mr. Condon would have been taken to jail—but I—"

She threw out her hands in a gesture of despair, and her eyes filled with tears.

"We followed Condon before," said Templar, "and we caught him. We can follow him again and get to him before your father does. Who has an idea where he would go?"

"Down the river as fast as he can paddle a canoe," suggested O'Shay.

"He'll double straight back across the mountains like a hunted fox," said Templar.

The girl shook her head.

"He has McArdle along, and you mustn't forget that," said she. "He couldn't make McArdle face those mountains so soon again."

"You tell us, then," said O'Shay. "You worked this trail out faster than the rest of us once; you can do it again."

She looked to Templar with appeal; O'Shay stepped squarely in front of his friend.

"He's nothing to you now," declared O'Shay. "And you're nothing to him. You're Hong Kong again; you're on the trail like an Indian. Play that part, and start in thinkin'."

His bluff, cheerful tone set her smiling; and all at once she said thoughtfully: "If I were Condon—running for my life—I'd take the canoe across the lake, I'd set it adrift where I went on shore, and then I'd start up the valley, and plan to break across country through the mountains."

"I know them," said O'Shay.

"We'll play suppose," said the girl. "You draw a map. Draw a map of the upper valley and the mountains both sides."

"Here we go," said O'Shay, and, with a pencil, he began to draw on a large sheet of paper which he took from his pocket and unfolded. "Here it is north. The Little Brother comes in here. Sometimes you can ford it and sometimes you can't."

"This isn't high water; they'd ford," said the girl. "Go on!"

"Here's the Atwell Creek comin' in from the left."

"They'd keep to the right bank, I think. They can't waste too much time. They've got to cover miles."

"Good girl. I think you're right. They go up the valley. The walls of it soften down a little—"

"Into rolling country?"

"Rollin'? You might call it that. Looks like breakers more than rollin' waves, though."

"Where does that lead?"

"Onto big trees and more rough goin'."

"They'd turn to the right, there, I think," said the girl. "I've followed Mr. Condon so long I think I know how he works. He takes the hardest course almost always. He hopes those behind him may make one mistake—and follow the easiest way!" Then she added: "Is there any short cut from here to those hills—where the valley walls break down?"

"Sure," answered the big man. "Look how the valley winds! But if you cut straight across through the back-country—"

"Let's try it, then!" cried Elizabeth Crane. "We have a ghost of a chance! If we've guessed the way he would go, let's follow on and try!"

"Go back with her to Tolman," commanded Templar. "I'll take up this trail. Elizabeth, will you go back with Danny to the town?"

"No savvy," said the girl, and her eyes were as dark and blank as ever before.

CHAPTER XLII

They tried no longer to persuade the girl. For that matter, no matter how hard the trail, they doubted that she would hold them back very greatly. First of all they left the old mill-house and tested the theory of Hong Kong by hurrying down the bank of the lake. Where the waters gather in the race below the pool, they found the canoe, sure enough, caught broadside in the overhanging branches.

They managed to reach it with a broken bough, and drew it back to their side of the stream. Even so it would have been of the little use to them, had not the great carelessness of the fugitives left a paddle in the boat. With that in the mighty hands of O'Shay, they drove the little craft across the current, landed on the farther shore, and struck straightway across the hills with O'Shay setting the course and leading. Then followed Hong Kong; and Templar came as rear guard.

They had in fact no cause to regret the coming of the girl, where she could not match the longer strides of the men, she broke into a dog-trot, swinging easily along, with never a stumble of weariness. And Templar, watching her through the starlit night, felt his heart swelling with pride and with joy.

He and big O'Shay strode along with rifles in their hands, and the weight of revolvers to hold them back, to be sure, and yet they made the miles fall swiftly behind them. Avoiding the rougher country, they were led by O'Shay along a high ridge, which swung snake-like back and forth and carried them, gradually mounting, through the loftier ranges which pressed up on either hand, half seen during the darkness, but then, as the night wore away, lifting black and vast into the dawn light. Like a drawing worked on by ten million hands, dimness became thronged with vague, gigantic forms; huge mountains were slashed across by chasms of blackness and lines of brilliance, and then, as the drawing was made almost complete, the colorists began to work, first tenderly, cautiously, with pastel shades, sweeping in valleys in transparent blues, and tinting heights with mauve, with pink, with faded rose; but then, growing bolder in art, the richer, deeper dyes were piled on the canvas, and crimson, and royal purple, and gold turning to fire burned everywhere across the mountains.

The three travelers, unpausing all those hours of journeying, lifted their faces to the bright skies and glanced aside at one another, for they were filled with hope.

The ridge along which they had walked, as along a rough rod, now dwindled and passed into a steep slope up which they climbed slowly, and so came to the crest of a pass between two broad peaks. They looked down on a sea of lower hills.

Now, with the sun well up in the East, they made a brief halt beside a spring, and there they first drank, and then ate some jerked beef and hard tack which Hong Kong produced. She was a little pale, but there was no sign of her strength or her resolution diminishing. Yonder, among those big hills, was their last chance to find the quarry; and, when they had made that small breakfast, they started ahead once more, making rapid time down the slope.

Angling up the slope of the hills, and dipping straight down on the farther sides, they worked on for at least two hours. The morning had become hot and brilliant, and the hills were covered with the strange loneliness of mountain silence, mountain sun and rock and forest.

They came toward the top of a very steep slope and heard, somewhere from the broad bosom of the valley which they had just left, the lowing of a cow, borne loudly up to them upon the wind.

"We're on a lost trail!" said Templar gloomily. "We'll never find them!"

On the very heels of that speech, they heard a dry, brittle sound, like the breaking of a great board beyond the slope; slowly, afterward, loud echoes and small crept around them. They stared wildly at one another, full of the great surmise, for each of them had recognized the report of a rifle; that report was followed by a fusillade, and they broke into a run.

When they topped the ridge, they had the picture clearly beneath their eyes. There was a narrow valley, steep sided, with a small stream leaping in a zigzag course through its middle. In the midst of that valley were two knolls, which looked like nests of rocks. From one of these, two men were fighting; from the more northerly clump of stones, a single marksman was firing from time to time.

"It's my father," said the girl. "He's come down and cut them off! But how did he ever guess! How *does* he know so much?"

Even as she spoke, one of the two leaped to his feet and spun around, and then dropped on his side. O'Shay, his glass fixed upon them, said briefly: "That's McArdle. He's lying on his side, now, and keepin' up a bluff, shootin' into the air, now and then. That cur, Condon, is desertin' him!"

They clearly could see Condon slipping through the rocks and out of sight beyond the knoll of stones; but he reappeared almost at once, mounting the steep slope of the ravine on the farther side, where his course was sheltered, by thick shrubbery, from the view of the enemy up the valley.

"Drop him, Johnnie," urged O'Shay. "I'm no good at a distance like this. But drop him before he gets up over the ridge!"

Templar hastily caught his rifle to his shoulder, but then lowered it with a little exclamation.

Half way up the farther cliff there appeared to be a narrow ridge or shoulder and, when Condon reached this, he turned onto it and began to run swiftly along it, only ducking and dodging, now and again, as though taking advantage of cover to screen himself from the watchful eyes of the man in the valley beneath him.

"What's he doin'?" asked Templar vaguely. "What

does he mean by that trick?"

"Shoot, shoot!" exclaimed O'Shay. "Drop the dog and ask him when he's dead!"

The rifle went again to the shoulder of Templar, but the trigger fell with a dull and muffled click. The cartridge had proved a dud.

The ejector, also, stuck for a moment, and, by the time he had a fresh bullet in the chamber, Condon no longer was running forward. He had dropped to one knee and unslung the rifle which he had carried over his back during his climb. His goal was plain enough now; it was that single form lying amid the rocks of the northward knoll.

"John! John!" gasped the girl.

And Templar, steadying his hand, fired.

He knew that he had missed—high and to the right—even as he pulled the trigger, and he pumped in the next cartridge and drew his bead, lying stretched out flat. He saw Condon wince away from the shot, which must have struck the rock face very near him. Then, realizing that he was mysteriously under fire, Condon whirled and leaped for the shelter of a small bush which grew on the edge of the shoulder. The bush, accordingly, Templar used for a target, and fired again.

They saw Condon reel up from his new found covert. He staggered backward, stumbled on the edge of the cliff, and then fell headlong down the slope, his rifle flashing down, in rapid circles, before him, and the satchel which contained his wealth bumping behind him; for it, also, had been lashed at his back.

It was not a sheer fall, but a sort of run of sand and gravel such as Westerners are fond of calling a "devil's slide." A cloud of dust rose behind Condon; big stones were seen starting down before him, bounding high into the air, and landing with a white crash in the waters of the stream, which here twisted in close to the ravine wall.

His impetus had reached an almost hopeless point when the satchel strap, of new, strong leather, caught in a bush that jutted from the side of the slope. The descent was violently stayed. Into the face of Condon poured the stream of gravel and small stones which his passage had loosened. Then, with no dust to obscure the vision, he was seen working for a foothold, clinging to the bush with one hand, and waving the other hand high. In that hand there was a flutter of white. Plainly he was surrendering, and begging yonder terrible marksman to fire no more.

"All right—all right!" gasped Templar, as though his voice would be able to ring across that great void of thin mountain. "I won't shoot. Good God, I wish him luck!"

"Crane is going to shoot!" exclaimed O'Shay suddenly.

Seeing what had happened, the man in the northerly rock-nest had risen to his knees and trained a rifle on the form which struggled on the cliff face. But the shot was not fired. No matter what bitterness of fifteen years of torture was in the hard heart of Crane, he played the game as a sportsman should, and would not fire at a helpless enemy.

So all the valley waited; even the wounded McArdle had dragged himself to the top of a rock on his own knoll and stared at the struggle of Condon.

Now, his feet well entrenched, the latter took a closer grip on the shrub and began to draw himself up, slowly, but the moment all the weight was bearing upon one foothold, it gave way with a telltale little spurt of sand, and Condon lurched down at arm's length. The shrub itself, though it had borne the infinitely greater shock of his first fall, now was seen slowly dragging from its place. One root seemed to break, and Condon jerked downward several feet. Clinging to the bush with one hand, with the other he worked desperately in an endeavor to make hand or foothold; and sand and gravel flew beneath his efforts.

Luck was against him, and the girl bowed her head and covered her face as the bush jerked quite loose and sailed down the slope, leaving Condon scrambling for a hold like a cat clawing at the too smooth surface of a treetrunk, or running wildly on a treadmill. So with hands and feet he struck at the sliding soil, gained a brief resting place, and then was seen slowly moving downward again.

His efforts had loosened a considerable body of the soil, and now it gave way with him. The impetus increased; the body of ground dissolved in dust-puffs and gravel-showers; and Condon dropped rapidly down.

His struggles had not been utterly in vain, however. Just above the stream, where its waters had eaten away the bank and left a lofty overhang, there was a dense fringing of brush, and through this Condon cut rapidly until he was at the very verge.

There again his grip gained some purchase. With raw palms and naked tendons, no doubt, he labored; but he hung now, swinging back and forth like a pendulum, on the edge of safety if he could draw himself up.

Luck again checked him. A dropping tide of loose rubble, which his fall had started, now washed over the brush and crashed full down upon him, and Condon fell into the white streak of the water.

Those three watchers on the other height started wildly. It did not seem possible that that keen, cunning, remorseless brain at last had ended.

No, the vitality of a very water rat was in the man! They saw two arms flung wildly out of the white rush of the stream. They clutched a projecting rock, and there he remained, clinging desperately, buffeted and screamed at by the water, and covered with stinging, shooting spray which sometimes blotted him out from the sight of the watchers.

In the meantime, casting old enmity behind him, Crane had run to the edge of the stream, and now, wading knee deep into the tugging current, he reached his rifle butt towards the fugitive.

Condon reached for it, seized it. What happened then, exactly, no man could tell. It might have been sheer accident, but it seemed rather the venom and despair of Condon, who saw himself saved, at best, for only a few wretched days. At any rate, the trigger was pulled by his touch, and, with the explosion of the rifle, Crane fell back dead upon the bank of the stream, while Condon was snatched down the white water.

CHAPTER XLIII

They buried Crane among the rocks of the knoll where he had intercepted the flight of his arch enemy and given him, at last, to the bullet from Templar's rifle. They piled the stones high above him, and then they started to hunt for the body of Condon.

It never was found, and the leather bag which contained his wealth was gone with him. Somewhere the foaming jaws of the creek held him and his, but a two-day search did not reveal a trace of him. So they turned back through the mountains and made a long, slow march to Tolman, their pace regulated by the strength of McArdle, who had been shot through the fleshy part of the shoulder.

McArdle, from Tolman, went back to the prison which he had so lately left; and the crime of fifteen years before had swept the boards clean of all its participants and of its victim, as well. Only one thing had been achieved, and that was the clearing of the name and the fame of Crane.

"But that was worth everything," said Mrs. John Templar to her husband.

"He did the great thing," said Templar gravely. "He stopped Condon and held him for us."

"And if he had lived," went on the girl, "I think his soul was embittered forever, and hardened. But he died in a great act of charity, John. He died in a great way, and I think he would have lived as a great man, if it hadn't been for the fifteen years of prison."

And she was right, thought Templar. In fact, he felt that in all ways she was inspired with the greatest wisdom, and every day of their married life made him wonder that so pure and lofty a soul could have designed to notice such an unimportant person as himself.

He asked her once, as they walked among the trees of his Long Island home, when she first had noticed him.

"When I saw you breaking Snyder like dead twigs!" she answered.

"Hong Kong, you love fighting," said he. "That Snyder, though—he was the worst of the lot! A poisoner, too!"

"Of course," said the girl! "McArdle was paying him on the side; and after you killed Larry of course the grand thing was to get rid of you in any possible way. Snyder thought of poison."

"But a squirrel stepped in between."

She was silent.

"Still," said Templar, "though you may call it chance

if you like, I think it was something else."

"What, John?"

"Something behind—pulling the strings—juggling good out of evil. For the criminals, death or poison, my dear. For a brave man, a clean name. For you, a penance, poor dear. Only for me a colossal reward a thousand times beyond my deserts. And—tell me what did you do in the forest that night I trailed you from Condon's house?"

"I went to see Father."

"And when you got into the kitchen and caught up the cleaver—if you'd had a split part of a second before I caught your arm, wouldn't that have been the end of young John Templar?"

She looked at him with a faint smile.

"Hong Kong no savvy," said she.

They came into a clearing. It rang with enormous blows of an axe, and there was mighty O'Shay swaying the tool as if in a fury.

"Look!" murmured Templar. "What a man! He's getting his exercise."

"Not at all," answered the girl. "He's killing a tree."

Center Point Publishing
600 Brooks Road ● PO Box 1
Thorndike ME 04986-0001 USA

(207) 568-3717

US & Canada:
1 800 929-9108